DRY TORTUGAS

by

AFN CLARKE

CLARK*e*-BOOKS

First paperback edition published in 2006 by PublishAmerica as *'Dry Tortugas by Anthony Clarke'*

First eBook edition published in 2012 by Clarke-Books LLC as *'Dry Tortugas by AFN Clarke'*

This paperback edition published in 2016 by Clarke-Books LLC

Cover background beach image © Misterlez | Dreamstime.com
Cover foreground photo © Clarke-Books LLC
Cover design by AFN Clarke

ISBN: 978-1-938611-24-7

CLARK*e*-BOOKS
www.afnclarke.com

For my Daughters

Dry Tortugas

"The inaccessibility and solitude of the islands were a metaphor for the desolation of a soul stranded in a desert of indecision, self-pity and deceit. Monroe stared at the drifting fragments of his own mortality and slowly turned away, unable to face the horror of his own extinction."

From "The Conch Collector" by Jake Kimble

Dry Tortugas

ONE

May 23rd 2002

Hurricane Joshua was early. A month early, catching the meteorologists by surprise at its sudden appearance, with little of the slow build-up across the Atlantic normally associated with tropical storms.

Local fishermen had sensed it days before and tensed with a foreboding they could not readily explain, but Jake Kimble was not thinking about the stirrings of unease he had heard before the voyage - as a quiet whisper circulating through the anchorage - he was watching in awe as the waves rolled towards him, some of them tumbling over themselves, lunging across the dark menacing bulk of the sea in a lazy pounding curl of surf that raced down the blue green face of the wave.

He watched with a rising sense of euphoria as the white foam snarled past the boat, snatching and grabbing at anything loose or badly fitted that the hungry ocean could tear away. But Jake trusted the yacht, and Peter's skill as a boat builder, to deal with the vagaries of the unpredictable ocean. And he trusted his skill as a sailor learned over the years, and his past experiences on the ocean that were a constant reminder of the power of Mother Nature. Disappointed at finding nothing to take away into its green blue depths, the wave swept past the smooth hull, growling indignantly. Jake glanced up again at the darkening sky, knowing that this unpredictable storm was going to be particularly violent. Away in the distance, lightning crackled and flared, sometimes arcing down to the ocean in an ear splitting crash, at other times flashing horizontally through the clouds as if the entire sky was on fire, followed by a thunderous explosion.

Earlier the VHF Radio antenna mounted atop the mizzenmast had blown away with a vicious squall, the winds rising to seventy-five knots, blasting horizontal stinging rain across the deck. Then it was gone and the fifty-knot steady blast from the approaching storm front seemed a gentle breeze by comparison. The wildness of the storm winds and majesty of the ocean advancing in huge mountains of constantly changing liquid mass filled his heart with a wonder he could not explain. There was no room for fear, just awe at the enormity of the storm at work and the sheer inconsequence of humankind in the face of such power. It was not belittling; it was inspiring.

Frankie struggled up the companionway steps, slid back the hatch, slipped out the top board, scrambled into the cockpit, replaced the board and closed the hatch. Hooking the safety harness to the specially reinforced padeye she took over behind the wheel, her olive skin pale, eyes wide with fear. Looking around at the foaming ocean it was worse than she thought and an involuntary shudder ran through her already shivering body, not sharing Jake's sense of wonder at the terrifying scene.

"THIS WAS NOT MY IDEA OF A PLEASANT FEW DAYS SAILING. NEXT TIME TAKE YOUR MISTRESS AND IF YOU DON'T HAVE ONE, I'LL FIND ONE FOR YOU," she shouted above the screeching wind.

Jake grinned, unclipped his safety harness from the padeye in the cockpit, leaned over to the windward side deck and clipped it to the jackline that led forward to another secure padeye by the forestay.

"KEEP HER INTO THE WAVES. I'M GONNA RIG THE PARA-SEA ANCHOR."

Frankie nodded and watched him crawl along the foredeck to the anchor locker and retrieve the bulky parachute sea anchor. Its twelve-foot diameter canopy would dig into the waves and keep them steady in the snarling ocean, allowing the waves to sweep past the yacht as she lay bow towards the storm.

Jake struggled with the three hundred foot length of chain and nylon rode, secured it to the samson posts then double checked the swivel before heaving the package over the bow just as a wave reared up and broke over the top of him, sweeping down the length of the shuddering deck. The parachute sea anchor dumped back on top of Jake and he set about once more to untangle the mess and heave the package over the bow, succeeded this time and paid out the thirty feet of chain watching as the canopy gradually opened under water before it was swept from his view, the line running smoothly through the fairlead until it reached the extent of its length and snapped tight, stretching as the canopy dug in and held.

Jake tied off the trip line and strained his eyes to see the tip of the small marker buoy rising and falling on the waves in unison to the rise and fall of the yacht. Satisfied, he crawled back to the cockpit and slumped beside Frankie, breathing hard. With the deployment of the para-sea anchor the motion of the yacht was less chaotic as she presented the smallest surface area possible to the oncoming waves.

Frankie leaned forward, grasped the knurled nut on the side of the steering pedestal and tightened it, locking the rudder in position, then sat back and rubbed her eyes. She looked at her hands, wrinkled by exposure to the salt water and dug out a pair of gloves from the pocket of her foul weather jacket.

"DID YOU TRY THE SAT PHONE?" Jake shouted.

She nodded, not finding the energy to speak.

"AND?"

Frankie shook her head. "Nothing. Couldn't get through," her voice barely audible in the rising cacophony.

"GET BELOW. REST. I'LL STAY ON WATCH."

Frankie was not going to argue. Slipping from behind the wheel, she pulled out the companionway boards, unclipped her harness and clambered below into the comparative warmth and quiet of the saloon. Turning, she saw Jake take up position behind the wheel before slotting the boards back in place and slamming the hatch home, shutting off the outside world before more of the ocean could pour into the saloon. Bracing herself against the roll of the yacht, she crossed to the navigation desk and flipped the switch on the bilge pump, straining to listen while it emptied the sea water from the bilge, then, satisfied that the bilge was empty, flipped the switch off and collapsed onto the settee without bothering to remove her foul weather clothes.

One moment she was awake, the next asleep, exhaustion overcoming the fear that kept her conscious. But it was a sleep filled with flashing images of the past, present and perhaps, she thought, the future. A future full of hazy figures and disconnected images without form. A lazy, surreal, chaotic pattern. Then she was awake again as if no time had passed.

Not sure what had woken her, she sensed rather than was aware of the approaching wave. The sound changed, the roaring crash of the waves deepened and there was an ominous silence amid the constant clamour. Deep inside her psyche, she knew it was the sound of Armageddon. The end of the world as she and Jake knew it, and strangely she felt at peace.

In the cockpit Jake felt it too.

Pale sunlight filtered through the thick swirling clouds fading with the creep of night and advancing waves became dark monsters beyond the range of his vision until they swooped down and roared past him. Then the light was gone and darkness enveloped them in an instant, their world reduced to a small hollow in the ocean as the wave bore down upon them, blocked the sky and became their entire universe as it reared up as a massive vertical mountain in front of the yacht.

But he felt no fear.

If this was the end then so be it. And a calm descended over him as he tipped his head back, watching as the wave reached its ultimate height.

Slowly the yacht began to climb the face. Thirty degrees became forty, became fifty, became sixty until she was at almost ninety degrees, heading up the face of the wave that towered above her.

Shuddering under the enormous load of the boat, the parachute sea anchor held as the crest of the huge wave fell over itself and descended like a giant hand reaching down to pluck the fragile yacht from the sea and crush it within its palm.

For Jake it was as if everything were happening in slow motion.

He could see individual fingers of boiling foam reaching out towards him from the curling lip of the wave, and the nylon line stretched taut as a bowstring.

Water sprayed out of the fibres as the line snapped out above the surface, straining to hold the yacht on the smooth, vertical, dark green body of ocean before it entirely engulfed the yacht in hundreds of tons of water that smashed onto the deck, driving it beneath the surface.

And Jake marvelled at the overpowering size and speed of the rogue wave as he braced himself against the wheel, hugging it tight to his chest, knowing that this was how the ocean often claimed its final payment from those who dared venture upon its restless back.

*   *   *

Sixty miles away to the east, rain, blasted into millions of horizontal stinging barbs by the wind, hammered relentlessly as Owen struggled with the storm shutters. Doggedly fixing them in place over the windows of the small bar that had been his livelihood for the past forty years, as Hurricane Joshua stretched out its sinewy fingers from where its eye hovered one hundred miles out in the Gulf of Mexico turned and screamed towards the Florida Keys. It had changed course during the afternoon from its northwesterly movement and a little over five hours ago abruptly aimed a direct hit on Key West.

He could feel its awesome power already, but he was not thinking about himself or the bar, he was thinking about Jake and Frankie, alone, right in Joshua's path. Wondering where they were and whether or not Jake had realised that the storm had changed direction and instead of passing them by to the southwest, was now on a collision course with the yacht and the Keys.

The heavy shutter banged up against the window barely missing the glass and jammed Owen's fingers against the edge of the window frame, his sharp cry of agony whipped away in the wind. Grimacing against the pain of the lacerated, broken and already swollen finger, he slammed the shutter home, snapped the catches in place, then turned for the last one.

"I should'a listened to my instincts," he muttered, "they never should'a gone out. I knew it."

Grunting under the weight of the last shutter and the vicious wind that threatened at any moment to rip it from his grasp, he manoeuvred it gently into place being careful to keep his fingers clear this time, completed securing the latches and leaned against the wall to catch his breath just as a battered Jeep slid to a halt beside him.

Mary Slaney, mid thirties, a little heavy but surprisingly agile and

11

quick, jumped from the seat, pulled the storm jacket tightly around her and struggled against the wind over to where Owen stood.

"Heard anything?" The wind snatched her words away before Owen could hear them, but he knew what she was asking.

Grasping her arm, he staggered to the front door, wrenched it open and thrust her forward, following quickly as another violent blast shook the building. Inside it was as if the storm didn't exist and the noise and vibration separated from the cosy warm interior of the saloon.

Mary peeled off her coat and shook her head, raindrops spraying from her short hair.

"Got a towel?"

Owen leaned behind the bar and tossed one to her, then sat down nursing his broken finger, face grey with pain.

"Does Nikki know?" Mary finished towelling her hair and glanced at Owen. Her gaze slipped down to his hand and the blood trickling from the lacerated finger. "What did you do?" she scolded gently.

"It's nothing."

Gently she took his hand and wiped away the blood. Owen winced in pain.

"It's broken and you need stitches."

"Pour me a scotch, would you. A stiff one."

He watched as Mary went behind the bar, poured a scotch and rescued the first aid kit from behind a crate of sodas. She placed the scotch within his reach and searched through the first aid kit.

"No I haven't called Nikki. Not yet. It's not the right time."

"When *is* the right time?" she questioned irritably and then triumphantly held aloft butterfly sutures, two tongue depressors and a small bottle of disinfectant, all of which Owen eyed mistrustfully as he downed half the scotch in one gulp.

Mary pulled up a stool opposite Owen and once again gently took his hand in hers. As an afterthought she moved the scotch bottle closer to his elbow.

"This is going to hurt. A lot."

"Thanks."

"You're welcome."

Carefully, ignoring Owen's gasps of pain, she cleaned the wound, applied the butterfly sutures and manipulated the bones together. Using the tongue depressors she bound the broken index finger to the middle finger and looked up at Owen's face. The scotch had helped, but his skin was pasty grey beneath the tan, and pain lines stretched from the corners of his eyes.

"Tomorrow morning it's a trip to the hospital and have it set properly."

He nodded and poured another slug of scotch. Mary knew that the pain would prevent him from getting too drunk, and that he would stop drinking once the alcohol had taken the edge off the throbbing agony. Owen never drank the profits.

"So. Nikki," Mary said determinedly.

Owen sighed deeply, closed his eyes and sat back, nursing the damaged hand. "She's got enough to worry about right now. Anyway, we don't really know anything. We haven't heard a thing since the hurricane turned. Nothing. Jake's last message said the seas were twenty feet and getting bigger. We can't even raise them on the radio anymore."

He knew she was right. Deep down in his gut he knew they were in trouble and that Nikki needed to know. Slowly he reached over and pulled the telephone across the bar, lifted the receiver and dialled.

*   *   *

The house was quiet, just the way Nikki liked it. Smiling quietly to herself she plumped the cushion behind her back and settled down to read Jake's new book that had arrived special delivery that morning. She knew it had been a labour of love for him, a painful twelve-year journey of intermittent work through a past strewn with emotional minefields distilled into eleven hundred pages of close typeface. But he had finally finished the novel, and the reviews Nikki read suggested it was his best.

For most of the day she had left it on the coffee table in the conservatory, as if teasing herself by denying the pleasure she knew she would feel when at last she settled down to read. So she worked slowly around the house, doing odd little jobs, moving awkwardly as the baby settled inside her, preparing for its first glimpse of an unsettled world. Neither she nor Peter had wanted to know the sex of the child, but she felt sure it was a boy, and knew how delighted Jake would be, although she was sure he would try to hide his joy beneath his usual scowl. Finally as the long afternoon drew towards evening, she lay back on the cane settee, adjusted the pillow one last time and with a glass of fresh lemonade beside her, took up the hardbound book.

The cover was simple. A tropical coral island, a sailboat and the title:

THE CONCH COLLECTOR
by
JAKE KIMBLE

She opened the cover slowly, savouring that special new book smell and read the neat writing on the flysheet.

> *Nikki*
> *You were right my darling daughter. It is just a*
> *book that will gather dust on a shelf and crumble*
> *in time to be forgotten, but you will live on. Love*
> *your child, that is all that matters. I am proud*
> *to be your father.*

She saw, on turning the page, that he had dedicated the book to both her and to Frankie and she smiled, feeling the sudden emotion constrict her throat and a tear start in the corner of her eye.

Slowly she turned each page as if it were made of fine delicate gold leaf until she reached the first chapter. Still wanting to cherish the moment of anticipation as long as possible, she took a sip of lemonade, sighed contentedly as the baby moved again and began to read.

> *Monroe steered the twenty-eight foot, flat-bottomed Sharpie*
> *through the shallows as if in his sleep. His mind following the*

14

usual pattern of lost thoughts that began every new day. The wooden boat seemed to have a mind of its own, following the narrow shallow channels unerringly, homing in on his favourite conch beds. Once there, he would begin the daily ritual by furling the sails and dropping anchor, letting the boat swing and drift until it held and settled in the quiet morning.

He liked it here, where mangroves curled gnarled roots into the mud-sand beneath the water, thrusting fat boughs upwards in short stumpy arms, motionless while mosquitoes buzzed, a constantly moving cape over them.

Monroe stretched, picked up the flask and uncorked it, tipped it to his mouth, gratefully tasting the liquor as a gift from the Gods to the start of his new day. Then he slept for an hour or two in undisturbed peace, away from the clamour of the town, constant gossiping tongues and staring eyes that accused him in silence without once charging him with anything.

If he were guilty of a crime, then it would have been wishing for solitude. He was guilty of desiring his own peace, which he found in his secret conch beds.

Nikki read carefully savouring every word, letting herself drift back to the Florida Keys, feeling the hot sand under her bare feet, hearing the lap of gentle surf against the shore and the rustling breeze through the scrub pine and palm trees. And she longed to go back with her baby, to see the light in Jake's eyes at his first glimpse of his grandchild.

Monroe bent to the task, feeling through the sand beneath the layer of sea grass, eyes closed, allowing his sense of touch to locate the ring. He knew it was here where it had slipped off his finger the day before as he dived on the conch that crawled across the bottom.

The air in his lungs was rapidly being replaced by carbon dioxide as his body absorbed the oxygen. If he could just last a

15

moment longer; then his fingers touched the small white gold band and closed around it, but he didn't head for the surface immediately. The rising panic of a second ago disappeared with the joy of finding the ring and he relaxed, opened his eyes, stared at the band and slowly rose to the surface thirty feet above, air dribbling from the corner of his mouth.

For a few moments he was suspended between realities, a visitor in an alien world that felt strangely comfortable to him. A time without end until his head burst the surface and fresh oxygen filled air rushed into his starved lungs. He held the ring high watching as the sun glinted off the metal and laughed, his voice ringing purely in the still emptiness of the lagoon.

She let her eyes drift from the page and the book fall onto the cushion, the smile still on her face as if she fondly remembered the fictional incident as if it were her own. An incident in the distant past that no longer held the stark edginess of reality, but was cloaked partly in illusion.

For two hours she lay wrapped in a comfortable tropical paradise with Monroe, until a distant sound brought her back to the Narragansett Bay with a rush.

"Honey?" Peter's voice rang hollowly through the hallway into the conservatory, followed by his slow footsteps, deck shoes squeaking on the polished wood floor.

Looking up from the book, she watched as he entered the conservatory. Tall lean, with a shock of unruly curly hair and still with wood shavings clinging to his clothes, his smile radiating the boyish enthusiasm she hoped would never leave when the cynicism of old age crept upon them both.

"How're you doing?" He leaned down to kiss her carefully so as not to disturb her position. She could smell freshly cut wood, epoxy and paint that still clung to him. In the last twelve years he had transformed the small, ramshackle wooden boat-building yard into a thriving business.

"I'm good. Jake's book came this morning." She held it up for him to see as he crossed to the table and poured himself lemonade from the jug.

"He finished it? Good for him. "

"Yup."

The telephone shrilled suddenly, disturbing the calm of the moment. Peter sauntered into the hallway to answer it. Nikki could hear the murmur of his soft voice but not the words and an inexplicable feeling of dread invaded the quiet of the house with a sudden draught of cold air.

She closed her eyes and when she opened them again Peter was standing by the window looking out across the Bay.

"It's Jake isn't it?"

"That was Owen. There's a hurricane in the Gulf. Just turned towards the Keys. It's way too early for a tropical storm. It just brewed from nowhere," he was rambling half to himself and half to Nikki, still trying to understand how a storm could be this early.

"They were sailing to the Dry Tortugas. Just like they always do this time of year," she said quietly.

"Owen said they had a message over the radio five hours ago and haven't been able to raise them since." Peter turned from the window and knelt down beside the settee, taking Nikki's hands, looking into her eyes. "Jake's good. The boat's strong. I built her to take anything the ocean can throw at her. They'll make it."

Slowly Nikki shook her head. Deep inside she knew that they wouldn't. "Maybe not this time."

"Lots of sailors make it back after they've been reported lost at sea."

"Lost at sea," she whispered, the words seeming to float in the air, touching off a memory that now seemed so long ago, as if in another life and she turned her head towards the Bay and watched the sailboats beat back against the wind, headed to the marina and a safe haven.

As if triggered by a remote signal, the baby moved and Nikki felt her body contract in a startling spasm completely beyond her control, the pain forcing a gasp from her.

"Oh. Oh," Nikki gasped, feeling her waters break. She knew what that was but there was another sensation, something that didn't feel right. She looked down and saw a dark stain of blood seeping through her dress. "Oh my God."

For a moment Peter stood transfixed and then Nikki looked up at him, her eyes glazed in sudden shock and fear.

"Call the doctor."

Stung into action he hurried back into the hall as the contraction passed and Nikki lay back. But another spasm cramped her entire body in an intense pain that seemed to blot out the entire world, spinning her conscious mind into a dark whirlpool of agony and fear.

She was aware of noise around her.

Of the sound of garbled voices and distorted images of faces.

Of giant hallways that seemed to go on forever and ever and waves of agony that swamped her soul.

*   *   *

The vision of Nikki lying, hovering between life and death, played like an old movie across Jake's mind as he wedged himself tightly into the corner of the cockpit and let out a primal scream, challenging the forces of the ocean to do as they wished. In his heart he knew the ocean understood as the curling wave smashed into the boat, and when it seemed that the force of the ocean would throw the yacht over backwards, the para-sea anchor held the bow.

For a long heart stopping moment the yacht hung suspended, bow pointed directly skyward. It was as if Nature and God were conferring, deciding what should happen next as Jake stood awestruck at the seeming insignificance of his existence. A vision of his daughter appeared before him, her arms outstretched and as he reached out and took her hands in his, the yacht plunged through the top of the wave like a surfacing submarine, shuddering for a second or two in mid-air as the ocean dropped away beneath the hull, before slamming down onto the back of the wave.

All the while Jake stared into Nikki's face and held onto her hands, sensing that she too was struggling for life. And he thought he could see the conservatory in the house on the Narragansett Bay as Nikki fought to give life to her baby. Saw the vision as a hallucination playing on the surface of the boiling sea.

And at that moment, Jake knew neither his nor Frankie's lives were insignificant. He knew God existed out here on the wild ocean, because there was nothing else that could have created such awesome power.

Gasping for air as the water emptied out of the cockpit through the oversize drains, Jake stared at the back of the retreating wave. *'There are very few times when you are given a second chance'* he thought and spoke quietly into the storm. "Yeah though I walk through the shadow of the valley of death, I will fear no evil." He looked into Nikki's eyes as the next monstrous rogue wave reared up ahead of the boat and held her tightly. "I am here my daughter, take my strength. Take my strength and Live."

*   *   *

Fifteen hundred miles away, Nikki heard her father's voice in her mind and held onto his hands as she felt the life slip from her body. And as she gripped tighter and stared into his face, she felt his strength surge into her, taking over her body as the bleeding stopped and a thin cry echoed through the conservatory.

The Doctor straightened and let the nurse mop the sweat from his brow. Peter stood pale and frightened beside the settee, Nikki gripping his hand tightly. Then he felt her grip loosen and a calm come across her pale face.

"Doc?" he said tentatively.

"The bleeding's stopped. She's weak but she'll be fine." The Doctor leaned back against the wall. "It's pretty close to a miracle."

Tears poured down Peter's cheeks as the Nurse placed the swaddled now sleeping baby in his arms, and Nikki opened her eyes.

"I saw him," she said weakly. "I saw Jake." And her eyes closed again as she drifted off into a dreamless sleep.

"Who is Jake?" the Doctor asked quietly.

"Her father," Peter muttered, voice shaky with emotion. "He's missing at sea."

"Oh," was all the Doctor could say. "She'll be fine now and so will the baby."

Peter sat down beside Nikki, stroking her forehead and holding her hand, tears staining his cheeks. "He'll make it my love. I know he'll make it back, I know he will. But you have to think about our son. It's what Jake would have wanted."

But Nikki could not hear Peter's voice, her mind was in fast rewind, as images from the past ran backwards in time, until she was a four year old child who suddenly realized that her father was never coming back to her.

And she felt the pain and confusion of that child.

And again the images spun in her mind, moving forward until she was twenty years old, then flickered to normal speed and she saw a funeral casket.

Then they changed again and at the centre of her illusions spun a hypnotic white light as if reflected off a silver disc.

Gradually the pain eased. The world steadied and she drifted as the out-of-focus images came and went with distorted faces, until slowly a face she finally recognized solidified and somehow she was twelve years younger, stepping into the past as easily as if passing through a door into another room.

TWO

May 1990

Staring down at her mother's body, Nikki felt a chill of fear and a spark of annoyance. Fear from seeing death close-up for the first time and annoyance because of the way the mortician had combed her thinning hair down across her forehead as if trying to hide the liver spots that had appeared a few years earlier with the onset of premature old age hastened by alcoholism.

Leaning forward, Nikki flicked it away from the mask-like face, tips of her fingers drawing faint lines in the powder that covered the dead skin. Wafts of formaldehyde and decay drifted from the coffin, a cloying, sickening odour that would take days to wash away. Clearly visible beneath dried gossamer skin, so thin Nikki felt she could just blow it away with a gentle breath, she could see the creamy coloured bones of her mother's face. Even the most skilled illusionist could not hide the inexorability of death from her careful scrutiny.

There were other odd little things.

The pillow slightly stained just beside Eve Kimble's left ear, her body unusually shapeless beneath the pure white dress.

Nikki wondered idly whether the Valium she had taken half an hour earlier had given her some extra perceptive sense; or perhaps anaesthetised her from the true presence of death. This was not how she remembered her mother. Death had a way of disappointing those that saw it first hand; especially when the mortician had decided to exercise his frustrated artistic talent by unsuccessfully producing an altogether inappropriate Mona Lisa-like smile on the face of the dead woman.

The coffin was undoubtedly second-hand. Her mother was not the first, nor would she be the last to reside in it, and for a fleeting moment Nikki had the image of the body being removed from the coffin, then tossed into the incinerator by bored crematorium workers.

It was a little sordid.

A little sad.

Her hand moved down towards the dead mouth and smeared the dull red lipstick upwards into a grin. Now her mother's face had the appearance of a circus clown.

Sam turned his head away feeling the nausea rise; then risked a glance back at Nikki. She was young, nineteen years old, beautiful, and now immensely wealthy having inherited the bulk of her mother's family fortune along with the mansion set against the background of the Narragansett Bay. The 'Old Money' Sam had coveted for so long was within his grasp, so he considered his feeling of disgust a small price to pay for the opportunity to share in the millions.

Slowly she became aware that they were not alone and straightening, looked past Sam to the thin figure of the mortician, clad in an ill-fitting black suit, standing, waiting, a counterpoint to the soft cloying music that filled the dimly lit parlour. His gentle cough barely made a sound, but carried sinuously across the room to fill the dead space for a moment before fading.

"I don't want to be indelicate at this most distressing of times, but there is the question of when the cremation should take place."

His well-rehearsed smile was as thin as the rest of his body.

Nikki stared at him for a moment. "I'll let you know. You can keep her on ice can't you? Money isn't a problem."

He blanched. Maybe it was just a momentary spasm of emotion in his pale waxy face, an unusual display in an unusual moment. Directness bothered him, ruffling the perfect order and timing of his day. Nikki saw the alarm in his eyes before they resumed their dead look and felt a little better. For her it was a minor victory in a black week.

Sam leaned forward, whispering softly.

"Why can't you wait for a few days? There are papers for you to sign and, as one of the Trustees, I am responsible for carrying out your mother's wishes."

"She wanted me to find my father. That's what I'm going to do."

"It's been nearly fifteen years since he left."

"So?"

"Jake's dead."

"What?"

Shock gave way to anger. She felt stifled by the oppressive low light and dark drapes and sweeping past the Funeral Director, ran out into the gloriously beautiful day. Without sunglasses, the bright light hurt her eyes. A cooling breeze blew up the Narragansett Bay as low, fluffy, high-pressure cumulus clouds drifted in a clear blue sky. Walking back to the car, Nikki was not aware of the beauty surrounding her, as confusion crowded out almost all sensations except one of complete and utter loss. Beneath the numbing reality of her mother's death, she could feel the distant heartbreak and sorrow. Her world was spinning out-of-control like a top beginning to wobble off balance. But she did not feel loneliness, she had been lonely all her life and for a moment she wondered if her father was indeed dead.

Maybe Sam was right.

Anger flared again. Where was Jake when she needed him most?

A confused maelstrom of surreal images swam before her eyes, so that she had to steady herself against the car door to prevent from falling. The metal, warm from the summer sun, was somehow comforting, a solid link to a reality she did not feel. She was a child again, marvelling in the warmth of the metal touching her tiny fingers.

Then the moment was gone.

*   *   *

The car slid to a halt on the loose gravel drive, askew, rear wheels on the grass leaving churned dirt and sprayed gravel across the lawn. Torpor wound around her energy and strangled the desire to do anything except lay down and sleep, so she allowed the sound of the 'door-open' beeper to drift into the background of her consciousness and disappear along with the other unpleasant things in her life, deposited in her closet of dusty memories, slumbering like a hidden monster waiting. Always waiting.

Unlocking the front door, she stepped into a house that still echoed with those memories.

Ghostly sounds.

The shrill laughter of children and whispered giggling of teenagers arriving back late from a party. A deliciously exciting kiss from a local boy expressly forbidden to enter the house by her mother, followed by the confused, frightening excitement of that first venture into the world of adolescent sex. Now the house was a strange mausoleum that made her shiver with the same chill of fear she felt in the funeral parlour.

A quote from her father's novel jumped into her mind, unbidden, annoyingly clear, yet strangely comforting.

> *For him, Death could not be the black clad figure that so frequented the paintings of the Old Masters down through the Ages. Death was a friend. Death was an escape from Hell. Death was a splintering sunburst, a fiery explosion of bright light. The sudden sweet smell of fresh cut foliage and the exultant, screaming last gasp before peace and tranquillity purified the soul forever.*

In the house, her mother's influence was everywhere. In the furnishings and offbeat paint schemes. Faint smell of her perfume still hanging in the air. At any moment Nikki half expected to hear her staggering footsteps on the stairs as she invariably headed for the wet bar in the Victorian styled conservatory.

Standing looking at the view across the lawn towards Narragansett Bay, Nikki absentmindedly rubbed the leaf of a small lemon tree that grew in a pot by the French windows, savouring the smell. It was a motion reminiscent of the same act she would perform as a small child, when loneliness, confusion and the sight of her mother collapsed across the cane settee in a drunken stupor, combined to isolate her in a cold world.

From the hallway the telephone shrilled loudly, shaking her from her reverie. For a moment she was tempted to answer it, until the answer machine took over and the strained voice of one of her friends echoed mechanically with well meaning condolences falling emptily on the marble floor. Suddenly the house became stifling and an overpowering desire to leave gripped her, before exhaustion flooded through her body and she lay down on the cane settee and slept. And he was there in her dreams, the smiling handsome man who so excited her body and whose face remained so tantalizingly obscured.

She knew who he was but could not match a face to the body. Sometimes the fiction of the dream carried into the reality of her consciousness and stayed with her for hours after she had awakened; and always when she dreamed, shadowy figures hovered in the background, even though she thought she knew who they were.

> *A small, exquisitely made silver pendant spun in a shaft of bright light, reflecting dazzling rays from its gleaming surface, a tiny smiling Buddha, hand made by a blind Vietnamese boy in the back room of a small, cramped, stifling sweatshop in Saigon.*
>
> *Even as the war had raged on around him, the little boy had made the Buddha from memory.*
>
> *From the memory before the grenade had taken his sight.*
>
> *Burned in his mind in that instant, he had treasured the memory and brought that sacred treasure to the moment when his sure hands had crafted the tiny pendant statue.*

Swirling in the light, a face appeared.

Monroe's.

He was young, handsome, strong, sensitive and bold, humanly flawed and yet somehow perfect. She saw him naked holding the pendant and smiling. Then she was with him, wrapped in his arms, holding him tight, feeling his erection rise against her and she kissed him passionately, tasting the blood on his lip and then drew away as the noose slipped over his head and he smiled at her. It tightened with a twisting creak, jerking him into the air, and she felt a sense of overwhelming love and peace that mingled with the awful terror of the moment. Waking with a start, her conscious mind filled with horror from the nightmare, she involuntarily felt for the chain around her neck, touching the silver Buddha pendant, holding it up to the sunlight shafting in through the conservatory window.

It spun reflecting the light.

Breathing deeply and evenly she let the last vestiges of the nightmare empty from her mind, then went to the downstairs bathroom and splashed cold water on her face, staring into the mirror at the hollow eyed yet still beautiful young face, before ascending the stairs to her bedroom.

She stood in the doorway and looked at all the familiar things that seemed so alien now, as if the room and its contents belonged to someone else. Some other little girl; teenager; young woman. The bed, dressing table, bookshelves and pictures on the walls. Teddy bears and dolls, all consigned to a shelf of childhood memories.

Rummaging through the closet she found the shoebox she had kept hidden away from her mother's prying eyes. Packed neatly inside were tattered photographs and faded news clippings of a time before she could remember clearly, along with battered paperback copies of Jake's two books.

There was no need to open the books, because she could quote passages quite easily. Many times since she had first stumblingly read the novels as a small girl, she had hidden herself away in the closet or down by the shore, reading the books repeatedly. Closing her eyes and imagining Monroe beside her.

> *Drifters blew into town with the first waves of the hurricane season, searching for what little work there was and Monroe watched as they walked aimlessly, the men leading the women with whining snivelling children following along behind.*
>
> *He turned and bent down again to arrange the nets in his boat so that he could easily cast them when the time came. At least that's what he told himself.*
>
> *The truth was that he wanted to hide from their stares and pretend that they did not exist in his world, so that he would not be obliged to feel any sense of guilt for his own well being. Guilt was a luxury he did not want and even if given freely, he would have refused to accept the gift.*

The front door slammed, the sound rushing up into the bedroom with the clatter of footsteps echoing on the wooden staircase.

"Nikki. Damn you." Sam's voice like some vague theatrical cue, and she giggled suddenly at the ridiculousness of the situation. She was still giggling when he opened her bedroom door. Standing in the entrance, slightly out of breath, face flushed with anger. Innocence and purity emanated from the room, acting as a catalyst for his emotions, turning anger to lust and the need to possess her body.

Slowly he crossed the floor taking her in his arms, crushing her mouth with his, while his tongue forced open her mouth, his hands roughly ripping open her blouse and feeling crudely for her breasts. At first she resisted, but he was stronger than she, forcing her back onto the bed, his hands searching for her beneath her dress.

Her knee found his soft groin with a vicious snap that forced the air out of his lungs and his body off hers. Swiftly Nikki lurched to the corner of the bedroom and stared coldly down at Sam, his six foot three inch slim body and handsome face screwed into an ugly grimace of pain.

"Oh wouldn't mother be proud of her lover now. Get out, you son-of-a-bitch." Quietly, calmly, her voice carrying an authority she did not feel. "God I wish Jake was here now."

He turned his head away gasping in pain. "He's dead, I'm all you've got."

"I don't believe you. Get out." She left him lying on the floor and crossed to the bathroom, locking the door behind her and standing in the shower for a long time, allowing the tension and the sensation of his violent groping seep from her body, until she felt she had cleansed herself thoroughly.

*   *   *

Dust billowed up spiralling in the sun's rays shafting in through the open garage doors as she stripped the dust cover from the Ferrari. Although it was nearly twenty years old, monthly visits from the local mechanic had kept the car in almost perfect condition. Always fuelled and oiled, battery fully charged. It had been Jake's car and a macabre monument her mother had kept to a failed marriage.

Nikki remembered the times she had sneaked the keys while her mother was away from the house, and taken the Ferrari for a joy ride with her friends. Again there was a brief recollection of youthful hot summer nights. Targa top stowed and the wind blowing in her hair while music mingled with the uninhibited laughter of her friends crammed into the passenger seat. The mechanic had known, of course, but he kept the secret to himself and always ensured that the brakes were in good order.

Nikki stared at the Ferrari 308 GTS Quattrovalvole knowing that it was almost as old as she, and as she stared she knew that her father was still alive. Not from any physical evidence, she had not known whether he was alive for most of her life except for the press clipping seven years ago. She just knew, as if in some way the car had given her a psychic sense.

Her own car was still standing in the driveway, door open, warning tone bleating annoyingly, devoid of an audience. She parked it in the garage, and crossed to the Ferrari.

"Nikki, please. Let's talk." Sam stood in the doorway as if nothing had happened, flicking his hair away from his eyes, smoothing it back behind his ears and trying to maintain his composure.

"There's nothing to talk about. That was a lousy stunt you tried to pull and I'm out of here."

"Where to? This is your home."

"To find Jake. You're not all I have."

"He's dead. You're wasting your time."

She rounded on him, anger flashing from her eyes. "How do you know that?"

"Eve told me."

"I don't believe it. I know he's alive."

"Suppose he is. Where would you find him? You've no idea where to start."

There were times in her life when she was speechless. Incapable of the withering remarks her mother could always find, invariably leaving her adversary smarting under her verbal attack. Nikki thought that maybe verbal insecurity was something she'd inherited from her father, but how could she know that.

Taking the newspaper clipping from her purse, she slowly opened it so that Sam could see the photograph. He glanced at it, seeing a young Jake Kimble standing beside a marlin strung up on the quayside. In the background was a sign, '**Key West Sport Fishing**'.

"You really think I'm that dumb, Sam?" she said slowly.

"So you find him and let's just say for argument's sake he is alive and not a name on a tombstone. What then?"

"I'll be away from here. Before she died, mother told me to find him She gave me this." She stared at Sam, noting the confusion and shock on his face, before folding the clipping and stuffing it back in her purse, slamming the car door and reversing out into the driveway, scattering gravel.

*   *   *

The shock of seeing her mother's body in the morgue, anger at her absent father and the revulsion created by Sam's behaviour had almost caused her psyche to overload and the safety valve of sanity closed, shutting off thought, dealing simply with the practical task of driving the car.

As she drove to an uncertain future, her thoughts strayed back to Sam. He had been her psychological lifeline for such a long time, perhaps even a surrogate father. Tears sprang suddenly and she swung the car too fast into a curve. Tyres protested, but the pedigree of decades of racing translated into a smooth interaction between the road and the sophisticated suspension, allowing her mistake to go unnoticed. She was used to the car and the car was used to her.

East Greenwich came and went and before she knew it, she was on Interstate 95 headed southwest through Connecticut, sweeping along the coastline with its myriad bays and inlets. Past towns whose names evoked the seafaring romance of the past. Mystic. New London. New Haven. Bridgeport. All came and went in an unrecognisable blur.

THREE

Jake paused and peered closely at the hole in the shell. Two inches long, located between the second and third row of horns, exactly opposite the delicately coloured pink and cream mouth, where the foot of the conch could be seen tucked back, almost out of sight.

Waiting.

Uncertain.

Sure that he'd made the opening in the right place, Jake laid down the heavy knife and picked up a thin, lethally sharp steel blade, inserted it into the hole and sliced backwards and forwards until he felt the muscle give.

His whole being was concentrated into removing the stubborn conch that, though mortally wounded, refused to the very last second to give up the struggle for life.

To Jake, this was a fair fight.

A death to give life, for the conch would provide him with enough meat to sustain him for the rest of the day.

For the most part he was careful how he harvested the conch. Not for any altruistic motives, he had given those up years ago, but simply because he liked to see them moving slowly about the ocean floor and when some of them died, of natural causes, he would have yet another fine example for his collection.

It should have been a perfect life for him.

A sun soaked tropical paradise, where turquoise waters lapped pristine white sand beaches and civilization a stone's throw away. But beneath the seemingly carefree perfection of his existence, he could feel the inexorability of his past creeping towards him with the passage of time.

He reached for the flask. The need to beat back the demons with a shot of rum was, to him, not an excuse but a necessity. Besides, sour conch salad was always better when fortified by the dark liquor.

A Buccaneer's drink for a Buccaneer's meal.

As the liquor burned down his throat, followed by the brown sex organs of the conch - a succulent delicacy only enjoyed by true conch gourmets - the past slowly receded. He had brought most of the ingredients with him in the small cooler and sat down to prepare his meal. It was a ritual every time he came out to the small beach and sat by himself in the peace and quiet.

The white meat, about the size of his palm, he sliced thinly and tossed in a small wooden bowl with chopped Serrano chillies, a small tomato, garlic, cubed cucumber, salt, black pepper, a small diced shallot, thin slices of lime and the juice of two sour oranges. The taste was pure enjoyment, a perfect ending to an afternoon that was the precursor to an almost boringly beautiful sunset.

It was only when Jake sat back after another mouthful of conch followed by a long pull at the flask, that he felt the heat burning through his light cotton shirt. Sweat dripped down his arms and onto the sand, disappearing quickly without trace. He turned his blue eyes towards the sun as it lay low in the sky reaching for the horizon, and looked around at the beach. Surrounded by palm trees, the invasive Australian slash pine and mangroves afforded the tiny cove total privacy.

That was why he had bought the lot, even though he knew the price was exorbitant. But that did not matter. Peace and solitude were worth any price.

At forty-five years old, he was still slim and had not yet succumbed to middle age spread.

Rum had seen to that.

Vanity, that had been the vice of his youth, was now relegated to a distant memory.

Rum had seen to that also.

Standing, he walked slowly back to the battered rigid-inflatable dinghy pulled up the beach a little way, secured with a seven pound Fortress anchor, wavelets lapping at the transom with the receding tide. He carelessly tossed the cooler into the bow and sighed, not feeling like dragging the weight of the dinghy back into the water. But the thought of Frankie's smooth body and a promised return chess match with Owen, lent strength to his tired muscles.

With the boat in the water and engine ticking over, he took a last look around the deserted palm fringed beach and gunned the outboard, swinging the dinghy out towards the reef and the open ocean beyond.

*   *   *

At the time Jake was rounding the headland on his way back to his anchorage, Nikki awoke in a motel room in Georgia. Having driven through the day and night to escape the ghosts of the mansion on the Narragansett Bay, exhaustion had finally forced her to find a bed with clean sheets and a hot shower to wash away the memory of the previous day.

But the memories persisted, some real, some invented and some just a patchwork of incidents from childhood crowding her sleep.

Nikki could see her mother, drunk, staggering down the hallway as she stood in the bedroom doorway a folded piece of paper in her hand, tied with a ribbon. She held it out towards Eve, a present from a six year old.

Her mother stared, tore off the ribbon, roughly unfolded the paper and laughed crudely. "It's blank. There's nothing here you silly child," she slurred the words and staggered away.

But it *was* something to a six year old. It was a book with a story like her father's; and to her the blank paper was covered with writing and pictures as far as her imagination could take her. Why couldn't her mother see that?

She cried in her sleep, small childlike whimpering sounds as the scene changed and her mother was sober, kind and loving. Gathering her up in her arms, talking softly and soothingly as she read Dr. Seuss. Nikki could see *Horton the Elephant* and the *Cat in the Hat* and all the other whimsical characters. Image piled upon image, until she woke in a cold sweat, as the face in the coffin suddenly smiled and the skin split open.

Cold air belched into the room from the clattering air conditioner.

Shivering, she pulled the bedclothes up over her shoulders. The room began to close in on her until she could bear it no longer and packing her tote bag, dressed and stepped out into the humid heat of the

Georgia day.

Sam was right. What was she going to do? Having simply driven away from her home with no thought or plan except that of escape and a vague notion of finding her father. She watched the motel desk clerk prepare the bill and push the credit card slip across the counter for her to sign. Gradually her mind settled and she began to think about what she was doing.

A ten-year-old newspaper clipping and the final rambling exhortations of a dying woman, whose mental state was questionable, were the only slim clues she had to the very existence of her father. Jake? Monroe? The images in her mind were interchangeable, both fictional.

> *Azure streaks across the stratus clouds changed shape with the shifting winds.*
>
> *Monroe lay on his back staring until the world began to spin and he felt for a moment he might be tossed off the earth into space. The simple beauty of the sunset at odds with the crackle of gunfire and acrid stench of cordite and stale blood.*
>
> *His blood, he thought lazily...*

Sitting in the Ferrari for a long time staring at the ocean and the sail boats that moved along the Intra-Coastal waterway, she knew that the only thing to do was to begin the search at Key West and go wherever the trail led.

It was an exploration of her past and her future, an adventure into an unfamiliar world far from the secure cocoon of the mansion on the Narragansett Bay. But rather than frighten her, it gave her life a sudden meaning. The money from the trust fund was more than sufficient to keep her comfortable for a very long time and there was nothing else that consumed her every waking moment as much as the obsession to know her father.

To know Monroe.

Suddenly the day seemed full of purpose and promise, with the targa top stowed under the hood, her dark hair blowing in the wind, the

Ferrari settled comfortably into a high-speed cruise.

If she was aware of the speed, or that her hair was tangling into a mass of knots, she didn't show it. Even though she plummeted headlong towards an uncertain future, it was a relief to be clear of the claustrophobic atmosphere of the beautiful mansion on the Narragansett Bay and the responsibility of her sick mother. A blood red sun settled into a golden ocean beyond the low lying Keys, like a familiar painting she had seen many times before and now simply ignored.

Twenty years of resentment, bitterness and anger distilled into a single star that burned brightly in a refreshing feeling of sudden empowerment. Throwing her head back, she laughed in a heady rush of adrenaline.

Glancing briefly in the rear view mirror her face stared back accusingly.

Young beautiful clear blue eyes an interesting contrast to her dark hair. A Celtic look betraying her ancient ancestry.

Reaching up, annoyed by the sight of her own face, she altered the angle of the mirror until she could see the straight road behind reaching out of sight. Pinpoints of lights where other vehicles had switched on their headlamps speckled the descending blackness.

Thoughts settled on her mother and she felt the accusations rising again. Eve's death had given her a sense of relief and it angered her and again she shifted the emphasis to the obsession that had held her in its grip since she was a little girl.

One half of the spider's web she had been caught in all her life had dissolved away. But the other remained, with freedom still just out of reach.

Ahead, a small town lay sprawled along the seashore, languidly basking in the twilight, devoid of tourists at the moment. Easter break over and the obnoxious college kids back in school in controlled chaos, but Nikki slowed just the same.

Glancing at the fuel gauge hovering just above empty, she pulled into a brightly lit gas station where an elderly woman sat outside the office in an old rocking chair. A large electric fan positioned in front of her, watching as Nikki slowed to a stop.

By the time Nikki had climbed out of the car and opened the fuel tank cap, the woman had risen to her feet with difficulty and stood with the nozzle poised ready.

"How much?" The old woman's voice was soft, belying the almost ferocious look of her deeply tanned face.

"Fill it."

Nikki walked away a little, not wishing any conversation and stared down the road.

The woman looked her up and down. From the bare feet, jeans and tee shirt, to the Ferrari. Her face betraying nothing.

A mosquito buzzed and settled on Nikki's arm. She slapped and then scratched without seeming to notice.

"Best not scratch. Leave them be."

"What?"

"The mosquitoes. Just kinda ignore them. Better that way."

Nikki scratched again and slapped at a second and then a third, oblivious to the woman's advice. Then turned to see the woman replacing the nozzle.

"Cash or charge?"

"Charge."

The woman took the offered card and walked slowly back to the small clean office, Nikki following.

"This lotion'll keep the mosquitoes away." The old woman pointed to plastic bottles of 'Skin So Soft' on the counter.

"No thanks. Just the gas."

The old woman shrugged, shook her head slightly and wondered at the pride and arrogant ignorance of youth that would rather suffer than accept good advice.

Within two minutes, the Ferrari was up to speed again, and the old woman back in the rocking chair in front of the fan, watching the night steal across the Keys with the speed of a blanket being pulled across the land, leaving the islands as low silhouettes that momentarily disappeared until the moon rose to bathe land and sea in a soft silvery glow.

*   *   *

Jake settled into his routine at Owen's bar as tourists gathered outside clutching their cocktails and beer glasses to watch the sun descend into the ocean, hoping to catch sight of the flash that sparked across the horizon when the sun finally sank from sight.

The illusion was so slight that only a few saw it, but it didn't spoil the ritual of the sunset gathering. And every night without fail the faithful congregation gathered and worshipped the departing of the day. It was almost a religious experience.

And so was Jake's nightly routine.

The faded sign outside the bar proclaimed it *THE FISHING SMACK*, a corny name that had remained, and inside the decor indeed reminded its patrons that there had once been a thriving sponge fishing community in this area. But with the increasing tourist industry, small-scale commercial fishing was in decline and so was the bar, as the sport fishing boat owners had taken over and moved to the marinas.

The local clientele liked it that way.

It was a throwback to the old days before the Keys became a chic place to live. Before *'alternative lifestyles'* had taken over and moneyed power and sail boat owners ventured south between the hurricane seasons to race and indulge themselves in every excess known to man. That was the way Owen felt, and refused to install air-conditioning, pin ball machines, a jukebox or any other mechanical and electronic toys that may have increased his business.

And the local clientele liked the atmosphere.

It had the air of a seedy run-down reminder of a seedy run-down past. Indeed it had been the watering hole for many writers and artists, most of whom were long since deceased, and it was back in those days that Jake had first visited the establishment. Then he had been an outsider and his talent and youth mistrusted, but time and the vagaries of the artistic community had eroded the barriers and he was now a monument to what had been.

And the local clientele liked that too.

Owen was seventy-five, bald and beginning to succumb to the fat that old age and little exercise ravaged on a body that in its youth had been vibrant and athletic. His bright grey inquisitive eyes had seen just about everything and everybody pass in and out of the bar. Hemingway had been a friend, but such was Owen's reticence that very few people knew and those that did, never questioned him about the relationship.

Owen kept his friends' affairs to himself.

And the local clientele liked that best of all.

Faded photographs still adorned the walls; dollar bills pinned with the customers' names scrawled across them together with the date. It was a ritual from the days when fishermen, never knowing when they would get paid, would pin up the bills so that when they were impecunious, they would still have enough for at least one drink. Now it was just fun and gave the bar a homey atmosphere. It was comforting to the regulars to see their names and the dates on the bills, even to those that only frequented the bar once or twice a year as a pilgrimage, to sit quietly, hear the murmur of conversation and watch the slow inevitable game of chess.

Jake stretched over and moved his bishop across the board, removing one of Owen's rooks, then leaned back and absentmindedly stroked Frankie's arm as she stood behind him, looking down at the board.

Like the others in the community, Frankie kept very much to herself. Fleeing the dark misery of a life as the daughter of a Pittsburgh steel worker who liked to beat his wife and fondle his daughters. In Key West Frankie had found a niche where she could bury her painful past.

A Mulatto with a natural beauty that did not require make-up, she had the fine bones of her Norwegian mother and the light ebony colour of her Jamaican born father. Silver earrings were the extent of her vanity, for as the owner of a restaurant, she had many opportunities to watch the rich painted ladies that frequented Key West from their communities in New York, and had no desire to be like them.

She and Jake had met at her restaurant and drifted into a long-standing relationship that held no ties on either side, yet the very nature of their unspoken agreement was itself a commitment. Jake liked that she was quietly feminine, yet independent. She liked that he demanded nothing and gave friendship, love, laughter and a measure of emotional security.

It was also well known to those who frequented the bar that their healthy sex life ensured that nobody could come between them. But if they knew, they never spoke of it, for that too was one of the taboos of the bar. Everyone helped each other without question and everyone preserved each other's privacy.

"Check mate in two moves." Owen smiled and moved his queen into striking distance of Jake's king, removing a knight.

Jake studied the board.

He was in no hurry.

He never was.

A dozen eyes watched the game quietly, enjoying the balmy night air and the quiet companionship.

Jake lifted his glass of rum and sipped.

It was that time in the evening when he felt relaxed enough just to sip the liquor and enjoy Frankie's presence and the sight of the beautifully carved antique pieces on the polished board. The ceiling fan hummed quietly, creating a slight breeze to cool the skin in the heat of the night.

He held the bishop, feeling the smooth surface of the mahogany piece and with his other hand, splashed more rum into his glass. There was a gleam in his eye as he moved the bishop across the board taking a pawn.

"You're right. Check."

Owen stared at the board and moved his king one space, looking up into Jake's eyes as if daring him to go one better. Jake was still smiling and suddenly there was an air of quiet expectation in the bar.

Jake moved his rook and sat back contentedly, smiling broadly, eyes bloodshot, glass in hand.

"Check mate."

Owen stared at the board and then up at Jake.

"Never."

Frankie grinned and moved around to sit on the arm of Jake's chair.

"Oh yes," she murmured, her voice as soft as a gentle breeze in the rigging of a sailboat.

Owen rose like a volcano about to explode and stared down at the board.

Bar patrons smiled quietly as the nightly ritual drew to its close.

"Luck."

Jake laughed, a clean, clear, happy sound. "Chess is a game for lovers and poets, my friend. And you are neither."

Grunting in disgust Owen carefully stowed the pieces back into the felt lined box.

"And you are full of rum and bullshit, Jake. When you die. And I hope that will not be for some considerable time because my retirement depends upon your patronage. But when you die, I'm going to varnish you and stand you in the corner as a warning to others who want to beat me in my own bar."

Good-natured laughter echoed in the room as Owen crossed to the bar stowing the pieces beneath the row of liquor bottles.

"Stop bitching and bring another bottle," Jake said gently.

For a moment, a look of fleeting pain travelled across Frankie's face as she glanced down at Jake. He caught her eye and smiled fondly.

Owen banged a bottle on the bar. "I should have thrown you out years ago. You're a bad influence on my customers."

"Yeah right, Owen."

Again laughter rippled around the bar as the customers warmed to the ritual of the nightly banter. It eased the burdens of the day and prepared the way for a sleep where dreams were pleasant and plentiful, and the demons of the dark found no room to play. It was the friendly banter of two long-standing friends who knew each other's weaknesses and simply accepted the inherent decency they saw in each other.

At ten o'clock the bar slowly emptied. Jake and Frankie made their unsteady way along the street to the quay where the dinghy sat silently waiting amongst the other yacht tenders at the dinghy dock.

The moon had risen above the distant anchorage bathing the town in its silvery light, buildings taking on the appearance of an old Bogart black and white movie, Victorian houses ghostly in the night.

"The moon like a widow on a lonely vigil, pale and shivering, stares out across the vast unknown expanse, untouched by all that glistens; by all that pukes in protest." Flinging his arms outstretched in supplication, he staggered and nearly fell.

Frankie held on to him tightly. "My, my. We are cynical tonight aren't we?"

"I'm a Florida Conch Killer."

"What?"

"Nothing. It doesn't matter anyway."

For a moment the demons had surfaced and stolen Jake's safety net, before the alcohol drummed them back into the forgotten recesses of his mind.

"Don't even know what I'm talking about anymore."

But he felt a chill steal over his body in the warm night air as if a ghost had run its clammy hand across his back.

He laughed suddenly, stopped and took Frankie into his arms, holding her face and staring into her eyes with a ferocious intensity. But his voice was soft and loving.

"I'm a cranky drunk. Pay no attention." Holding her at arm's length and looking over her body with satisfaction. "And now I just want to jump your bones until the pelicans cry 'enough'."

Frankie giggled, breaking away from him, dancing seductively, her hips swaying to a silent rhythm. "Baby, I'll be lucky if you stay awake long enough to take off your pants."

"It's never been a problem."

She laughed quietly and swayed back to him, kissing him softly, rubbing her body against his.

"Mama's secret method, that's why."

*   *   *

The fifty-foot wooden ketch, based on a design by L. Francis Herreshof, that swung to its mooring a little way separated from the other yachts, was Jake's home.

The fact that he didn't fully appreciate the lineage of this vessel, with its sweeping sheer, clipper bow and classic long shallow keel, meant that he simply did not know much about L. Francis Herreshof.

Based on the Mobjack design drawings, the builder had modified the layout, converting it to a centre cockpit and aft cabin with little damage to the original design. Built in the Chesapeake Bay, by a builder who prided himself in his skill to meld traditional wood design and craftsmanship with modern techniques, she was the perfect example of using two different building methods to create an ageless beauty.

Thin strips of western red cedar, cold moulded in three layers, the first two at forty-five degrees to each other, the last, horizontal, sheathed in fibreglass comprised the hull, which had then been painted and polished to perfection. Yet one big error by the builder would prove fatal. He had reduced the keel depth by a foot and increased the ballast weight in order to be able to ply the shallow waters of the Florida Keys. And one small error in the starboard garboard planking, where the keel met the under-body, had gone unattended. Laid by an apprentice, the epoxy mix had been the wrong ratio and the adhesion of the planks along the length of the keel under-body joint, were not as secure as they might have been.

On the surface everything had seemed perfect but, over the years, these errors had time to weaken the keel structure.

That was sixteen years ago. Now the hull needed a new coat of paint, brightwork restoring, steering chain and cables, cutlass bearing and flax packing replacing, not to mention lines, sheets, some blocks and sails.

In spite of all that, she was still a commanding sight. Like Jake, the yacht was worn, faded, yet could still turn heads. The elegance and pride of the past could still be seen beneath the battered exterior.

Slipping alongside, Jake allowed the sides of the inflatable to slide carelessly along the hull, until Frankie stretched up and secured a line to a midships cleat, then climbed aboard. She stood on the side deck and looked down as Jake pulled up the outboard, then looped a line from the transom to a stern cleat. Tonight he wasn't going to lift the dinghy to the davits; the effort would be too great. Besides he had other things on his mind.

Looking up he watched as Frankie slowly slipped out of her dress, allowing the thin material to fall to the deck. Her breasts pushed firmly against the white cotton brassiere and Jake could see the swell of her womanhood beneath her panties. Her thighs were a little heavy, flaring out into firm hips, curving into a waist that had once been a little slimmer.

Watching her moving to the sound of the silent rhythms that were a part of her heritage; hips swaying in the moonlight; breasts, freed from the cotton brassiere quivering hypnotically before his eyes he was a prisoner of her eroticism, rum and the moonlight. The yacht, warm ocean breeze and her naked before him, captured his body and froze his mind as no drug could possibly achieve. Swirling, swaying, her image seemed to pulsate. Astern in the clear night sky, the moon melted into a dazzling dancing light, at one with the ocean and his senses, transporting him from this time, this place, to a suspension of his very soul.

Reality was unreality.

Time, infinite.

She knew that his erection was growing as he looked at her, and she enjoyed the image in her mind and the butterfly flutters in her groin that always pre-empted sex. This was the moment that they both looked forward to the most at the close of day. To feel the warm night with a cooling air that flowed across their skin and the freedom to stand naked and unashamed before each other.

This was more than physical, more than emotional. This moment transcended the earthly plane and their human needs and desires. This moment was joined to the infinite, to the universe, to a point where the sky met the ocean in an explosion of life.

Standing silent shadows on the gently moving deck, they kissed, then Jake led her down into the saloon and back to the aft cabin where he lay her on the berth, slipped her panties from her legs and gazed at her for a long moment.

There was something about the sight of her naked before him that was deeper that simply sex or the need to procreate; it was a joining of themselves; an abandoning of all their safety nets and displaying to each other their complete trust.

Love and sex were merely words. What they experienced transcended definition, became a truth without the boundaries of mere words; but it was bittersweet, because she knew that the moment could be repeated whenever she wanted, but so could the disappointment.

Their mutual orgasm was long and satisfying and then Jake fell immediately to sleep. Frankie stared at him for a long time, until the moon passed by the port-light and his face drifted into shadow and then she lay back and closed her eyes.

This was not the perfection she had dreamed of as a child, or as a young woman, but after the experience of all the past unsatisfactory relationships she'd had, this was safe, satisfying and she knew deep in her heart, lasting.

Age and experience had taught her that the knight in shining armour was a myth best preserved in storybooks. And for a time, she'd deliberately sought not to have children to save them from the disappointment of puberty, and the disillusionment of maturity.

Perhaps she did not believe that, and yet perhaps she knew that the scars of her abused childhood would never heal completely, and the fear of creating a child that would suffer the same way was strong and undeniable.

Unskilful surgery to abort a ten-week foetus by an inexperienced and greedy doctor had solved the problem in the most terrifying way possible. The memory of the pain and misery still haunted her and guilt remained as an unwelcome guest in her soul.

At times such as these, after she and Jake had made love and he was sleeping softly, the rum ensuring a dreamless sleep, she thought of what they might have had together. But she knew it was her dreams made flesh and the natural urge to procreate with the man she thought she loved.

If there was emptiness in her life, it was manifest in the dark of the night, echoing with the lap of the water against the hull as the tide rose with the passage of the moon.

She was with him because he was safe and she trusted in her ability to control him easily with rum, sex and a power that she had been aware of since early childhood and only practiced occasionally. But she did not admit that to herself. It was here in the silence of the night and in the long moments before sleep forced away the unpleasant thoughts that the Truth nearly caught up with her.

*   *   *

As Frankie gradually drifted off to sleep, the red Ferrari slowed to a crawl.

Nikki, tired and irritable, drove quietly through the town past the airport and into Key West proper, looking for the area that was in the faded press clippings. A slight breeze carried the fragrance of frangipani and hibiscus. Banyan trees appeared ghostly in the car's headlights, silhouetted by faint yellow street lights, looking like giant wooden webs as she drove through the streets of Old Town Key West looking for the harbour, glancing at the press clipping to get the image set in her mind. Even at this time of night, the heat and humidity hung like a cloak between the houses, caught in the thick foliage. Things had changed and the harbour was different, but the boom where the Marlin had hung was the same, preserved as a monument; painted now, but the angles silhouetted against the skyline were unmistakable.

Parking the car and retrieving the targa top from beneath the hood, she spent twenty minutes sitting on the sea wall looking out across the quiet anchorage of Man-of-War Harbour. Then returned to the car and slept fitfully until dawn broke without fuss on a town waking to yet another sun soaked day.

All the sand from all the beaches in all the Keys seem to have blown into her eyes overnight and her joints were stiff from twelve hours cramped in the sports car. There was some movement on the quayside as the men who made their living from the ocean, trudged to work. Casual fishermen sat at the end of the pier and cast their rods without any real confidence, enjoying the rhythm of the exercise as a pleasant way to greet the new day.

Nikki wandered over to where a couple of older men sat watching the sun rise, plastic travel mugs full of hot steaming coffee in their hands. They looked as if they belonged to the Keys and to the ocean over which they stared, a permanent reminder of the past.

"Excuse me."

Both turned at the sound of her voice and looked at her without expression; waiting.

Nikki slapped at an early morning mosquito and scratched. Both men shifted their gaze to her arm.

"I'm looking for a man called Jake Kimble. I believe he lives here but I don't have the address."

The elder of the two tipped back his baseball cap and smiled briefly, then pointed across the anchorage to Jake's boat.

"It's the ketch. The Herreshof," he paused and nodded to her arm where she was still rubbing the now bleeding bite. "Best not scratch."

Nikki ignored the advice and looked out across to the yacht.

"How do I get out there?" she demanded rudely.

Baseball Cap had lifted the coffee mug to his lips, and was cautiously sipping the scalding black liquid. His friend nodded absentmindedly and peered up at Nikki.

"Reckon you're gonna have to wait for Peter."

"Peter?"

"Right. Water taxi Captain. He'll be starting his rounds 'bout seven. Good boat builder too," he offered, contemplating the anchorage with a furrowed brow and scratching his head. "Picks up Frankie first. Then Harold. Should be on time," he chuckled and turned to Baseball Cap as if sharing a personal and very obscure joke.

Baseball Cap wheezed asthmatically. "Should be."

Soft chuckles rose with the steam from their coffee as Nikki walked back to the car, anger in check, waiting to have Peter the water taxi Captain pointed out to her. She had waited fifteen years and could wait a little longer.

Gradually the town came to life as the sun climbed higher. Nothing that would tell much except that the working day began early, while the tourists woke with hangovers and contemplated another day at the many beach bars. Sleep overcame her again and she dozed restlessly, unaware of the whaler as it cut through the water of the anchorage, slowed and stopped alongside the ketch.

A woman jumped down into the boat and it sped off across the calm water to a smaller yacht and picked up another passenger.

Laughter close by woke Nikki. She stared blearily as a young couple skated past on roller blades. Switching her attention to the quay she saw a tall, lean, handsome young man talking with Baseball Cap, who pointed without looking as Nikki locked the Ferrari's doors and walked across the parking lot.

Peter was in his early twenties, with long blonde hair tied back in a pony tail and when he grinned it was with an open boyish friendliness. A Londoner who had washed up in Key West five years earlier, having worked his passage across the Atlantic with a yacht delivery skipper on a forty foot catamaran, he had applied his skills building ten foot wooden sailing dinghies in his spare time while operating the water taxi and working at the repair yard. He ambled slowly across to Nikki.

"Hi. Norm tells me you want a lift," his voice was soft with the hint of laughter.

Nikki stared past him expressionlessly. She had her mother's ability to intimidate. "How much to take me to Jake Kimble's boat?"

"Two bucks," he paused. "If I could take you."

Her blue eyes stared at him disconcertingly direct. "And why can't you?"

Peter felt a chill suddenly sweep over him and for a moment was thrown off balance. The boyish grin faded from his face and the two old men began to take an interest, sensing the sudden hostility.

"Jake doesn't like visitors. Likes to be left alone. You don't get there without an invitation."

Nikki's eyes never left his face. "He's expecting me."

Peter watched her coolly, realizing that he was attracted to her and yet wary of her overt hostility. "Never told me 'bout it. I'd be expecting you otherwise."

Nikki drew her wallet from her bag and flipping it open, flashed the driver's license under his nose. He reluctantly took his eyes off her and glanced down.

"I'm his daughter."

Peter stared at the photograph and the name then slowly lifted his eyes to hers. "I guess you are." He grinned suddenly. "It's still two bucks."

But the comment was wasted. Nikki was already halfway down the steps towards the whaler.

Peter glanced at the two old men. "That, as they say, is a daughter with an attitude."

They grinned and chuckled as he followed her into the boat.

*   *   *

The whaler sped away from the ketch in a plume of spray, Peter watching her standing on the foredeck and appreciating her silhouette against the rising sun.

Nikki waited until it was almost back to the quay and then turned and climbed into the cockpit. She slid back the companionway hatch, opened the short narrow louvered double doors and climbed down the companionway steps into the saloon.

Her heart begun to beat a little faster, and the palms of her hands were sweaty with an unwanted and unaccustomed nervousness. Now she was here she felt she would rather be anywhere else instead, but the whaler was already at the quay and Peter gone to check his messages and work on a wooden trawler that had run up on a reef and needed six planks replacing.

"Hello. Anybody home?" she said falteringly, her heart beating rapidly.

The boat swung quietly to its mooring, creaking slightly. It was the first time Nikki had ever been aboard a sailing yacht like this. Her experiences confined to small powerboats. She stared around the saloon, taking in the clean but untidy space.

The interior was a beautiful example of the cabinetmaker's art. In love with the look and feel of exotic woods, the builder had designed and crafted the cabins to be a testament to his skill.

Galley to starboard, equipped with a three burner Propane stove, fridge/freezer run from two DC Compressors and double stainless steel sink, complete with pressurized hot and cold water and a foot operated sea water pump. Inch square white ceramic tiles graced the counter tops.

To port, a short narrow passageway led to the aft cabin, past the navigation station from which someone had removed all the electronic navigation aids. The chart table was piled high with old manuscripts, some in padded envelopes. Yet in spite of the evidence of life, it was as if the person who slept here did not *live* on the yacht, simply *existed* there.

Beams of sunlight shone from one of the starboard port-lights, highlighting a framed photograph, dusty and askew on the forward bulkhead.

A photograph Nikki knew well.

It was strangely comforting and the tension that had rolled her stomach into a tight knot eased as she stared at the faces in the picture; dust coated the glass, smearing away beneath her fingertips to reveal a young looking Jake standing beside the Ferrari with a tiny baby in his arms. Beside him, a woman that could have been Nikki, so closely did she resemble her mother.

Suddenly irrational anger again gripped her. "Hello. Hello. Anybody here?"

She banged open the door to the forward cabin, turning sideways to pass through. Another door to the right led to a small head with teak seat, stainless steel shower fitment and stainless steel sink. The counter top tiled in the same way as the galley.

Then she turned her attention to the empty double V-berth spanning the width of the boat and tapering to the bow. There were books on the shelves and women's clothes in the lockers. Nikki fleetingly thought they were a little garish, not her style.

Returning to the saloon and walking on through to the aft cabin, she failed to appreciate that beneath the dust and untidiness, was exquisite woodwork. It showed in the carefully inlaid strips on the saloon table and the way the drawers and doors opened without a murmur once the safety catches were tripped. Settee cushions were a deep sumptuous maroon colour that fitted perfectly with the teak wood.

It should have been dark inside. But the white painted coachroof, many opening brass port-lights and an overhead butterfly hatch, kept the interior surprisingly light.

The door to the aft cabin was open and as she entered she saw Jake sprawled across the berth that lay along the centre line of the boat, a full queen size, the bedclothes barely covering his naked body.

Seeing him was a shock. The memory of a four-year-old child reinforced with ancient photographs, had burned an image in her mind of a young and vital man, instead of the head of greying hair, beard and lined face she saw before her.

This was not Monroe.

For the second time her resolve began to weaken and she nearly turned and walked quietly away, but there was nowhere for her to go, and again, anger burned brightly. Reaching forward she shook his shoulder roughly. Jake stirred slightly, turned onto his side and, mouth open, began to snore very gently.

Nikki shook him again, wrinkling her nose from the smell of stale rum, but he was deeply asleep, the residual effects of the alcohol delaying consciousness for a little longer.

Thrusting her chin forward, just as she had as a little girl, she turned, went back into the saloon, found what she was looking for in one of the lower galley lockers and filled the plastic jug from the cold water tap; then stepped back into the cabin and looked down at Jake and emptied the contents of the jug onto his face.

Consciousness drifted back as if he was walking along a dark tunnel to a pinpoint of light. Then suddenly Jake was awake, with the sour taste of stale rum in his mouth and slight pounding at his temple. Gradually he realized that the strange sensation he felt all over his body was water.

Opening his eyes, he stared up blearily at the face above him, focusing slowly on the face of a young woman framed by dark hair, looking down at him seriously.

"Christ. Eve? Is that you Eve? Shit."

Nikki stared down at him feeling a growing surge of disgust and contempt. "You don't even know me."

Jake rubbed his eyes not knowing whether he was awake or still asleep and dreaming. "Eve?"

"She died last week." Nikki turned and stepped out of the cabin.

Jake stared after the apparition. "What?"

Rubbing his eyes again he knew that this was not an apparition, but the image and reality were confusing, the past living and breathing in the present.

"I'll make coffee," Nikki called over her shoulder.

"I hate coffee."

The voice and image were real and there was a growing dread inside him, as the demons suddenly appeared, marching from his subconscious into the cold light of day.

"Where's Frankie?"

"That your dog?" Feeling mean, she slammed the kettle onto the stove and lit the gas. Then rummaged through a locker for a couple of clean cups as Jake pulled on a pair of short pants.

"Who the hell are you? What are you doing on my boat?" Jake tripped and almost fell, then sat down for a moment to ease the pounding in his head, before stepping into the saloon.

"I'm making coffee." She turned and looked at him as he stood eyeing her, tousled haired, bloodshot eyes, bent over slightly as he leaned against the saloon table.

"Told you. I hate coffee. Who the hell are you?" He knew, but still it seemed like a dream; a dream he wanted to wake from and have everything return to normal.

"Don't you recognise your own daughter?"

What he saw was her mother as he had always remembered her.

Beautiful.

Cool.

Distant memories of passion and lust rose in him and appalled him with their insidiously creeping insistence, their sudden strength as if the past had become the present and the smell, emotions and sounds of the bar in Honolulu had invaded the yacht and changed his world. Appalling in their clarity and power.

Shaking his head, trying to fight down the passion of the past in the hope that this was not real. "Nicola?"

"I always hated that. My name is Nikki."

For a long moment they stared at each other and the years fell away as if only separated by a gossamer drape. The girl, the mother, the baby, his daughter. Images like flash cards dazzled before his eyes until he had to turn away and reach behind the settee for the bottle of rum.

Nikki watched as he crossed to the sink and searched for a glass amongst the soiled dishes; found one, rinsed it roughly, sloshed rum into it until the liquor threatened to overflow, steadied his hand, tipped the contents down his throat then refilled the glass.

She watched him swallow the second full glass and cough. "You have to drink at this time in the morning?" It came out before she could stop it and she saw the flash in his eyes.

"You don't like it you can leave."

"Thanks for the warm welcome."

Jake shrugged and filled the glass again. The pounding in his head was easing, his vision clearing.

"What are you doing here anyway? Didn't think your mother even told you 'bout me."

Lifting the kettle from the stove, she poured water into two cups, then replaced it carefully. Residual heat from the ring brought the kettle back up to boiling again and made it sing softly, gradually dying away as it cooled. For a moment she didn't know what to say; didn't know what she was doing here except that she had to be here.

"She died. You're all I've got." It was a little girl's plea and she was angry with herself for sounding so lost and alone. "I can see why she left you."

"Is that what she told you?"

Nikki turned away, hiding the pain that suddenly crossed her face, not wanting to show him any weakness; but he saw it none-the-less and cursed himself.

"She always kept track of you. When I asked her, she told me I should find out for myself."

"That's always a disappointment. Like finding out Santa Claus doesn't exist."

Suddenly a scene of her fourth Christmas jumped into her mind, startlingly clear. She had woken in the middle of the night seeing Jake placing the presents at the bottom of her bed; white beard slipping and she could clearly see his face. In the background a sound of giggling, and framed against the hallway light in the doorway, her mother swaying and nearly falling, recovering her balance and giggling softly.

Jake sniggered as he placed the presents and then he stopped and looked down at her.

She was sure he could not see that her eyes were just the littlest bit open, because he suddenly looked very sad and reaching out, touched her arm softly, stroking the tender white skin, then quickly slipped the beard back into place and left the room. His expression had stayed with her, and so had the bewilderment she felt.

"I remember. I was four years old."

Jake nodded. His memory wasn't so good, but for a moment they had a link. A solid connection; if only he could remember. But the rum and his need to forget had eroded his memory, and her bright excited eyes made him uncomfortable.

He turned away. "How did she die?"

The moment was gone. Nikki dropped her gaze, then looked up and out through the companionway hatch at the blue sky.

"Just died. That's all. Brain tumour."

"Oh. She suffer?"

"I don't think so."

"Good."

The casual word stung her, anger returning as she swung around to face him.

"Why should you care?"

He shrugged, the movement an attempt to show his unconcern.

"You're right. Why should I?" He crossed to the companionway hatch and looked out across the harbour. "You seen Frankie anywhere?"

Anger boiled over and as he turned she swung her fist, catching him flush in the mouth, sending him backwards into the companionway steps and she felt an exhilaration followed by a sharp misery, the mixed emotions running out-of-control through her.

Jake's head bounced off the steps and for a moment the whole saloon swung in a lazy arc before stabilising, reality returning with the pain as his lip swelled and he could taste blood in his mouth.

"Christ."

"She thought the sun shone out of your ass. Boy was she ever wrong."

"She teach you to punch too?"

Nikki took another swing, but Jake caught her small fist in his hand, feeling the smooth soft young skin, the first time he'd touched his daughter in fifteen years and the pain of the last time struck deep inside him, converting to anger as they faced each other.

"Once I let you get away with. Not a second time. I don't know why you've come, but if you think you can walk into my life and beat up on me, you're wrong."

As the words poured out, he knew that the anger was really directed at himself, at Eve, at the whole mess they'd fallen into all those years ago. Dropping her hand he turned, looking for the bottle and the glass, found them and poured another generous shot of rum. Then sat down at the saloon table and looked up at her.

"I didn't choose..." His voice trailed off. He was confused, not wanting the conversation to go in that direction as he stared down into the rum, noticing small black flakes floating along the bottom of the glass.

"Choose what?" Nikki intuitively sensed that the truth was close.

But Jake shrugged and his eyes closed, shutting out the world for a moment, wondering if the image before him would disappear. "It doesn't matter," he muttered, the confusion of the unreality of having his daughter here and the unrelenting hangover blending into a seemingly impossible hallucination.

"Maybe it matters to me."

There was a constriction in her throat, but Jake just opened his eyes and kept staring fixedly at the bottom of the glass.

After a while he slowly raised his eyes to Nikki, seeing her clearly for the first time since he had woken. She was the spitting image of her mother and Jake felt both the joy and the pain together as he looked at her young beauty.

"I didn't mean... What I mean is... Look... Why don't we start this again?"

"What?"

"Well, you go out and come back in again. I mean... Hell I don't know what I mean." Suddenly he felt very uncomfortable, voice tailing off echoing his awkwardness, and she felt a softness steal into her heart as she looked at his blue eyes.

"Hi Nikki. You're all grown up," he said at an attempt at lightness, then looked away, embarrassed, uncomfortable, not knowing how to behave or what to say. "I'll just get cleaned up."

She watched as he shambled back to the aft cabin and closed the door. Nikki stared at the door, tears in her eyes.

"Hi Jake," she whispered and then angrily wiped away the tears.

FOUR

Beneath the surface of dust, where his hand had wiped the metal clean, the paint was as bright as the first day he had taken delivery of the car two decades ago. He stroked the smooth curving lines as if he was touching the hips and thighs of a woman. There was a beautiful strength that was common to both, and there were fractional moments of memory that he felt as he looked at the Ferrari.

Eve's smile.

The sound of her voice.

A faint soulful fragment of a familiar but long forgotten song.

Even the momentary smell of that day was suddenly strong in his nostrils. It seemed silly that a machine had brought those emotions back to him, but at the time it had been a symbol of his success and of his decline, and he knew now as he walked around the car, that it really only meant that back then he could afford to spend the money. It had simply reflected the size of his bank account. Nothing more.

That was why he had left it in the garage when the marriage was over. Now it was as it should have been then, just a startlingly beautiful object. A credit to the car manufacturer's art, and he enjoyed seeing it once again.

Nikki watched him as he studied the car, lost in his own world. Her mother was an abstract link that tenuously held them together, but the car was physical; it was here; a solid object that connected them from the past down the years to this moment.

She felt a slight adrenaline rush. A nervousness that both pleased and annoyed her. "Mom kept it in the garage. She wouldn't drive it. Wouldn't let anyone drive it." She laughed suddenly without humour at the absurdity of her mother's obsession. "Every month she had a mechanic check it over and a car detailing service polish it."

It *had* been an obsession, not just an absurd obsession, but a sick obsession. When she was growing up, Nikki viewed it as amusing, then boring, then annoying, now it seemed sad that this woman who never wanted to hear her ex-husband's name mentioned, should keep the car as a perverse monument to their failed marriage. There was something sinister about it.

"I thought you'd like it back."

Jake had completed a circuit of the car and looked up at her, smiling.

"It's yours. I have no use for it. Hell, I haven't driven a car in ten years."

It sounded absurd, but it was the truth.

"I thought it might mean something to you."

Jake's eyes clouded over and he looked away, the memories painful.

"It did. Once. It's yours."

"Thanks," she said without enthusiasm.

Jake glanced at her quickly, feeling the connection and not knowing how to deal with it. There was an enormous feeling of deja vu as he looked at her standing beside the car. Suddenly he was back on the driveway at the mansion on the Narragansett Bay and Eve was standing beside the car, holding Nikki in her arms. Jake had set the camera on a tripod and focused the lens before sliding on the fifteen-second timer and running quickly to stand next to Eve, Nikki and the car. He could almost feel the boyish exuberance of that moment. Even taste the delicate smell of wisteria blossoms and the orange shampoo Eve had used that morning. The memory made him short of breath, and as he looked at Nikki and saw Eve. It was a confusing unwanted emotion.

"Hungry?"

"Sure."

As they walked along the street by the harbour, Jake explained the eccentricities of Key West as if he were a tour guide with a stranger. In a sense he was, for they were strangers, held together by dusty memories and a name they both shared. She listened with polite interest as he explained his own philosophy of living in Key West and she began to feel the atmosphere he created in his novels that she knew so well and for a moment it was as if Monroe was speaking from the tattered pages of the books.

"To be a drop-out in this town requires money. It's sixties attitudes with nineties economics, but for the most, the struggle's worthwhile for the satisfaction of living in a part of Paradise. Even though the mosquitoes, 'no-see-ums', heat and humidity take a lot of getting used to."

He looked at the bites on Nikki's arms and legs that were so numerous they were beginning to blend. She had forgotten them in the emotion of the moment.

"Get you some cream for those and try not to scratch. Best if you don't scratch."

His voice faded into the background as she turned the pages of his book in her mind, still searching for Monroe.

Monroe pasted the cream over the parched skin, speaking softly to the woman who lay shivering in the heat in the bottom of his boat, staring up at him with wide sun burned eyes that could barely see. Seven days in a life-raft in the open ocean had shrivelled her skin, and the sun and salt combined to reduce the tissue to red raw oozing pustules that caused her to shiver violently.

Although she watched as Jake bought the cream from the elderly pharmacist and they exchanged pleasantries as Jake explained that Nikki was his daughter, she paid no attention. She was still embroiled in the novel and the sudden image of Jake and Monroe as the same person. What she saw was a contradiction. The actions were that of Monroe, but not the vision she saw before her. Both images collided in her imagination and jumbled reality into an uncertain, uncomfortable sensation.

However, for some inexplicable reason, she began to feel a certain sense of well being as she walked with him, seeing the local people smiling and greeting him, surprised that she was his daughter, but the comfort was tinged with sadness and a disconcerting confusion. Jake was trying to keep the conversation light, impersonal, away from areas that would hurt and dredge up the dark past. Oddly and annoyingly, the Ferrari had partially opened tender wounds that the demons waited to bring forth and he fought to prevent their return.

Unconsciously he steered her towards Frankie's seafood restaurant, the front of which was open to the harbour, with tables behind a low, white, wooden picket fence. An awning saved the customers from the direct heat of the sun. The name on the sign above the awning said simply *'FRANKIE'S PLAICE'*, a tongue-in-cheek play on words that Frankie had thought amusing, but went completely over the heads of most people who thought she just couldn't spell. Nikki did not see it and followed Jake to a table where they could watch the parade along the waterfront.

Mary, Frankie's business partner, strolled across to them smiling.

"Hey Jake, what's goin' on?" She stared at the purple swelling on his lip. "You run into a door again?"

He touched his mouth suddenly and then grinned at her. "Hi Mary. Nothing much. What's the special?"

Mary tipped back her head and laughed happily. "You kiddin'? You know there's no special."

She glanced quickly from Jake to Nikki and back to Jake. Eyebrows raised, a quirky smile on her lips.

"Mary. This is my daughter Nikki."

Mary raised her eyebrows higher and looked across appraisingly at Nikki.

"You're his daughter? Have you got a problem or what girl," she laughed again before turning back to Jake. "Frankie's in back. You want the usual?"

Jake nodded.

"You honey?"

"Oh. Lemonade. Thanks."

As Mary started to walk away, she glanced over her shoulder with a mischievous grin. "I'll tell Frankie you're here. Back in a minute."

Nikki looked at Jake with mock surprise, a sudden and violent feeling of jealously invading her consciousness.

"Frankie's not a dog?"

He looked confused, not knowing quite what she was talking about, then followed her eyes as Frankie approached the table.

Nikki turned to look at Jake.

"Frankie?"

"Frankie."

Jake motioned to Nikki by way of introduction.

"This is Nikki."

"Nikki? Your daughter?"

"The same."

Familial instincts pounced to the surface and Nikki grinned maliciously. She hadn't intended it so and some detached part of her watched and was appalled.

"I was just telling Jake I thought you were a dog."

Frankie's eyes grew cold, her smile fading like snow on a hot plate.

"Really," she said softly, her voice barely above a whisper and turned to Jake, her eyes glistening like black coals. "Enjoy your meal. The catfish is excellent."

Like Nikki, some part of her watched and wished it could be different, but the turmoil she felt at this first meeting and what she perceived to be a snub, was too much. Possessiveness shut down her warmth and chilled the moment, but even as she walked away she cursed her stupidity.

Nikki watched her go. "I didn't mean it like that. I meant..." Her voice trailed off and she looked helplessly at Jake who had closed his eyes. It was the start of the nightmare he had hoped he would never have to face.

Hell, Jake hoped he would never have to face anything more challenging than a hangover ever again.

"Who would you like to insult next?"

"It wasn't intentional."

"Just comes naturally you mean?"

This was not going the way it should. Slowly, persistently, she was distancing herself from the one person whom she had sought to find and get to know.

As if to echo her thoughts, Jake's question lanced into her mind.

"Why did you come? It wasn't just to deliver the Ferrari."

"I had to see for myself just what had become of my father. It took a year to trace you," she lied, trying to make him feel guilty.

"A year huh?"

"Mom didn't die last week. She died last year."

This time the lie caught her.

"No she didn't. She died on the 20th. Last week," Jake said quietly, his eyes boring into her.

She felt the flush start up her neck and spread to her face. "You knew and you didn't bother to contact me?" she countered hotly.

Guilt welled up in his soul, the demons taking advantage of his weakness.

"Shit. Of all the great families in the world, I had to be born into this one." It was a childlike comment to make, but right now she felt like a child.

Why did Jake make her feel this way?

Sam was the same age as Jake and yet he had always made her feel like a mature adult.

But on reflection, that too had proved to be a lie.

And as she sat there, she felt alienated and the stranger she didn't want to be. There was a confusion she didn't understand. A longing to stay and desperation to leave.

Mary stood ten feet away, wondering whether to interrupt the family debate, deciding that in her experience it was not a good idea to mess between father and daughter.

Jake caught her eye and signalled for another badly needed drink.

Mary placed the drinks on the table, gave Jake a warning look and walked away.

"Yell when you want to order."

Grasping the glass like a man dying of thirst, he drank half the rum without pausing, feeling the liquor burn as it went down. Nikki watched from beneath lowered lids. To her it was the same thing she'd seen every day of her life until her mother had died and a resolve hardened in her heart. As yet she had no idea in what form that resolve would take, but she knew she couldn't live with a drunk.

"So you know Mom died in a sanatorium?"

"It was in the obituary."

"What else?"

"How do you mean?"

"What else do you know?"

Jake looked up, not at her, but at a couple of middle-aged ladies who had just entered the restaurant, their jewellery gaudily out of place at this time of the morning and in this setting.

"How was that Swiss school?"

"I needed a father more."

Jake didn't respond. Briefly they locked eyes before he turned away again, watching the ladies discussing at which table they should sit. Finally they decided and, grumbling about the weather, the mosquitoes and the lack of decent food anywhere in town, sat down.

"Why?"

"I cared."

"That was big of you."

"How come a cute little four-year-old became such a monster?"

"Maybe she's just like her father."

"I don't think I like you very much."

As soon as he had spoken, he was sorry, seeing the pain show briefly in her eyes as she looked down quickly at the menu.

Silence as tangible as the heat of the sun rising higher in the sky stretched between them. He searched for something to say to ease the tension.

"Listen. Why don't we eat later? I'll show you around. Okay?"

She moved her head slightly to one side, without looking up and for a moment he saw the four-year-old and he wanted to reach out and crush her to him, but he did not know how.

"Sure. Kinda lost my appetite anyway."

Jake downed the drink and waved to Mary who nodded and concentrated on the two little ladies.

*   *   *

White sails dotted the ocean as father and daughter motored around the headland. Further out, coastal sailors were taking advantage of the steady breeze and enjoying a day of sailing without the burdens of landlocked trivia.

Nikki found relief in the cooling wind, although her skin burned through the sunscreen smeared across the top of her shoulders.

They didn't talk on the half hour trip around the headland to the beach, but when she saw its gently curving pristine white sand, with palm trees swaying slightly against a backdrop of slash pine, she fell in love with it immediately.

The small lagoon was shallow; dark where the sea grass grew; turquoise where the sand was bare; a darker brown where the coral reef barred the entrance to anything but shallow draft boats.

Silence flooded the deserted lagoon as Jake cut the engine. The only sounds were the gentle lapping of wavelets on the beach and rustle of palm leaves in the breeze.

They dragged the dinghy up the sand a short way and she watched as Jake took the small anchor and dug it into the beach, testing the holding power with a couple of quick pulls.

Satisfied, he turned and walked along the deserted beach to a lean-to shack, partially hidden behind the palm trees, backing onto a thick grove of slash pine. Nikki followed feeling the hot sand on the balls of her bare feet.

The lean-to was a fairly substantial hut, with shelves containing many of the conch shells she had seen on the yacht. They smelled of dead fish and she wrinkled her nose in disgust. Jake ignored her and opened a small chest, rummaging around before passing her a pair of flippers, mask and snorkel.

"Ever snorkelled before?"

"Once or twice."

"These should fit."

"Frankie's?"

"Does it matter?"

She shrugged and Jake turned back to the chest, taking out a set for himself.

Nikki was looking out across the beach. "It's just so beautiful."

"Nobody comes here. It's the best place for conch in all the Keys." He shrugged as she glanced at him unbelievingly. "Well I like to think so."

"I've never seen live conch."

Jake closed the chest and walked down to the water's edge.

"Guess that expensive education was just a complete waste of time then." The accusation had no barb to it, the tone faintly scolding, gently mocking. "They like sea grass. Kinda like cows. They're slow and they eat a lot."

He waded into the water, spat into the mask and rubbed the glass with his fingertips, then rinsed it out with seawater. "Helps keep it from misting."

Nikki did the same. "Is this all you do all day?"

"As opposed to what?"

"Work."

"Oh that." He rinsed the snorkel and wet his hair down before pushing it back from his forehead and fitting the mask.

"Gave that up years ago. Nothing but ulcers, taxes and problems."

"So what do you do?"

"My home is paid for. I've money in the bank and my wants are very few and inexpensive."

"Except for the booze."

Jake rinsed the flippers and checked to see if there were any breaks in the rubber as Nikki busily adjusted the straps on her mask.

"It's just a simple pleasure."

"It killed Mom," she said meanly. She did not want the conversation to go this way, but something drove her, rationalising that it was his fault and that he brought out the worst in her. But it was a lame excuse for her inadequacies and confusion. "I found an old Time magazine article about you. That's how I found you."

"Pretty long shot."

"It worked."

Strangely he remembered the incident from so long ago. Somehow the reporter had found him, quickly snapped a photo and run before Jake could react. It took a few phone calls to some old friends to find the newspaper, but even then it didn't stop the article from appearing.

"Clever."

"Mom kept all your clippings."

"So you said."

"She loved you."

Again there was little response from him as he screwed-up his eyes against the glare of the sun.

"Why did you leave?" she probed, not wanting to break the communication.

"To get away from questions like that. You sure you're not a reporter from Newsweek?" he glanced at her carefully, a little fearfully. "No. You look too much like your mother."

"That's what everyone says." She struggled with the strap of the mask.

"But you behave like me. You're pushy." He took the mask from her tightened the strap and handed it back.

"I learned that on my own. It was a question of survival."

"You coming in or not?"

"I don't have a swimsuit."

"Improvise." Sitting down in the water, he lifted his feet, sliding on the flippers, then paddled slowly out towards the beds of sea grass they had seen as they motored into the lagoon.

Slipping self-consciously out of her tee shirt and jeans, revealing a scant white brassiere and skimpy panties that left little to the imagination, Nikki quickly looked about. They were the only ones on the beach, and the sailors on the ocean were too far away to notice.

Déjà vu invaded his calm again and the unsettling feeling returned as he saw Eve and quickly averted his eyes from her breasts thrusting towards him as she splashed through the shallows.

At first the salt water stung the bites she had scratched, but the sensation vanished quickly, replaced by a feeling of wonder at the underwater world that slid beneath her as she glided along to where she could see Jake diving down in about twenty feet of water.

Now she was aware only of the sound of her breathing, hollow and strained through the snorkel. Spread out below her was the incredibly beautiful world beneath the surface.

Jake swam slowly up to the surface, bubbles dribbling from his mouth, wobbling upward, his face contorted by the rubber mask, eyes wide, exaggerated by the slight magnification of the glass. In his hand he held a conch, the outer surface rough, covered in algae. Nikki could see the underside and the foot visible in the smooth curve of the shell. Pure milky white and pink colours of the shell interior, in complete contrast to the dull unattractive topside.

Water dribbled into the mask as she smiled involuntarily.

Jake let the shell go and they both watched as it drifted slowly to the bottom, settled into the grass almost visibly sighing in relief. Here Jake was in his element; it was familiar and comforting and at times he felt that he need never take another breath, he could simply stay here, floating weightless amongst the conch, the reef fish and the eagle rays that occasionally joined him. Diving again, he swam along the bottom, stopping to watch the creatures move slowly through the sea grass and he felt content and at peace.

A movement above and to the side caught his eye. He looked up to see Nikki diving down beside him, her eyes screwed up in pain pointing to her ears. He held his nose and simulated blowing. She followed his movements and nodded as the pressure equalised, then headed for the surface, out of breath; Jake followed and they surfaced together.

Spitting out the mouthpiece she grinned, images of the wonderful world she had witnessed still swirling before her eyes.

"It's fabulous."

Her enthusiasm was infectious and he was glad she shared his sense of wonder. "I thought you said you'd snorkelled before."

She had the grace to blush, but it couldn't diminish the wonder she felt. In spite of all her mother's wealth, they had never taken vacations, and Nikki's only experience of foreign travel had been the finishing school in Switzerland. At this moment it all seemed so very far away.

"Come on, I'll show you the reef." Turning, he put the mouthpiece back between his teeth and headed towards the reef, Nikki following.

They were both like a couple of kids. He perhaps more than she, because he had never shown anyone other than Frankie his private world and it was a novel experience for him to be finally sharing it with his daughter. He felt the child in her, the child he'd known and yet he saw a beautiful young woman, whose body so exactly mirrored his memory of her mother's that the conflict of emotions awash within him was almost overwhelming.

For this tiny fleeting moment, they were in another world where the past existed as the present; where sea anemones and sponges grew in the living beauty of the reef; where multi-coloured fish swam all around them without fear, a dream-like counterpoint to the reality of the present.

Jake tapped Nikki on the shoulder and she lifted her head. He took out his mouthpiece. "Don't go anywhere near the wavy cream and red stuff. It's fire coral and it'll make a real mess of you."

As he dove, she followed, seeing where he pointed to the fire coral that looked so beautifully delicate, so innocent.

> *Long thin red welts lanced diagonally across his lower back, beneath his arm almost reaching up to his right nipple. Fire coral welts that stung as if he had been bullwhipped as the length and character of the welts suggested. They were a badge of honour, a payment for the pleasure he took from the reef every day. It was just and righteous and Monroe gloried in the smug self-satisfaction of his pain.*

Slowly she felt she was being drawn into the fiction of Monroe, into his world for a short time living inside the novel and she marvelled at the wonder of the reef, almost forgetting that she was running out of air and feeling a sense of panic when she looked up at the surface so far away.

Paddling hard to get to the air, breaking the surface and gasping for breath, laughing with joy her anger and fears momentarily forgotten.

For nearly two hours, they swam, dived and floated, watching the life of the reef dwellers, unaware of the tiredness in their limbs and the sun burning their backs. Their entire beings were concentrated through their eyes.

But it could not last forever and slowly, regretfully, they paddled back to shore and walked up the beach, sinking onto the sand looking out across the lagoon, the sights still vivid in their memories. Gradually the euphoria left Nikki and reality crept back, Monroe retreating back to fiction creating a void again. She saw Jake as a stranger once more, watching as he took the diving gear back to the lean-to shack.

He was a middle-aged man she did not know; an older image of the photograph, but not the man she had held in her mind for so long. Trying to equate the figure she saw before her to the novelist she'd read about in the clippings from nearly two decades ago and to Monroe whose strength of character so pervaded his novels seemed impossible. Monroe was Jake and yet he wasn't. Once again confusion created an irrational anger. White salt crystals formed on her drying skin and she could feel her back burning.

Jake returned with her tee shirt and jeans. The cotton felt rough on her skin where salt had formed an uncomfortable barrier. He sat down beside her, placed a beautiful conch shell on the sand, pulled the flask from his pocket and tipping it up, swallowed a slug of rum. An unconscious act, unaware that she was watching him disapprovingly.

"Why do you drink?"

"I like it."

"I don't believe that. Monroe drinks too, but he doesn't like it."

"Monroe is fiction."

"Mom said the same thing."

"Maybe we did have something in common after all."

Anger, unwanted, uninvited, surfaced again. She felt she wanted to hit him again and shout and scream at him and somehow make him stop, but all she said was, "I don't think I like you very much either," and continued to stare out to sea, watching the sails in the distance as yachts tacked along the coast. "I wanted to get to know you."

"Why?"

"I don't hate you."

Looking at her profile he saw Eve so clearly that it disturbed him more and more with each passing moment. The strength of his initial attraction to Eve reborn every time he looked at Nikki. So he looked away trying to settle his mind on the four-year child he remembered.

"I wasn't a good father. It was the wrong time and the wrong woman." Glimpses of the past, like snatches of old black and white film, rapidly flickered across his memory.

"I was twenty years old and for the first year of your life I only saw you in photographs." He paused. "I wasn't... good."

"I don't remember it that way."

"Children never do."

"What happened?"

Film frames jumped and flickered in Jake's memory, incidents he'd tried to expunge from his mind over the years, suddenly leaping to the forefront frighteningly clear; erased quickly with a shake of his head and a shot of rum.

"Forget it. Go home. Get on with your life and let me get on with mine." The anger in his voice surprised him. He hadn't meant to sound like that.

Nikki stood and walked away a few paces, on the verge of tears. He slammed his hand on the sand.

"Shit."

Hearing him walking up behind her, she hurriedly brushed away the tears, determined that he not see, then felt his hand momentarily on her shoulder.

"I'm sorry. That was unnecessary. I didn't mean it that way. Not the way it sounded."

Nikki slipped back into her shell, retreating to the safety of the cocoon she'd built around her emotions, but this time she was unable or unwilling to close the door completely and the pain of impending loss tied a tight knot in her stomach.

"You're right. This is a waste of time." Anger flared, her stubborn genes asserting themselves, demanding that she not just give up and fade away.

"I don't need a drunken has-been for a father. What possible help could you be anyway?"

"I guess I deserve that."

Her anger evaporated as suddenly as it came, leaving her emotionally drained. All the events of the past week had wrung her out, left her like a limp rag almost devoid of feeling so that nothing seemed to matter anymore.

"Maybe you can buy me dinner. One I get to eat this time. If that lady friend of yours doesn't scratch my eyes out."

She walked away towards the dinghy, leaving Jake standing, swamped with feelings of futility, uselessness and guilt.

*   *   *

At the yacht they showered, changed clothes and as Jake cleaned up below, Nikki sat on deck amid the stray sheets, lines and fenders, enjoying the breeze and the sense of distance from the claustrophobia of the shore.

Little did she know that it was one thing she and Jake had in common, it was why he'd bought the boat. Father and daughter shared the same feelings of isolation and Jake had long ago come to terms with his need for solitude, but for Nikki it was confused with the loneliness of the mansion on the Narragansett Bay.

Brand new yachts, their crews colourfully dressed, sailed past towards the marina at the end of their regatta, some waving to Nikki, the sound of their happy voices carrying across to her as the bows sliced through the water, sails cracking as some tacked towards the marina. She waved back and suddenly a feeling of insecurity and discontent crept over her as she sat in the sunshine.

She felt alienated, a stranger out-of-place and unwanted.

Pain from sunburn shifted her thoughts to her skin, stinging, dry, feeling like a sheet of scorched parchment. She was thinking she wanted to stay and yet there was seemingly nothing here for her. No way to connect to her father.

Jake was not as she had imagined and that was both disappointing and annoying. How could she tell him about her feelings? About emotions that she didn't fully understand herself. The woman and the child alternating within her, both demanding equal attention. She was afraid that he would disappoint her.

In her subconscious she was beginning to resolve the problem, but as they ate dinner and she looked from Jake to Frankie, she seemed to drift further and further into a morass of loneliness.

Jake was more drunk than he had been for a long time. It had not been intentional as usually he was capable of remaining at least relatively cognisant of his surroundings. But not this time; this time he was descending into oblivion; maybe he just wanted to resolve his problem with unconsciousness as just another easy escape.

Frankie tried to maintain polite conversation as if she were acting in a vacuum. Protective of Jake and yet angry. Loving him and hating him at the same time left her somehow powerless to act, to prevent him from destroying himself and she wished she had been strong in the past and helped him kick the addiction. The result was a bad melodrama in which she had unwittingly become the key player; a role she had not ask for and didn't want and since Nikki's arrival, their spiritual connection had been severed, the umbilical cord that held them together for so long seemed to be a memory.

Jake leaned across the table, reaching for the rum bottle, but Nikki got to it first, snatching it out of his hand. He barely noticed.

"You've had enough," she snapped.

Frankie seethed with irrational anger. "He knows when he's had enough."

Nikki stared at her as she might stare at a petulant child. Their roles reversed for an instant. "You have to be kidding. He doesn't even know what day it is right now."

Jake could hear the conversation as if he was a distant onlooker, not a part of the play, simply a detached spectator. The rational part of his mind that still managed to function despite the rum, observing in sadness and shame, so much so that it propelled him from his seat and out into the street, stumbling past several tables and disturbing the occupants in his haste.

Frankie leaned across the table, her anger barely controllable.

"Who the hell do you think you are? How do we know you are who you say you are? How do I know you're his daughter?"

To Nikki it was an absurdly stupid question. She had always known that Jake was her father; there was no question about that at all.

"And who the hell are you? His wife?" Hitting home exactly as Nikki hoped.

Frankie stared at her, words failing to come, as her fears about her relationship with Jake, of losing him, were suddenly clear and manifest in this beautiful young woman.

"No, you're not his wife. You're a bitch in heat."

Nikki was in full flow and had unconsciously borrowed Monroe's phrase.

The slap came as a surprise. Shocked customers stopped eating and a palpable silence fell as they stared at Nikki reeling from the blow.

Smiling with no hint of humour, she seemed to triumph at having forced Frankie to hit her, revelling in the sting of the slap.

"He's my father and you're killing him," Nikki hissed, rose and left the table to join Jake outside as Frankie sat immobilised, appalled at herself, frightened at her need to inflict pain.

Perhaps the girl was right. Perhaps that's exactly what she was doing. Over the years, a routine that seemed normal had insinuated itself into their lives; alcohol blurred the days and nights, mellowing the evenings of playing chess and staring at the sunset; dispersing their inhibitions so that sex was somehow dreamlike and vague; isolating them from the reality of their daily lives and the need to examine their relationship. There had always been tomorrow and when tomorrow came there was always another tomorrow. The girl had simply held a mirror for her to look into and she didn't like the image.

Jake walked with Nikki, unsteadily, watching as she unlocked and opened the car door. It could have been a scene from one of his novels, and maybe for him, that was exactly what it was at that moment.

"Sorry it didn't work out. Like I said. I would have made a lousy father." He steadied himself against the fender as Nikki glanced across at Frankie.

"Too many distractions?"

Jake didn't hear, just shrugged. *'It's not real'*, he told himself. *'This is a dream, a nightmare.'* And secure in the unreal illusion he had created he *could* let her go, for it *was* a dream and she did not exist.

"Take care of yourself."

She slipped into the driver's seat an idea already forming in her mind.

"Send me a conch, Jake."

71

As he watched the tail lights disappear he seemed to have forgotten what had happened. As if he did not want to face the reality of his weakness, he had erased the evening from his mind.

Frankie took his arm, "I'm sorry."

As if he was an old man with Alzheimer's he allowed her to lead him to the dinghy and they motored slowly out to the yacht.

"You okay Jake?"

It was a question that he chose to ignore. He wasn't listening, just tipped the empty flask up to his mouth and threw it overboard without thinking.

Frankie struggled to help him onto the deck, secured the dinghy to the stern davits, hauled it out of the water and spent half-an-hour getting Jake into the berth. When she'd finished, she stripped off her sweat soaked clothes, sat down on the berth and watched his sleeping face.

"I can't take any more of this Jake. I really can't."

Emotional exhaustion swept over her and she lay back against the hull, staring out through the port-light at the dark expanse of ocean.

*   *   *

While Frankie drifted off to sleep, Nikki slowed the Ferrari, headlamps sweeping across the slash pine, mangroves and palm trees, and turned down a narrow dirt road that ended in a mangrove swamp. Beyond she could see the ocean.

For a long time she stood staring through a gap in the mangrove, oblivious of the mosquitoes that buzzed around her and speared their needle proboscis through her skin, to taste her blood. She was considering her course of action, justifying what she had decided to do. Forming a plan into a heroic act to save her father and recover her lost childhood. There was an irrational logic to her thoughts and finally, mind made up, she stood and went back to the car.

The town was rowdy in the tourist section, the nightclubs and bars full, people walking in the street laughing and joking as she drove to the quay in the less popular part of town. She parked, locked the car, and clutching her small tote bag containing clean clothes, found a small wooden rowboat next to the sea wall.

Jumping down, loosening the painter, she fitted the oars into the brass rowlocks, pushed off and sat down on the oiled teak seat. This was the first time she'd ever attempted to row a boat and the first few strokes were nothing less than dismal, succeeding only in turning the boat around in a circle and bumping back into the sea wall.

At last she got the boat headed in the general, if somewhat erratic, direction. It was a long way; the onshore breeze making the work hard and soon she was panting with exertion, turning every now and then to see how far there was to go.

Bumping and scraping noises against the hull woke Frankie. At first she thought it may be still in her dreams, but the crick in her neck told her that she was laying across the berth, head against the cool hull and dreams had given way to a waking headache.

The scraping sound came again with another bump. Stumbling into the saloon, snapping on a light she looked up at the open companionway hatch; she was sure she'd closed it after she'd laid Jake on the berth.

Nikki watched her from the doorway of the forward cabin, flare pistol held in her hand. Whether the gun was loaded, or indeed how to use it were both inconsequential thoughts. Threat was all she had in her mind, but she did have the sense to keep her finger away from the trigger.

Watching Frankie's naked buttocks brought a hysterically nervous giggle to her lips, a mean sound, the beauty of the ebony skin firing her jealousy.

Frankie spun around at the sound, her heart pounding erratically, coming face-to-face with Nikki and the pistol.

"Keep right on moving."

"What the hell are you doing?"

"Just climb the steps."

"JAKE."

"You think that'll wake him? A hurricane couldn't wake him. Christ.

He drank enough to keep him unconscious for hours."

She waved the pistol erratically and Frankie backed up the steep companionway steps into the cockpit.

Nikki giggled; it was as if someone else was doing this and she was observing from a distance. As she let her eyes wander over Frankie's naked body, she felt mean and bitchy.

"Jesus. The alcohol must really have dulled his sense of perception. Now walk up front."

"Why are you doing this?"

"Walk. You know. The pointed end."

Frankie backed away, her eyes firmly fixed on the pistol pointed unwaveringly at her stomach.

"Listen. I know we didn't hit it off, but this is ridiculous."

Nikki ignored her, pointing to the mooring line. "Untie that rope."

Frankie glanced down and slowly the meaning began to dawn upon her. "You have to be kidding."

"Just do it." Nikki smiled as the mooring line slid into the water and the yacht began to drift slowly. "Back to the cockpit."

They walked slowly until they were abreast the cockpit on the side deck.

"Stop there."

"Let's talk about this."

"Jump."

"What?"

"Jump."

"No way."

As Nikki lowered the pistol Frankie felt a surge of relief and her legs weakened as the threat diminished. She closed her eyes briefly and didn't see the fist coming, connecting on the side of her head, knocking her over the lifelines into the water. Nikki leaned over and looked down as Frankie struggled to the surface; then sure she was okay, jumped into the cockpit, turned the key, momentarily startled by the warning buzzer that suddenly blared before she pushed the starting button. The engine coughed into life, settling into the dull rattle of an old diesel.

Nikki slammed the gear lever forward and pushed open the throttle as Frankie lunged for the passing boat, but it sped by and she could only tread water and watch as the yacht surged forward zigzagging across the harbour before finally settling on course, heading towards the open ocean. Hysterical laughter burst from Nikki in a fountain of release, mixing with the bubbling water from the wake and evaporating rapidly in the heavy air.

Gradually, excitement and hysteria diminished into an unwelcome anti-climax with the heaving unbridled ocean swell. Nausea, rising with every pitch and roll of the yacht, settled into her stomach. Determined not to succumb, she fought down the insidious creeping torpor, focusing on the need to continue with the plan, but doubt began to crowd her every thought.

Frankie watched as the yacht grew smaller in the darkness, then swam back to the quay; reaching the steps in what seemed like moments, although it was a half mile swim, still dizzy with a dreamlike feeling of detachment, wondering if she would wake and discover Jake lying beside her. Dragging herself up the steps, oblivious to her naked state, she walked back to the restaurant.

At this time of night, the streets were deserted, tourists still in the nightclubs and bars, and those that weren't still too drunk or concerned with their own activities to notice anything.

Somewhere in her subconscious a car horn blared, headlights swept across the street and then the illusion vanished and she was on her own again, climbing the stairs to her small apartment. It consisted of a living room overlooking the bay, kitchen, bathroom and single bedroom. Her needs were minimal; taste sparsely Bohemian.

Standing beneath a solid spray from the showerhead, she washed the harbour water from her body trying to rationalize what had happened, then reaction set in and she knelt in the tub shaking and sobbing; but soon anger replaced shock and gradually she stopped shaking as her mind began to clear.

Drying herself slowly, reflectively, she looked out through the window across the darkened harbour. Clouds blanketed a sad moon so the mooring where she was so used to seeing Jake's yacht was obscured by an impenetrable darkness.

In that moment a chill stole through her body. An unfathomable chill as if the ghosts of a million suffering souls were crying out. For a long while she paced the living room, debating whether or not to call the Coastguard, but in the end, didn't; partly from anger and partly because she knew, deep inside, that Nikki needed to be with her father.

Alone.

Either instinct or intuition told her that events beyond their control were shaping the course of the future and it was best not to fight, for there was nothing she could fight against. It was a dangerous conclusion, but somewhere in the depths of her psyche, the history of her ancestors controlled her thoughts and told her to allow the drama to play out its ragged course. Here existed inevitability, formed in the arena of the intervening years and now it was time for the play to begin in earnest.

Whatever happened now would affect her life forever.

FIVE

For five hours, the yacht sailed out into the open ocean. Warm rain fell, clearing almost immediately, allowing the sun to rise at the start of another tropical day. Nikki leaned against the wheel, euphoria long since evaporated as seasickness took hold and racked her body with dry retches. Gradually that too eased and she looked around the yacht and the ocean, taking stock.

Land had long since been left behind along with the excitement of her piracy. All around lay empty ocean, the water now deep blue as the shallows close to land gave way to the deeper waters of the Gulf of Mexico; and instead of the short waves of the bays, the swell of the Gulf came in long sweeping passes, powerfully lifting the yacht in a slow, smooth rolling motion.

Lockers in the saloon revealed all the booze Jake had stored out-of-sight. Bottles of rum, whisky, gin, wine, brandy and a case of beer. The not so secret supply of a serious alcoholic; a pathetic testament to the degree of his addiction.

Tucked away in a hanging locker in the forward cabin, Nikki found an empty black tote bag that she spread on the saloon sole and filled with every bottle she could find. Occasionally she checked on Jake, and found him sleeping soundly, oblivious to everything except for the meanderings within his own dream reality; then she returned to the saloon and dragged the tote bag up into the cockpit.

One-by-one, she opened the bottles and tossed them overboard; without anyone at the helm, the yacht motored around in a circle.

A last check of all the lockers in the boat, including the bilges beneath the floorboards, satisfied her that there was no more booze on board.

Then the engine quit.

It coughed a couple of times, spluttered on, coughed again and then died, the silence unnerving as the yacht drifted with the current and the wind.

Nikki stared at the instrument panel, then at the wheel and then up at the mast; a feeling of dread crept over her as she realized that without the engine she had no idea how to control the boat.

Back in Rhode Island her mother had kept a small powerboat on the private landing that Nikki took for wild rides, water skiing with her friends when her mother was sufficiently inebriated not to notice. And as wild and irresponsible adolescents, she and her friends had scorned the sailors who shouted things like, *'Ready about'* and *'Helms a-lee'*, seeming to spend their time working hard getting nowhere. Now, without the engine, she was completely lost and the yacht became a brooding monster she didn't understand.

The empty mansion was a thousand miles away and for the first time since leaving the safety of the Narragansett Bay, she longed to be back in her bed, listening to the wind in the trees as another winter storm howled up the Bay.

The swell was moderate and steady and the yacht took up an attitude slightly bow to wind and sea, lying a-hull, rolling as the waves moved under her. It was an unpleasant motion and again her stomach started to play games inside her body, as halyards clattered against the masts and the yacht creaked ominously, a discordant accompaniment to the sound of water against the hull.

What had seemed the perfect answer to her problem had now become a problem in itself and the feeling of loneliness she had felt before was compounded by the isolation of the deserted sea.

As she wallowed in the full extent of her misery, Jake struggled to consciousness through the blinding pain in his forehead. He wasn't sure he was awake as the yacht seemed to be moving differently and he lay back again and closed his eyes, groaning as his whole world seemed to turn and spin. When he opened his eyes again, he found he was staring out of the port-light.

Something was wrong.

Normally he would see the quay from this position, but all he saw was a wave as it swept under the yacht and rolled off into the distance.

"Shit."

Suddenly he was fully awake, ignoring the pounding in his head he struggled into his pants. The yacht rolled on another wave and he slammed into the port hull, steadied himself, closed his eyes for a moment, then searched for the flask, forgetting that the previous night he had thrown it into the harbour. Cursing and stumbling with the rolling of the yacht, he stepped into the saloon, looked up into the cockpit and saw Nikki, pale and unhappy behind the wheel.

"What the hell's going on? What the hell are you doing here? What the hell are *we* doing here?"

Unsteadily climbing the companionway steps he stared around at the horizon.

"We're at sea for Christ's sake," Jake exclaimed unnecessarily.

"It seemed a good idea at the time," Nikki muttered miserably.

"You did this?"

"The engine gave up."

"I don't believe this. I'm dreaming. Tell me I'm dreaming."

"I wish I were."

"I'm speechless."

"Me too."

Anger at Jake tinged her misery, as if it was his entire fault; and in a sense it was. The decision made twenty years ago had boomeranged through time to this defining moment. But Nikki was beyond the philosophical, and death seemed preferable to this existence as her seasickness rose and fell with the swell and the yacht rocked out-of-control.

Jake sat down in the cockpit, head throbbing wildly.

"Have you any idea what you've done? Do you know where we are? How long have we been out here?"

Rhetorical questions, none of which mattered. If he was waiting vainly for an answer, then it didn't seem to matter to either of them how long it took in coming.

Nikki glanced at her watch, the act of focusing her eyes on something so close making the nausea more intense. "About six or seven hours."

"Jesus Christ."

"I just wanted you alone, without Miss Cellulite 1950 hanging around."

Jake was either not listening, or just ignored the remark. "This boat hasn't been out of the harbour for five years."

"There's no time like the present."

Again Jake ignored her. "How did you get through the reefs?"

"There were reefs?"

It didn't really surprise her. Nothing surprised her now.

Another bout of nausea swept over her just like the occasional white cap that gently tumbled down the face of oncoming waves in the distance.

"Dear God. Why me?" Jake screamed to the sky, his arms outstretched in supplication. It was completely ridiculous but he didn't care and neither did Nikki, her only response was to lean over the side and dry retch, feeling only slightly better as the attack passed.

"Okay. So it was a bad idea. Now how about you get us back and I'll leave you in peace," Nikki whispered, grimacing at the taste of bile in her mouth.

"Just like that, huh? You any idea where we are?"

Shaking her head sent the horizon tilting crazily, stars spinning before her eyes and the aching soared to an almost intolerable level.

"You're the sailor, *you* figure it out."

To Jake, unaware and uncaring at this moment, she was not his daughter; she was a stranger, a threat to his very existence. Rage boiled inside him, fuelled by the hangover and the beginnings of the cravings for a drink. His expression as he leaned towards her, frightened her for the first time.

"I'm not a sailor. I've never been to sea. I bought this tub to live on where nobody could just drop by. To live on. Not to sail," he lied, sitting with his face inches from hers for ten seconds before shaking his head in disgust.

"You're kidding me. Right?" she said quietly.

It had never occurred to her that he, living on a boat, would not know even the basic rudiments of the mariner's art; it was inconceivable. That information had not been integrated into the plan. Once out at sea, her plan was that they would work out their differences and get to know each other. She would find her father and he would accept her and the scene would soften as if seen through a gossamer filter, the music would swell and they would sail away together.

But Jake was far beyond dream fantasies. He badly needed a drink to assuage the screaming demons that were beginning to make themselves felt. A drink would readjust the chemical balance in his body and allow him to work this out; it would also allow him to mellow a little and tell the truth that he did know something about sailing. But the mean side of him wanted her to suffer for her actions. He stepped towards the companionway.

"I need a drink."

A cough and low groan made him stop and look down at her. Blue eyes, very much like his own, a little bloodshot from seasickness and exhaustion, fixed guiltily on him.

"What now?" he mumbled tiredly.

"I threw it overboard. Dumped it."

Several emotions fluttered across his face, at first incredulity, then the anger of an alcoholic who suddenly felt his lifeline ripped away, filled his being. He stared around at the ocean, looking to see if there was a bottle floating out there, or maybe a trail that would lead him to where they bobbed, waiting; but there were just a couple of terns skimming across the water, concerned only with their own business.

"The booze?"

Nikki nodded slowly, wearily, not certain how he was going to react, suspicious of his anger, as if some sixth sense told her that he could be dangerous.

"All of it?"

She nodded again.

He sat back down, the shock like a physical blow, as if someone had wrenched his flesh and drained blood from his body.

Subconsciously she had thrown the booze away to supplant herself in his affections, but had instead become the enemy. The naiveté of her youth and lack of experience creating a void between them as his whole being focused on the lack of a bottle of rum. Even if he didn't drink from it, just to have the bottle to hold would have been a reassuring comfort.

81

"Why?" he said in bewilderment as the surreal scene played before him.

Before Nikki could answer nausea rose again with the swell, but not so bad this time, as if it was on the wane having given up the struggle to kill her and she felt a little more alive than she had an hour ago. "I thought I knew. Hell. What's it matter anyway? What does anything matter?"

If the yacht sank beneath her, she would not have worried, simply welcomed a certain death with open arms.

Jake clambered onto the side deck and started to walk forward.

"Where are you going?" she shouted, a feeling of sudden panic rising as she watched him walk slowly along the side deck.

He turned and looked at her mockingly. "What do you think? I'm gonna swim for it?" He raised his arms and shook his head. "Look, I just need a little space of my own for while if that's okay with you?" He staggered as the boat rolled on a wave and grasped the shroud, then carefully made his way to the bow, sitting down, back against the pulpit. What he was doing was the act of a little boy sulking, he knew that, but his head pounded and sitting in the cockpit with her confused and upset him. He felt an urgent need to hold her, hug her and tell her everything was going to work out fine, but at the same time, anger and frustration boiled inside him as his body screamed for a drink.

None of the emotions seemed to be able to co-exist within him at the same time. They wrenched and tore at his soul unmercifully and he knew that the demons had been let out of their cages and it would be only a matter of time before they ripped at the structure of his sanity in an attempt to destroy him.

Nikki watched him guardedly from the cockpit and if only he had known, the same emotions of anger, resentment, frustration and love also boiled inside her.

And why shouldn't they?

Weren't they flesh and blood?

The same gene pool?

The same chemistry?

The beauty of the ocean. The peace of the day. The noble yacht.

None of those things existed for them right now. The beauty and majesty of the ocean was simply a tranquil counterpoint to their own confusions.

When he returned from the foredeck an hour later and apologized meekly for his childishness, she felt awkward and embarrassed for him. He disappeared below mumbling about trying to find out where they were. There was nothing for her to do topside, so she followed him down into the saloon and watched as he rummaged through a locker beneath the port settee.

"I told you I threw all the booze out."

Ignoring her, he pulled out a well-made square teak box, laid it on the table, and dove back inside the locker pulling out several hard cover books. The dust covers had been long since torn away, he tossed them over to the starboard settee; having replaced the locker lid, he sat down and pulled the box towards him smiling.

"Somebody's got to find out where the hell we are and get us back to civilization."

"You call that civilization?"

"Where the hell did that cynicism come from?"

"It must be hereditary," she said nastily and regretted the comment as soon as it left her mouth. "The cynicism," she added to try and take the sting from the remark.

Choosing to ignore the comment, Jake stroked the aged teak box enjoying the feel of the smooth varnished wood. Then he unhooked the clasp and opened it with a boyish enthusiasm, the pounding of his head and slight stomach cramp forgotten as he looked inside.

"If you had been around maybe I wouldn't be so cynical," she snapped, angry again that he had ignored her, "besides, reading your books is enough to make anyone a cynic." She was digging at him again, trying to force a reaction, anything to be noticed; but Jake wasn't going to allow himself to be drawn, concentrating instead on the teak box. There, lying in a nest of maroon velvet the same colour as the settees, was an old brass sextant. The chassis beautifully tooled with scrollwork. Lens, mirrors and filters, shiny and unmarked.

Nikki frowned. "What's that?"

Suddenly the boat lurched and she fell backwards against the galley counter, gasping in pain as her hip glanced off the rounded wood corner. Jake looked up with concern, forgetting the sextant and the question.

"You okay?"

Rubbing her hip, Nikki returned to the table and sat down, wedging herself firmly in the corner between the forward bulkhead and the hull.

"I'm okay."

"Sure?"

Eager to divert the focus of attention away from herself, she pointed to the sextant. "You were going to tell me about that."

In spite of the pounding in his head and dizziness, he felt the uneasiness in her, and looked quickly back to the sextant, removing it from the box.

"This is the mariner's best friend. Along with a well-found ship and a fair wind. It's a sextant."

"Very poetic. You know how to use it?"

"No." It was a partial lie.

"What?"

Suddenly her attitude irritated him and he waved his hand across to the books.

"Books. Didn't you learn anything? Everything you could possibly want to know is between the covers of books. Einstein was once asked why he didn't know his own telephone number. His reply was, *'you don't need to know everything, just where to look for the answer.'* A bad paraphrase but you get the point. You want to cook a trout; read a book. Play golf, make a cabinet or examine the mysteries of the human mind; read a book. Likewise, you want to navigate a boat; read the books."

Putting the sextant down, he reached over and picked up a manual of Celestial Navigation. "Books."

"I read yours."

The remark caught him off-guard as she intended; his eyes swept across to her but she was studiously examining her nails. He waited until she flickered her eyes to him and for an instant they locked together, before he broke off and went back to the pages of the book in his hand.

"Learn anything?"

"Not much." She wanted to hurt, to break him down somehow. To do anything to connect on a real level and as she stared at him, she saw that a veil had dropped across his eyes, preventing her from seeing the disappointment that flared inside him.

"Is Monroe like you?" she asked suddenly.

Shrugging carelessly, he gathered the books, crossed to the navigation table, cleared a space and set them down.

"Maybe," he said carefully.

Next he picked up the manuscripts, carried them to the forward cabin and tossed them onto the berth.

"What are they?" she asked, noting in surprise the careless way he deposited the manuscripts.

"Wasted time mostly."

"Your next book?"

"There may never be another."

Effectively he shut down the conversation. Writing, especially his, was not an area he wished to discuss; there was too much pain, frustration and resentment associated with his books; at least that's how he justified his failure to write. The truth was simpler, she sensed that he was afraid to write another novel, burying himself in alcohol and was tempted to probe further, but instead watched as he sat at the navigation table and read through a book on basic sailing; then with little else to do and the confines of the cabin making her feel nauseous again, she clambered up the companionway steps to the cockpit. No answers to her predicament were forthcoming from the ocean with its seemingly endless expanse and she sat wrapped in a cloak of unhappiness, wondering how all this had come about.

Why didn't Jake behave as she had expected that he would? She didn't understand that she was learning a lesson in basic human nature and that her father was not just 'her father', he was a person; not that she saw him as an alien, but there was a confusion in her mind between the character of Monroe, and this strange, complicated, secretive man.

The creator and the character should, to her logic, have been the same, or at least similar, but there were no similarities.

Monroe was heroic. His flaws and insecurities making him whole and real, but Jake was the antithesis; his flaws and insecurities made him seem unreal and intangible.

Where Monroe was young; Jake was old.

Where Monroe was strong; Jake was weak.

She had no way of being able to reconcile the character with the creator.

From the moment she had decided to drive to Key West, the first domino had toppled, the sequence set in motion and both she and Jake were embroiled in the game whether they wanted to be or not. The ramifications of ignorance and bitterness would only cease when the last domino had fallen; and there was no way of knowing just how far away the last domino stood.

Wallowing in self-pity, she felt that she had been let down by everyone in her life. By her mother; by Jake; by Sam. Her world was a non-existent event, a tiny blip on the evolutionary scale because none of them wanted her.

Jake seemed to deliberately avoid her and only when they had been swimming and diving had there been a connection, but that had vanished as quickly as the drops of water on the sand. Her thoughts and dreams had been turned upside down as reality stood nakedly before her.

She turned as he clambered on deck.

"Okay. Let's get this tub moving," he said with an authority he did not feel, but there was a purpose about him now, a mood different from before. His personality chameleon-like, changing from boyish enthusiasm one minute to a closed brooding recluse the next. "Stay by the wheel."

Clambering along the side deck to the mast, he untied the sail cover; rolling it up and tossing it back into the cockpit before untying the sail stops and hauling on the main halyard. The mainsail sped up the first fifteen feet, then he inserted the handle into the self-tailing winch and set to work cranking the sail up to the top of the mast.

It flapped and cracked in the wind and the boat weather-cocked, bow to the seas, pitching up and down in the swell. Securing the halyard, he clambered forward on the pitching deck to the bow, wedging himself against the stainless steel pulpit on the bowsprit and uncovered the jib, tucked the cover beneath him as he untied the sail, then scrambled back to the mast, tossed the cover into the cockpit and set to work hoisting the jib.

Turning to Nikki, a smile on his face as he secured the halyard, he shouted above the sound of the flapping sails. "Books. Just read and you'll learn."

Paying no attention, she squinted towards the sun beginning its fall from the sky towards the distant horizon, as morning became afternoon.

Jake dropped back into the cockpit, gathered up the sail covers and disappeared below, returning a few moments later. He hauled in the jib sheet, wound it around the sheet winch and cranked the handle, pulling the jib tight until the bow fell off the wind and the flapping sail set. The main boom banged across the boat with a rattle of blocks, filled, and suddenly the awkward motion eased as the yacht, happy at last, heeled, put its shoulder to the ocean and began to move.

He crossed quickly to the wheel. "Okay. Move. I'll take it."

Nikki slipped out of his way along the cockpit seat. "Where are we headed?"

Jake looked down at the compass. "East."

"Guess we're bound to hit something, sometime." The sarcastic remark was lost on the wind as Jake checked the sails, remembering all he had read and all he had learned in the past. Gradually the classes he had taken so many years ago began to come back to him and he remembered suddenly that he should have hoisted the mizzen and staysail first, but until he was fully confident in what he was doing, he decided to sail the yacht as a sloop. It meant that she wasn't realizing her full potential, but then that was indicative of her crew so at least everything and everybody was compatible.

He motioned to Nikki. "Okay. You got us here, you can steer." She slid back behind the wheel, grasping the wooden spokes. "Keep that line on those numbers."

A flash of anger rose in her. "I know how to use a compass," she snapped.

"Okay. Okay," Jake muttered.

As he busied himself trimming the sails, she experimented turning the wheel to port and then starboard, feeling the yacht head up and fall off the wind, watching the compass swing with each movement. It was fun and relaxing and with something upon which to concentrate and with the easier motion of the boat, her seasickness had gone completely; suddenly things did not look as bleak as they had a few moments before.

After a while, Jake left her to the helm and went below to check the engine and batteries. If there was one thing he knew about on this yacht, it was the power and water systems. They had been essential for living aboard at a mooring without the conveniences of shore power and water. However both problems were easily solved.

There were two generating systems on board, feeding two 4D, 625 amp/hour Deep Cycle Gel Cell Marine Batteries. A third smaller series 27, 12-volt battery was used solely for engine cranking. The first system used a high capacity engine driven alternator and the second a wind generator mounted on the mizzenmast. There was a third; a water driven system used when sailing, but it hadn't been installed and right now it would have been useful. But like everything else in Jake's life since he had moved to Key West, it had drifted away with the days, the rum and the gentle pursuit of conch.

Once every six days he would run the engine for an hour to ensure the batteries were at capacity and for the rest of the time, the wind generator kept up with his modest demands.

The diesel fuel tank lived beneath the aft berth. Jake tapped the gauge in the cockpit and cursed softly; the needle didn't move from empty. Once they were home and the tank was filled, bleeding the fuel system would be a messy job and the entire yacht would smell of diesel for weeks afterwards. He stood up suddenly in anger and banged his head, cursing as he staggered forward.

A check on the electrical panel for the batteries indicated they were topped up, the only draw coming from the fridge/freezer compressor, which kicked in every now and then. Although the draw was high, the insulation was more than enough to keep the fridge and freezer at the proper temperatures for long periods of time.

Four 50-gallon fresh water tanks and an eighty-gallon a day Reverse Osmosis Desalinator solved the second problem, water. The Desalinator lived in the bilge just aft of the forward cabin bulkhead, accessed through a hatch in the cabin sole.

Jake knelt, lifted the hatch out of the way and stretched down to open the seacock, then flipped the switch hearing the hum of the pump and watching the gauges leap. There was no need to flush the system because he'd done that a couple of days ago and the lines were filled with fresh water. He studied the pressure gauges, then altered the settings slightly until the flow settled at a steady three gallons an hour.

A feeling of light-headedness swept over him as he sat back on the cabin sole, momentarily disoriented. He was not such a fool to fail to recognize that the sudden lack of alcohol in his system was making him ill; and withdrawal would come soon and get worse as the change in body chemistry sent conflicting information to his brain from every part of his body. With growing dread he knew what was going to happen. In one of the galley lockers he found four bottles of Sprite and opening one of them, drank greedily. The sugar would help for the moment. Then he lay down on the cabin sole. The light-headedness passed as did the stomach cramp, but he stayed where he was for fifteen more minutes before attempting to get to his feet.

Decision-making was beginning to become a problem, as a myriad of images flickered through his brain on fast reverse into the past. Shaking his head he tried to concentrate. There was much to do in sailing the yacht back to port, such as calculating their position and navigating in the right direction.

Sitting down at the table and opening the book at the first page, he set his mind on a single path to push back the demons. As he read and made notes, he forgot the present and the past, instead immersing himself in the complex world of altitudes, azimuths, sight reduction tables and lines of latitude and longitude that would finally result in a point on a chart.

A dot amid the depth lines on a sheet, that, apart from the small drawings of islands and the sweeping line of the Florida Keys leading up to the mainland; was empty. And that dot would indicate exactly where on the surface of the earth they were.

It was an ancient art that, throughout the centuries, had differed only in the sophistication of the equipment. As Jake read, he dearly wished he had installed the electronic equipment when the first flush of enthusiasm for the yacht and for sailing had been upon him; before his life had become a series of soporific days that had dove-tailed one into the other. A Radio Direction Finder would have been a perfect piece of equipment right now.

The VHF radio had been in the shop for two years along with the radar, depth sounder and log. The repairman had long since given up trying to get Jake to retrieve them. Paid for, they still lay on a dusty shelf, carefully wrapped, ready and waiting, his name clearly marked.

*   *   *

Nikki, like Jake, found her mind completely absorbed; in her case by keeping the yacht running on track and by the time the sun touched the horizon, her body ached from the constant adjustments she had to make to the wheel, as the sea pushed the yacht around at will.

Apprehension had turned to exhilaration and a surging feeling of power as the yacht plunged on, heeled on a beam reach. Abeam the yacht the sun sank from view and darkness crept across the ocean, the ocean's welcome deep blue colour turned black with only the phosphorescence, silvery blue in the spray kicked up by the bow and the wake trailing behind the boat, to capture her attention.

In the gloom, her apprehension returned. Approaching waves ghostly in the gathering gloom, eerie in the roaring silence, brought the monsters of her childhood creeping at the edges of the night. Waiting for a weakness in her will.

Navigation and spreader lights suddenly blinked on, relieving Nikki of her growing feeling of loneliness, then Jake poked his head up through the hatch.

"Can you cook?" he asked with forced enthusiasm.

"You have food?"

"A load of cans in the bilge and a fridge and freezer full of meats and vegetables. Enough for several months."

"It won't be a catfish meal at Frankie's."

"Frankie doesn't serve catfish."

"But I thought..." she began, then *'got it'* and lapsed into silence.

"See what you can do."

"Sure."

He watched her disappear below and moved across to the weather side of the wheel, reminding himself to make an adjustment for the angle of the compass reading in this position.

With the sun gone, the wind felt cooler and the bow kicked up green water every now and then, which sluiced across the foredeck and sprayed back to the cockpit. It was refreshing and he remembered the first time he had set out to sea on the yacht five years ago with an instructor on a two day coastal cruise. And he wondered why he had stopped.

Beneath the turmoil in his mind was a small area of peace, unrecognisable through the fog of confusion, but there none-the-less. He thought of Nikki, of how they seemed to be so close and yet so far apart, like the opposite poles of two magnets coming together and springing back as if propelled by an electric shock.

Was it guilt that prevented him from expressing his love, or the fear of that guilt? Or simply the fear of love itself. She was a beautiful girl and so like her mother at that age, which at times confused his alcohol soaked mind until he could see his daughter.

How could he somehow bridge the gap that the years had created and their closeness maintained?

Nikki was thinking similarly as she searched through the bilge, then the fridge and freezer, looking for something to prepare. She decided upon cheese omelettes, with a can of sweet corn and oven cooked French fries. It was quick, easy and hopefully edible.

What more could they want?

Besides, back in the Narragansett house, it was all she ever cooked when the occasion arose, which wasn't often. Mostly the local restaurants had a brisk trade in delivering gourmet meals, especially since her mother's illness and hospitalization.

Cooking was a challenge, with the heel of the yacht and the cooker seemingly immobile. Pans simply did not stay in place, until she noticed a bolt on the bottom holding the cooker oven in place. All at once the cooker seemed to have a life of its own, swinging on its gimbals, the top surface remaining horizontal to the earth as the yacht lurched.

She laughed suddenly, the absurdity of the situation struck her like a one-liner bringing a smile that stayed until she carried the two plates up into the cockpit, handing one to Jake.

"Looks good. Thanks."

"I thought it would be easiest," she grinned. "Truth is I can't cook much of anything."

Jake grinned back, turning and looking at the food he knew his stomach couldn't take; the cramps were beginning again and his joints ached terribly.

"Did your mother not teach you to cook?"

It was an innocent question, but the smile died from Nikki's face.

"Why did you do it? Why did you leave?" she asked quietly.

Shadows cast by the spreader lights concealed her eyes so he had no way of knowing what she was thinking behind the question. He stabbed at a chunk of omelette but missed, his hand shaking uncontrollably so that he had to steady it with the other. Then carefully stabbed at the piece of omelette again, succeeding this time in skewering the egg, put it in his mouth and recoiled at the taste. It was like blotting paper; greasy cold blotting paper that had been squashed into a wet pulp. He knew that it was only his body recoiling at the thought of food and somehow managed to swallow it.

"There were reasons," he grunted, avoiding her eyes and staring at his plate.

Violent, uncontrollable shaking suddenly gripped him, surprising him with its strength, even though the wind was still warm. Nikki looked at him questioningly.

"There's a sweater in my cabin. Left hand locker. Would you get it for me?"

For a fleeting moment she almost refused, then put down her plate and ducked below, returning half a minute later with the sweater. Jake struggled into it, but still the shivering persisted.

"Thanks."

"You're welcome." She sat, this time with the light on her face and watched Jake as he flexed his shoulders and stretched, trying to be nonchalant.

"I was like you."

"Oh?"

"Unpredictable. Got something into my head and just had to do it. No matter what." He smiled, but she remained expressionless.

"What you did wasn't just a whim."

Once again the demons were there taunting him, prodding his conscience with barbed pikes; he turned away, staring out across the darkened sea. Here was a moment for communication, a chance to break through the barrier, another opportunity he knew he couldn't take.

Anger flared quickly within her. "Why don't you want to talk about it?"

"Some things are better left unsaid." Then the first real spasm hit him, like a hammer blow to the stomach from inside and he grunted in pain, doubling over.

"Jake?"

It eased quickly and he straightened.

"You okay?"

Still staring out across the ocean he nodded slowly; as the pain left him, so the anger subsided in her.

"I should never have come." If she had hoped for a response she found none, as he remained staring out at the ocean. "You selfishly gave me life and then you denied me the right to live it fully," she shouted, her anger returning sharply.

The remark hit a raw nerve in Jake and he turned, the pain in his body fuelling the resentment. "You're no different from thousands of other children from divorced families. At least you had a comfortable home and an education. That's more than most have."

"And every day, I had to live in the shadow of a father I never knew." Words filled with resentment and pain tumbled out, spilling into the cockpit, her voice rising above the wind and sea. "You have no idea, have you? Mom and I had to live with you every day, even though you weren't there. It was like having a ghost in the house. Do you know why I read your book? I had to. It was in the syllabus at school. *'Images From A Locked Mind'* by Jake Kimble. *'The most promising young novelist of our time'* Jake Kimble. The *'where is he now'* Jake Kimble." Her tone dripped with sarcasm and she laughed bitterly. "At the very least you owe me an explanation why I was not at all important to you."

Irrational anger like an infectious disease overcame Jake. "Who gave you the right to judge me?" he responded.

"You did. The moment you walked out on the day before my fifth birthday. It gives me all the right I ever need."

There was no answer to that, and the demons of his mind mocked him quietly.

"I was wrong. You don't behave like me. You behave like your mother," he said quietly.

"Then perhaps I'm lucky after all."

It was a battle he could not win. "You're getting to be a real pain in the ass," he said, stood up and reached for the edges of the companionway hatch.

"I'm making up for lost time."

He peered back at her, at the beautiful upturned face with the cold blue eyes. "I'm going below. You're on watch."

"What does that mean?"

"It means you steer the boat and you watch. Anything big comes along, you shout. You see a lighthouse, shout. You see anything. Shout. Wake me in four hours."

And then she was alone. Again she cursed her big mouth and its inability to keep shut; its need to voice every emotion that coursed through her body.

Perhaps he was right. Perhaps she was the incarnation of her mother and maybe that was why he seemed so remote; and she cursed her mother too, for not being here; for dying; and she steered the yacht towards an unknown destination and an uncertain future, a ship of despair tossed on a blind ocean.

*   *   *

Jake crawled onto the berth clutching a plastic bowl as nausea swept through him, cramping his stomach. Bile rose in his throat and spilled out of his mouth in a wracking retch. When the vomiting eased he lay back, eyes closed, body shaking.

"Oh God. Oh God."

Whether this was seasickness or Delirium Tremens, he did not know. Maybe a mixture of both, but he did know that it seemed as if his life was ending.

Slowly he opened his eyes and stared out of the starboard port-light at the stars that now speckled the clear night sky, vanishing every now and then as a wave blocked the view. Typewritten pages of his book rolled across the screen of his mind as he began to relive the pain of the past, seeking as before, a catalyst to expel the demons. But they crept forward in his writings, words laid down so long ago remembered as clearly as the day they were written, etched in the sea and the sky through the small port-light.

> *And in the darkness, the snake rose from the belly of his fear and stood, hood flared, the twin horns of touch flickering out towards his conscience. And he could feel the breath. The stench of his terror reflected back from those amber eyes that so pierced his soul.*

His eyes grew wide and his voice was soft. "That's where it is Jake. That's where you lost it. In the pit."

He was beginning to ramble; lose control, to let the demons take over.

"No. That's where you threw it Jake. Like watching a diamond slip away into the ocean."

Turning away from the port-light he dry retched over the side of the berth, his stomach cramped as tight as a drum. When it was over, he lay back, eyes closed.

"Threw it away Jake. She thinks she knows, but she doesn't. How can she? How can she? Eve would never have told her. Never."

It seemed that half his consciousness was still fighting and the other half had already conceded; the battle swung from one side to the other as he regained control and then lost it again, knowing that this was the start of a harrowing and painful process and Fear pounced on the side of darkness and pummelled his resolve.

Sanity returned with thoughts of Nikki and beat back the Dark side, although it lay waiting in the shadows, waiting for any sign of weakness to pounce once more.

He slept fitfully, dreaming confused dreams, waking every now and then before sleeping again; but the sleep was restless and he awoke with a cry, tired and in pain. Nikki provided an anchor for his thoughts and for action and he fell off the berth and stumbled through the saloon and to the companionway. In the beam of the spreader lights she lay slumped over behind the wheel, sleeping.

Left to its own devices, the yacht plunged and reared out-of-control. Jake spun the wheel, bringing the bow through the wind until the yacht was hove-to; locking the wheel he fetched a thin blanket from the forward cabin, spreading it over Nikki's sleeping form. He sat down opposite her, shaking as the DT's tried to assert themselves, looking at her and seeing Eve; remembering the first time they had met when he had stumbled into the nearest bar when on R&R in Honolulu. He was tired, angry, lonely and afraid and when she had smiled at him it seemed that they were the only two in the world and the smoke and noise of the bar disappeared. The whores with their obvious looks and crude gestures faded into the background along with the drunken soldiers, sailors and airmen who had gathered in the bar to forget what horrors tomorrow might bring and to drink themselves into oblivion so that their dreams would evaporate in an alcoholic haze.

But Jake was sober, yet as he looked at Eve he felt lightheaded and drunk; and as she held his gaze she promised herself that she would seduce this young soldier and marry him and have his child. In later years she could not understand why she had felt so strongly that he was the one for her; even when their marriage was at its destructive height she found that she still loved him just as much. Their volatile chemistries had mixed and mingled and torched into a flame of all consuming passion that both had mistaken for true love. Her body was smooth, soft, giving and her lust matched and exceeded his, so that within a few days they were married and when he stepped onto the transport plane to return to Vietnam, she was carrying his child.

Nikki.

Conceived in lust; born in love; raised in rage.

And he still did not understand how it had happened; still felt those emotions of overpowering love and passion for Eve; feelings he had tried successfully over the years to obliterate, now stormed back.

But Eve was gone and the overriding emotion was one of helpless frustration and sadness that he had been unable to express to her his sorrow and his continuing love before she died.

There before him was the image of Eve, but it wasn't her, it was the confusion of his emotions heightened by withdrawal from alcohol. He shook his head to clear the pain and the unwanted memories; but they persisted even as he looked out across the water while the tropical dawn stole across the horizon as a welcome envoy of the morning sun.

SIX

Nikki held the watch in her right hand, waiting, pencil poised over the paper pad as Jake readied himself. He sighted the sextant at the sky, flipped the filter down, looking through the telescope trying to locate the sun, found it, then moved the handle until the sun came down towards the horizon. It was as the book said and it was fun as he stood leaning back against the mast. Something to do to take his mind off the agony of alcoholic withdrawal that had begun to storm through his body and his mind, that constant slugs of Sprite could no longer assuage.

He followed the instructions how to swing the sextant from side-to-side, moving the sun across the horizon in an arc to locate the exact point the sun's rim kissed the horizon to find the point of sight.

"Mark it."

Nikki glanced at her watch and wrote down the time to the second; exact Greenwich Mean Time that was not local time here in the Gulf of Mexico but on the Zero Degree Meridian, which happened to run through Greenwich in London England. It was something she didn't understand, even though he tried to explain to her that Latitude was distance and Longitude, time, but he seemed to know what he was doing, so she went along with it.

Jake clambered back to the cockpit, the boyish look back on his face; pain forgotten for the moment as he played with his new toy, carefully reading off the figures from the drum and the arc, before putting the sextant carefully back into the box. Ten minutes later he took another sight and again carefully marked down the exact time and the figures from the sextant. He shivered suddenly, although the temperature was in the eighties and continued shaking for ten seconds before the seizure that held his body, died away.

Nikki watched him. "Why don't you go and lie down. I can do this."

Shaking his head he took the pad from her hand and went below, Nikki following. The yacht was still hove-to and looking after itself.

"It's okay. I'll do it. You lie down."

When he looked at her, she was shocked by the pasty face and bloodshot eyes staring at her with a haunted look.

"You don't know how."

Snorting in disgust she picked up the book. "Books. Remember? Everything you want to know is in between the covers of books. I think my expensive education can stretch to English and Math." She tossed it back on the navigation table.

Suddenly Jake was very tired and did not want to argue with her anymore. "Okay. I'll show you how to work it out. You'll have to take another sight in a few hours." Spreading the chart out on the table, he opened the book of Altitudes, Azimuths and Correction Tables.

"These are sight reduction tables. Without them you're lost. It gives the time and altitude for every day of the year so that you can calculate the Latitude and Longitude. Basically a sight is giving you the distances and angles of a triangle, from the sun to the horizon to the boat."

For an hour he explained the straightforward but tedious calculations that had to be made, then showed her how to plot the position.

Nikki stared at the small pencil cross he had placed on the chart and related it to Key West away to the southeast. It astonished her how far they had travelled, until Jake explained that the prevailing wind and current had helped. For a time they forgot their individual problems and submersed themselves in establishing the position of the yacht and proposed plan to return to Key West.

Another spasm cramped his body, bringing a gasp of pain.

"Jake. You okay?"

"Of course not. You threw away all the booze. Remember? How do you think I feel?" he muttered irritably.

"Sorry."

"It'll get worse. You prepared for that?"

"It's okay. You go rest. I'll take care of everything."

So consumed was his consciousness with the pain and the uncontrollable shaking that now took over his body, he had forgotten to tell her about 'Dip', 'Index Error' and other factors affecting the sight.

"You better be up for this."

The dread of realization stirred in her. "I started this. Right?"

"Right."

She helped him to the aft cabin and onto the berth; covered him with a thin comforter, plumping the pillow behind his head, an action she'd remembered her mother doing when she, as a child, was ill. It was a mechanical comforting act. Next she found a washcloth, wet it and laid it across Jake's forehead before returning to the saloon.

'*Keep heading west,*' he had said '*until I'm able to turn the yacht around and head for land*'. It did not seem sensible to her, so she spent the next hour planning a route back to Key West.

Bringing the yacht about was not as easy as she thought, as the boom cracked across over her head and the jib sheet refused to wind onto the winch. What had seemed a good idea was rapidly getting out-of-control. To make things worse, when she tried to steer a course for Key West, the wind was directly on the bow, stopping the yacht dead in the water.

After two hours struggle, she gave up the unequal battle and reset the yacht back on its original course, the jib flapping because she was unable to winch the sheet in enough. Little did she know it was turned around the winch anti-clockwise instead of clockwise and so was jammed. She tied it off and sat back, holding the wheel, wondering where to go from here.

Uncomfortably the yacht jogged along out-of-balance, slow and difficult to steer. Eventually Nikki, exhausted by her efforts, locked the wheel amidships and left the yacht to her own devices. A school of dolphin danced through the ocean swell nearby, but she didn't notice, unaware of anything except the misery that overwhelmed her.

Rhode Island and the comfort of the house on the Narragansett Bay seemed so far from this spot on the ocean. When she was there, it had felt like a mausoleum, with only the memories of a tormented and unhappy childhood; and she had been glad when the Ferrari sped through the gates on the road south. Now the security of her own room with all the familiar objects she had collected over the years implored her to return.

As a way to forget the life she had left behind, she went below to check on Jake. She found him semi-conscious, sweating profusely and muttering unintelligibly as he lay curled up on the berth in a near foetal position, a mere ghost of a man. She fetched a glass of fresh water and forced some down his throat, but he vomited it back up again, so she moistened the washcloth and laid it across his forehead.

In the same way she had noticed the texture of her mother's skin as she lay in the coffin, so she noticed his skin. Lines at the corners of his eyes, small scars and the way the beads of sweat quivered with his movements trickling down the creases in his face.

Then she held him in her arms. "Don't die on me Jake. Please don't die."

He seemed to hear her voice, calming a little, the shaking subsiding to occasional violent spasms. After a while, he slept and Nikki returned to the cockpit, letting the sea breeze and the sun ease the aches in her body. The resilience of youth adapting quickly to the circumstances and accepting them, not without a fight, but accepting them none-the-less. She could only watch, listen and attend.

Nothing more.

*   *   *

He saw the worms.

Huge silvery white, slimy worms crawling from his arms, waving their pincer heads in the air as if sniffing, sensing their surroundings.

And he screamed in terror.

"GET THEM OFF ME. GET THEM OFF ME."

Brushing at them with his hands and backing away to the top of the berth, until he was curled up in the corner and still they crawled out of and across his skin.

And he screamed and screamed.

Nikki burst into the cabin and saw him, eyes wide in terror, scraping at his arms, fingernails leaving long red welts on his skin, in places drawing blood; and he continued to scream until she managed to cover his arms and calm him with her soft voice.

"It's okay Jake. It's okay."

Turning his eyes to her, unseeing, speaking in gasps his voice shaking, mind pinned in the past; trapped in his book.

"*'And in his mind. His Locked Mind, the demons strolled casually without hindrance, reaping the harvest of his fertile imagination'.*"

Tapping his head with his forefinger, he stared straight at Nikki, his eyes focusing on her.

"I know you're in here. I know you are. And you won't get to me. Not anymore. I won't let you."

Suddenly he lashed out, fingers like talons, missing her face by fractions of an inch. She stumbled back from the berth, fetching up hard against the bulkhead, frightened.

"Jake it's me. Nikki."

Turning away, shaking, curling up again into a foetal position, his knees drawn up to his chest, he stared at the port-light without seeing.

"*'The Soul of his Sin succumbed to the Darkness and without light, lost the colour of his life. The rainbow hues of his Essence carried away and laid out as toys for the Demons'.*" Closing his eyes, the pain showing clear on his face. "It hurts Eve. Help me Eve. It hurts."

His childlike plea shook Nikki from her fear and with tears streaming down her face, she crossed the cabin to the berth and taking her father in her arms, she rocked him gently, smoothing the hair from his forehead.

"I'm here Jake. It's Eve. It's okay."

Relaxing against her as the spasms eased again he spoke softly again quoting from his novel.

"*Guilt appeared as a smiling Angel, with wings fanning cool breezes that burned his skin...*"

Nikki remembered the passage and finished it as his voice trailed away.

"*...and the Face of God rippled, melted and vanished as he cried out in his pain. And the Demons gently mocked in quiet contentment.*"

Looking at his face she saw that he had fallen asleep again. Gently she laid him back on the berth. Waited to make sure he was sleeping soundly before stepping back into the saloon.

Taking his novel from the bookcase, she found what she was looking for and settled down to read, taking comfort in the familiar words.

> *But at the centre was a point of light. A spark so slight, so fragile, its glow was barely visible. But it existed. It survived. It hid in silent Hope and gentle Desperation waiting to be found. To be recognised and nurtured into flame. He felt it as a quiet whisper in the darkness and in his hopelessness, failed to understand, but reached out blindly to touch the source of his salvation.*
>
> *Then, in his mind, he saw the Truth that was the Light, and without touch, without sight, without smell or hearing, he found that he could experience its presence with all his senses and understanding. And Hope came with the knowledge of the Truth.*

She read on until the uncomfortable motion of the yacht brought back the seasickness, then closed the book and set it back into the bookcase.

After an hour sitting in the cockpit, the seasickness gradually subsided and she noticed that the seas had become smaller, the motion of the yacht less violent.

By nightfall, the swell was long and even, the wind dropping to a whisper. The yacht creaked as if sighing with relief, resting until the wind and the seas kicked up again. She checked on Jake who lay shaking every now and then in his sleep, deathly pale beneath the tan, his cheeks sunken, giving his face a skeletal appearance.

As darkness cloaked the yacht, Nikki made a cup of instant soup and sat in Jake's cabin reading in an effort to understand him.

Suddenly he sat up. Wide-awake. Staring blankly at the cabin door.

"Eve? Eve? Stay close. Leave the dragon alone Eve. IT'S COMING. I SEE IT COMING. I SEE IT." Voice rising to screaming pitch, he started to hit his own face and chest, flailing around on the berth uncontrollably. "NO. NO. NO."

Nikki wrestled with his arms, but he beat her away until exhaustion weakened him and he fell back on the berth, his face bruised and cut where he'd struck himself. Leaving him, she went back to the saloon and searched through the locker beneath the settee for a length of strong nylon line. Having found what she was looking for, she returned to the cabin, cut up a towel and using it as a pad between the line and his skin, tied his arms and legs down to the berth.

Staring at her blankly, mumbling incoherently, sweat pouring down his face, he allowed her to force a little water into his mouth.

It dribbled down the sides of his cheeks onto the comforter.

He seemed calmer, still lost in his own world, where the creatures of his imagination and his reality prowled the shadows, waiting for another opportunity to strike before sanity and reason could banish them forever.

There were moments when he thought he was back to normal, where the real man was allowed out of the cage to wander the chaotic streets that were the carnage of his mind.

As he walked, he saw glimpses of Eve.

Sometimes as an Angel.

Sometimes as the Devil.

And then his imagination would create the monsters that were the abstract fears of his subconscious, made physical. He knew he was lost and he knew he had to return, but the reason escaped him. Then oblivion by way of unconsciousness released him from the terror, until the unseen jailers forced him back to consciousness.

Nikki slept, curled upon the forward berth she had claimed as her own. Exhausted by her efforts, she was grateful for the calm that had settled over the yacht. Her sleep was long and dreamless, the sunlight lancing in through the starboard port-light waking her early, refreshed, ready to start the new day. For a moment she thought she was back at home and that she was waking from a nightmare, but soon the sight, smell and sound of the ocean jarred her back to reality.

Checking in on Jake, she found him still asleep, then clambered up onto the deck with sextant and watch in hand.

The ocean was calm, with a gentle swell and little wind, the sails flapping forlornly but still managing to provide some lift to the yacht, making slow headway. Sooty terns appeared close by, their beaks ready to spear the fish they searched for as they flew across the surface of the water. Nikki watched them circle the yacht then sweep away. She had no idea they nested on the islands of the Dry Tortugas some fifty miles to the south of their present position. If she did, she probably would have tried to head the yacht in that direction. Instead she 'shot' the sun and transferred the figures onto the pad she had ready to make the calculations.

On the horizon a squall approached as a dark cloud sweeping towards the yacht, carrying high winds and rain. For a moment she thought it was land, then dismissed it, returning to the saloon to work out the sight. She did not perceive it as a problem with the calm water that surrounded the yacht. By the time she had struggled through the math and arrived at a position, the squall had reached the yacht.

It hit violently, the wind knocking the ketch onto its beam ends until the rotten sails ripped to shreds under the onslaught of wind and rain, releasing the pressure, allowing the boat to roll upright again.

Nikki was thrown bodily across the saloon. Fetching up against the starboard hull, the wind knocked out of her as water gushed in through the open hatch. It seemed like hours, but it was only seconds until the yacht righted. Fifty knots of wind in the squall kept the seas small, but the noise terrified her. The howling screeching banshee sound of a thousand devils screaming in her ears as the wind tore through the rigging.

Under normal circumstances, to an experienced crew, the squall would have been a welcome relief, a way to clean the decks and replenish the water tanks, but to Nikki it was a moment of abject terror as ignorance fuelled her fears.

It passed quickly, sweeping across the ocean like an avenging angel leaving the yacht riding gently to the swell. But there was a different feel to the yacht now, not that Nikki was able to notice the change. The sudden violence of the squall had put a strain on the ballast keel and there was a slight crack in the starboard garboard, the planking directly adjacent to the keel joint, where so long ago that small error in construction had been made by that young inexperienced apprentice.

To most casual sailors, the keel was the least thought of part on a sailboat, simply a lump of metal hung on the bottom of the hull that got caught on sand bars at low tide. But without the keel the yacht would become an upside down floating marine hazard that would eventually sink. Years of ignorant neglect had finally enabled the ocean to find the weak spot and exploit it unmercifully. With each movement of the yacht the ocean began to explore its inexorable ability to destroy everything that was not prepared. Not that the yacht was in immediate danger, but left to its own devices the ocean would eventually claim another victim.

As it was the water began to seep slowly, drip-by-drip into the bilge through the crack. If Jake had replaced the electric bilge pump when it had corroded and ceased to function, the problem would be lessened, but he had ignored it as he had with just about everything else in his life, and the water seeped in very slowly like the creeping mist on a shoreline, unnoticeable until it was too late.

Nikki struggled to her feet, her back aching, sloshing through the water on the cabin sole that had come in through the open companionway, until it quickly drained through to the bilge.

Staggering to the forward cabin she lay on the berth for a full five minutes, crying softly, before rising and struggling up the companionway steps to survey the damage.

Shredded sails hung listlessly from the mast, flapping in the breeze.

The wind had claimed first blood and vent its fury before moving on, a short reminder of the power of the elements. But if she only knew it, the ripped sails were the key to their survival, for had they not given way, the yacht would have lain on its side with the ocean pouring in through the open hatch until it sank out of sight.

The only way to allay her fear was through action. As she had no idea what to do about sailing the yacht, she set about cleaning the interior, until the tables, counter tops, lockers, bilges and cabin sole were spotlessly clean and free from encumbrances. In the process of storing the various items into the lockers, she discovered Jake's shell collection, carefully wrapped in tissue and plastic bubble wrap.

These were his prized possessions.

Completely perfect shells, undamaged in any way, cleaned of all growths so that their colours shone through in an incredible array of bright crimson to soft pink, from black and brown to creamy pastel shades. The pink conch she held in her hand was nine inches long, the opening beautifully curved, the back of the shell almost like flakes of fibreglass, brittle to touch now that the creature was no longer living in the ocean.

Next was a Triton's Trumpet, nearly a foot long, a more cylindrical shape, with brown and white interrupted stripes turning to a very pale pink at the sharp point where the shell seemed to be twisted like the tip of an ice cream cone. She handled the shell carefully, turning it over in her hand before wrapping it and moving to the next, a series of small brown Florida Fighting Conch. They were plain by comparison, so she quickly moved on to the small one-inch long Bleeding Tooth shells, with their two protuberances on the inside that looked just like two front teeth, a swathe of red colour surrounding them. She went on through the Cowries. Slim pointed Augers. Smoothly wrapped Cone shells and the exotic Murex with their delicate spines and lacy fans. These were in separate boxes.

What each one was called and to which family they belonged, she had no idea. The difference between a Jujube Top and a Lettered Olive, or a Chestnut Turban from an American Star was immaterial, because each was exquisite in its own colouring and carefully sculptured curves. Some bore a resemblance to works by the sculptor Henry Moore so smooth were their lines. She had never seen such diverse and beautiful shells, or had any idea that nature could produce such incredible shapes, forms and colouring that were not simply random accidents, but deliberate design.

But the most astonishing emotion was that she suddenly felt closer to Jake than at any other time. Here were things that, because of the way each were wrapped and stored, meant a great deal to him. They were a reflection of a side of his personality she hadn't seen. A personality that could appreciate the subtle delicacy of each shell, from the tiniest, to the largest.

Here in her hands was the essence of Monroe.

Here was where fiction met reality with a thunderously silent collision.

Having replaced them, she returned to the cabin to check on him. He was struggling against the ropes in silent ferocity, his eyes wide with madness, the antithesis of the Conch Collector. Of Monroe. He turned to her as she sat beside him and wiped his forehead.

"It's gone. I've lost it. I had it and it's gone."

He held her eyes with his, a burning haunting horror deep inside.

"EVE. LEAVE THE DRAGON EVE."

Sinking back against the pillow, soaked with sweat, he returned to the depths of his novel.

"*And he peered as if from the inside of a bubble that floated in an endless volume of noise, whilst outside, the Order of Chaos and Confusion rattled and shook with cruel laughter.*" He turned back to Nikki and fixed her with the full fury of his insanity. "*Then the Devil in the Guise of a soft forgiving cunt, sensuously took his manhood and crushed his life with barbed teeth until the pain destroyed his will and cut off his right to give life. And all the while, the hungry lips slavered and pulsated insatiably.*" Then he spat at her with all his force, the saliva hitting her face as he screamed. "I'LL NOT LET YOU. FUCK YOU. FUCK YOU. FUCK YOU."

Stumbling from the cabin, horror and nausea filling her body, the sorrow of seeing the depths of his pain spilling over in tears of helplessness and grief as he screamed and screamed at her.

"FUCK YOU. FUCK YOU. FUCK YOU."

Two parts of Jake fought and battled. Sanity watched her leave and begged her to stay, while the alcoholic madness wished her death and wanted to dance on her tomb.

But throughout the raving, the sane part of him was gradually gaining strength, using her as a lifeline, slowly pulling himself hand-over-hand back to reality. And as he did so, he cried at seeing her hurt and confusion and begged to be allowed to be her father once more and she his little girl.

It was a cry in the wilderness, lost amongst the frenetic drumbeats of the past.

*　　*　　*

Gradually the sobbing left Nikki and she opened her eyes, seeing the flat calm ocean as she leaned over the rail. Beneath the surface it was alive with fish and a green turtle swam slowly by, diving suddenly with quick strokes of its flippers as it saw Nikki move. Then it was gone, lost in the depths, heading for an unknown destination. The undulating waves drew her hypnotically and she had the almost overwhelming desire to slip quietly over the side and drift down into the depths, soon to be forgotten.

Nobody would know and nobody would care.

She would simply be a memory in a photograph album.

A brief and chaotic smudge on the canvas of a dysfunctional family history.

Shocked by the sudden yearning for death, she pulled herself up and sat back, watching as two sooty terns glided past, then dove into the water, struggled up into the air and glided away.

Dolphins, curious about the object lying still in the water, came to look; silently, gracefully, effortlessly, slipping through the ocean, their smooth grey bodies and bottle-nose heads barely making a ripple until they jumped out of the water in the sheer joy of life. A baby swam with its mother, staying close, making little playful leaps and Nikki laughed.

It was as if the dolphins had come to take away her troubles and cheer her up and having worked their magic, slowly went on their way, leaving a feeling of peace and happiness, but they also sensed that here was a vessel in distress, with a crew incapable of functioning properly. But there was little they could do except stare and, in their own way, sound a warning in squeaks and clicks some of which were lost on the human ear.

Afternoon drifted slowly into night with the rising wind and the sea building into a long swell, the yacht bobbing dismally without power. A large floating marine hazard. But gradually its character merged with that of the crew, echoing their distress with each tiny drop that entered through the infinitesimal cracks in the keel/hull joint.

Nikki spoon-fed Jake a little soup, which he managed to keep down as his body shook with tremors and his eyes stared with a lost haunted look unseeing.

He was in a state of semi-consciousness, guided by instinct to swallow the food, allowing Nikki to clean him up, change the bedclothes and wash his face and chest. She could not bring herself to do anymore than that and took the soiled bedclothes to the deck, tied the corners to a line and let them trail behind the yacht.

From the depths of the night came a distant rumble, the smell of diesel fuel strong on the wind. Closer and closer drew the sound and turning she saw the distant lights of a freighter bearing down on the yacht. With the sudden panicky sensation of a shipwrecked sailor seeing salvation, she did not know quite what to do first, so she started shouting.

"HEY. OVER HERE. HEY."

It was, of course, a completely irrational act, as the engines and the distance drowned out her cries.

Euphoria gave way to dread as she saw the black bow headed straight for the yacht and she realized the freighter had no idea they were there. It bore down on them inexorably and all she could do was watch helplessly. To Nikki it seemed like a super-tanker, such was its size in comparison to the yacht, but it was a medium sized 'tramp', with the 'Watch' busy making a cup of coffee and the rest of the crew asleep. Like a moving cliff face, the huge rusty side of the ship was about to crush the life of the frail yacht.

It was nothing personal, just a blind steel machine that could not see the yacht on its radar because Jake had never had cause to hoist the reflector to the spreaders. Lights were on in the wheelhouse as the ship passed by within four boat lengths, the bow wave tossing the yacht from side-to-side, the hammering of the engines a screaming cacophony in Nikki's ears.

Then it was gone.

Out of sight, with only the navigation lights visible and the diminishing sound of the engines to tell that it was ever there at all.

"Come back. Come back." It was a pitiful plea of dismay that turned to anger as her survival system kicked into gear. "Who needs you anyway? Screw you." She laughed hysterically at her stupidity as she shook her fist at the now vanished freighter.

Jake had said to keep watch and now she knew what he meant. The silence and emptiness of the ocean could not be taken for granted, for somewhere out there was a tragedy waiting for the unwary.

She brought a blanket up from her cabin and curled up in the cockpit, staring up at the night sky with its millions of pinpoints of light and watched the constellations move around the pole star accompanied by the flaring trails of shooting stars as they flamed across the inky blackness.

There was a Weems and Plath star finder in the navigation desk, so she passed the time trying to identify the galaxies. Every now and then a cloud would drift across to obscure the view and when it had passed, the stars had moved. She thrilled at the shooting stars that seemed to display just for her, arcing across the sky in destructive abandon. A last glorious flaming spectacular exhibition, before vanishing forever.

Satellites drifted slowly by, tiny pinpricks of reflected light, blinking back signals from every part of the earth to every other part of the earth, captured by specific electronic stations and converted to scientific data, television pictures or simply a phone call between lovers across the divide of the oceans.

As she sat contentedly watching the night sky, Jake slept peacefully, the demons withering and dying through lack of nourishment, until they blew away in the dust of defeat.

In the middle of the night, he woke and stared up at the ceiling.

It was quiet except for the gentle clatter of a loose halyard and the rushing 'whoosh' of a small breaking wave as the yacht lifted and settled. He felt his body as a tired vessel, limping slowly back to port. The gentle movement of the yacht lulled him back to sleep again as his apprehensions vanished and he knew he had won the battle. His dreams were gentle and occurred in a paradise of his own making, where deceit, deception and horror had no place. Eve was there, smiling and he let her go, knowing she was at peace and that he too could find that peace within his own soul.

SEVEN

Nikki stirred the oatmeal, added a little more water and watched it boil, continuing to stir until it was the consistency she wanted before turning off the gas flame at the gas cut-off Jake had pointed out to her and pouring the cereal into a bowl. Unconsciously balancing herself against the roll of the yacht, she carried the bowl through to the aft cabin.

Jake was sitting up, took the proffered bowl and sheepishly looked at her. "How long?"

"Four days," Nikki said guardedly.

Jake looked at the oatmeal and felt very hungry. With none of the alcohol blocks to diminish his appetite, he grasped the spoon weakly and carefully dipped it into the bowl.

"Don't eat too much. You haven't had anything for sometime and your stomach's going to be a little shrunken." She paused for a second and grinned ruefully. "At least that's what the book says." It was a gently scolding comment. A play on his arrogance and Jake smiled softly at the remark.

"I don't remember much."

"Just as well."

They were uneasy with each other, Jake not knowing what had happened and Nikki wishing she didn't.

"Where are we?" he said more to change the dynamic of the conversation than to know.

"Somewhere in the middle of the ocean." She smiled but he didn't react. "How do you feel?"

Like a blind man who had suddenly been given sight, he moved his eyes slowly over to her, seeing her clearly, perhaps for the first time.

"Like the Dolphin's offensive line have just rolled over me, then came back and did it again."

She laughed and he liked the way her whole face lit up, brightening the cabin. "You got pretty wild."

"I say anything interesting?" he said lightly but fearful that he had said things he would later regret.

Looking away, she pressed down the corner of the blanket and he noticed her long slim fingers. And felt his heart falter. "Quoted from your book a lot."

"Worst thing about alcoholic writers, it makes them even more insufferable than they already are." He grinned, embarrassed. "If I do it again, shoot me."

She avoided his eyes and continued to smooth the blanket with her hands, studying the weave with a sudden intensity. "Might just shoot you anyway." She paused before continuing, not knowing whether to say what she wanted to say or lie because it was easier. "You called out Mom's name a few times. I think you thought I was her."

Then he knew that it was Eve in the form of Nikki that he had battled and he wondered how she had coped, but dared not ask. With Eve, he had found the way to peace, but with Nikki he had no idea how to proceed.

"I remember seeing her." There was a block that still needed removing, but until he could find out what it was, he was held back, straining against pride and guilt.

Nikki patted the bedclothes absentmindedly, turned and glanced through the port-light, looking anywhere but at Jake.

"I couldn't figure out the position. Tried a couple of times and found we were in the middle of Texas. The dolphins didn't agree."

"You take the sight, I'll do everything else. Just bring in the books and the clock."

Watching her leave the cabin, seeing her slim shape, boyish yet unmistakably female he wondered why she had not mentioned boyfriends. It shocked him to realize how little he knew about her and how little he had cared over all these years, hiding behind what he thought was a higher morality and now saw as a squalid, petty excuse. It also shocked him to see how much the alcohol had destroyed his ability to feel, but then that was why he had started to drink.

What he was really beginning to understand was that he had been a coward for twenty years.

The revelation was uncomfortable and gave him a sense of foreboding and self-disgust.

*   *   *

Braced against the cockpit coaming, Nikki sighted through the sextant telescope and moved the handle until the sun came down to the horizon. Swinging it as Jake had shown her, she made a couple of minor adjustments and smiled with satisfaction.

"MARK," she shouted for Jake to hear, then scrambled below and handed him the sextant. He wrote down the figures and gave it back for her to stow carefully in the box.

"How tall are you?"

"What?"

"How tall?"

"What difference does that make?"

"I need to know the exact height of the sextant above sea level. That includes the freeboard of the yacht and your height minus a couple of inches." From her expression he saw that she was not convinced. "It makes a difference."

"Five six. Five seven. Need to know my weight too?" It came out before she could stop it, but he just grinned and opened the books.

"What's the date today?"

"Twenty seventh. Wednesday."

"Year?"

"What?"

"Just kidding."

He wrote down the figures from the altitude tables, the Index and Dip corrections. The resultant figure calculated by simple math was the Apparent Altitude.

"Okay, now we look in the book for the refraction and semi-diameter corrections for today. Write it down, make an addition and there we have the Corrected Altitude," he explained slowly.

She stared at the figures that meant absolutely nothing to her. Just a bunch of chicken scratches on the page.

"Now we need the Greenwich hour angle. That's the time," Jake continued and followed with a detailed and involved explanation of the Greenwich hour angle that bored Nikki, but she stayed with it as he opened the Nautical Almanac at the back. "These are the Interpolation Tables. They give the minutes and seconds," he said making another calculation, and then writing down the latitude and longitude.

"So that's our position, right?"

"Wrong. That's the position of the sun directly over the earth's surface by an angle of ninety degrees. Gives us a distance as a radius from there. We could be anywhere on the circumference of the circle. There's more."

"More? Jesus."

Proceeding through the remainder of the calculations, questioning her until he thought she understood, he then sent her back up on deck to obtain another fix. When she returned they went through the whole procedure again, ending with a true position marked on the chart.

"You've done this before. I mean you didn't just pick this up overnight."

"Well, I had a few lessons years ago. That's when I thought I'd cruise the world. It didn't last long."

"You mean it lasted long enough for the booze to change your mind." She felt deceived and a need to strike back, to make him suffer just a little more. "You could have figured everything out on the first day. Couldn't you?"

"I guess."

"Last night we nearly got run down by a ship and all you can say is '*I guess*'? Jesus Christ."

The expression on his face was of a little boy who had been caught with his hands in the cookie jar and suddenly all the tension that had built up over the last four days exploded in laughter.

But Nikki didn't feel like laughing, she felt like hitting him with a baseball bat, but somehow the situation was too ridiculous for anger.

"How about you make us some coffee?"

"I thought you hated coffee?"

"You got something stronger hidden away?"

"Coffee coming up," she said briskly.

Jake struggled off the berth and stood, bent over for a moment or two until the cabin stopped revolving, then reached for his clothes, pulling on a pair of old shorts and a tee shirt. He felt as weak as a baby, yet surprisingly alert, his brain cleared of cobwebs.

Nikki turned as he came into the saloon and sat down at the navigation table, watching as he laid out the chart, took up the dividers and parallel ruler then plotted the position.

Taking the cup from her outstretched hand, he pointed to the chart.

"We're about forty miles from the Dry Tortugas."

"And they would be...?"

"Small group of islands that are the southernmost tip of the USA. Never been there, but I hear they're kinda pretty."

"Funny name."

Sipping the coffee he stared at the chart.

"We'll head for them. They're closer than Key West and it'll give us a break."

Nikki was silent, looking at the small cross on the chart and at the tiny islands that seemed like an oasis in the vast ocean. What should have been a feeling of joy was one of disappointment. "We have a problem," she whispered.

Jake looked up sharply. "Problem?"

Mystified, he followed her topsides into the cockpit and stared at the mess of hanging shredded sails flapping in the breeze. Astern were the bed sheets trailing behind the yacht.

"What's that?"

"Sheets. Yours. Needed washing."

There was no need to elaborate. He got the picture.

"They need to be rinsed in fresh water when they're clean, otherwise the salt crystals will keep them damp." He turned to look back at the sails. "Well they'll have to come down. Guess they were rotten. Not to worry."

"Not to worry?"

Reaching over, he touched her cheek softly and grinned. It was the first time he had touched her like that and she felt the confusion rising.

"We have spares in the forepeak. Never been used."

They set to work.

Jake loosened the outhaul, untying it from the clew as Nikki rinsed the salt from the sheets and strung a line between the main and mizzen shrouds on the starboard side to dry them. Then she joined Jake at the mast and helped him haul down the mainsail. The shackle pin was rusted tight.

"There's a tool box in the engine room. Open the panel by the navigation table. It's in there."

Scrambling below, she returned a few moments later with the toolbox, placed it at Jake's feet and watched as he sorted through until he found a shackle tool, then replaced the rusted shackle before sliding the remains of the mainsail from the boom.

Nikki rolled up the shreds as Jake busied himself loosening the jib halyard, then walked forward to haul it down, unfastening the sail hanks from the forestay as he pulled. Some were rusted and required the services of a pair of pliers and a Mole wrench. Again the shackle tool came in handy to remove the halyard from the head of the sail. Nikki rolled up the shreds and put them in the sail bags in the cockpit.

They repeated this procedure with the staysail and mizzen before she managed to force Jake to rest, as dizziness swept over him and he thought for a moment he would black out. Nikki fetched a glass of water.

"You tell me what to do and I'll do it. You're in no shape for this."

He had to agree. The last four days had taken their toll physically and it would be a couple more days before his strength returned.

"Got any vitamins stored away?" Nikki asked.

"I think so. Frankie takes them. Look in the aft head, may find some."

"They're for you."

"Anything you say." He was too tired to argue.

As she observed him for a moment or two, she wondered whether he would relapse into the monster of the previous four days, but he seemed a shadow of that other person. There was quietness, a meekness about him that she found disconcerting. It made it more difficult to maintain the anger.

Sure that he was okay, she turned her attention to the sail bags.

"Where do these go?"

"In the forepeak. It's the locker at the far end of the forward berth."

Hauling the old sail bags down she pulled the new ones from the forepeak locker. By the time she had the four replacement sails in their bags back in the cockpit, she was breathing hard.

"Right. Let's get the sails up and this old tub moving. I want to close the Dry Tortugas in daylight."

"Why?"

"Reefs. That's why. The last thing we need is a hole in the bottom."

For an hour she helped him replace all the old shackles and check the sheets and halyards. As they worked, he explained every part to her, what they did and the importance of each piece.

Very subtly they were becoming a team. She began to see the yacht as an organic being. A part of them. They needed the yacht and the yacht needed them. The problems between them taking a back seat whilst they worked together to get the yacht moving again and headed towards land.

As peace descended for the first time in a week, Nikki became aware of the beauty and spirituality of the ocean.

Perhaps even God existed out here in this emptiness, where the forces of nature moved, swirled and eddied, unhampered by any constraints. And His creatures slept, fed, procreated and played as they were intended.

Only *Man* fought to control the elements, even though the elements always won.

Man in his arrogance continually convinced that he would prevail.

But as she thought these things, she knew that somewhere, just over the horizon, Mankind was changing both the illusion and the environment's fragile structure forever, in the misinformed opinion that it was for the better.

And she had a sudden strange feeling of panic that was unexpected and unnerving. A thought that if they kept on moving, Civilisation would not catch up with them and they could exist as Father and

Daughter here on the ocean. Together.

Jake broke in on her thoughts. "Make sure the shackle pin's tight, then come back here and I'll show you how to attach the outhaul to the clew."

Once the mizzen was secured on the boom with the halyard shackled to the headboard, they repeated the process with the other sails until at last all sails were ready to be hoisted.

Jake sat down for a rest and another glass of water, whilst Nikki laid out the sheets and ran them through the blocks and organizers to the winches on the cockpit coaming. Then she sat down beside him on the coachroof and watched the dolphins at play.

"Would you have preferred a son?"

"Strange question." He looked at her carefully, but she was watching the dolphins. "The thought never occurred to me. I was glad that you had all the bits and pieces you were supposed to have. That's all that mattered."

"Jake?"

"What?"

"It doesn't matter. Can we get on with this?"

"Okay. Mizzen and staysail first. Then mainsail and jib."

He showed her the staysail halyard and while she was hauling the staysail aloft, he slowly winched up the mizzen. Once up, he trimmed them from the cockpit and the yacht began to move through the water. Nikki hauled up the main and jib, sweating to winch the mainsail up the last few feet, the new sail stiff, the slides needing some dry lubricant, but she managed it none-the-less.

With all sails set, the yacht leaned into the ocean with a delight Jake could feel through the wheel as all the components that had been designed so carefully, finally came together for one single purpose. Converting the power of the wind into forward motion.

But there was a sluggishness that had not been there before.

Nothing that a novice sailor would notice, but it was there in the way the yacht moved through the water as the ocean seeped very slowly into the bilge through the tiny cracks in the garboard planking.

Jake set the new course, heading towards the Dry Tortugas. He spent half an hour fiddling with the sail trim until the yacht steered herself, the wheel locked a little to weather. Job completed, he flopped back exhausted. Weak as a kitten. Mind floating as if a couple of feet from his body.

"Nikki," Jake said weakly.

Alarmed, she turned towards him from her position on the weather rail.

"I'm going below for an hour or two. The yacht will steer herself so don't worry. If there are any wind shifts, wake me."

"Okay."

Once below, he crawled onto the berth and even before his head hit the pillow, had fallen deep into an exhausted sleep.

*   *   *

He dreamed an alcohol drugged nightmare. But the dreams were unlike the fantasies he'd dreamed before. The settings were fantastical, the images vividly real. Colours sharp. Well defined. Over accentuated just as the trees, mountains and cities were clean and perfect. And amongst the perfection, Eve in the guise of Nikki wandered peacefully smiling, holding onto Jake's hand and he felt the sexuality of his wife, though he saw the picture of his daughter and his lust ripped apart his heart with love and yearning and as he took her in his arms, she became Eve and he made love to her with a passion he thought he'd lost.

And, as he lay back floating on a sickly sweet marshmallow cloud of contentment, she rose naked before him and pressed her hard nipples to his mouth and he drank. When she pulled away, he opened his eyes to see Nikki smiling down at him.

"You're good Jake."

It couldn't be.

He couldn't have.

He sat up in the berth, but it wasn't a berth.

It was a bed and Eve lay down, opening her legs for him and he was drawn towards her sex, but when he looked up, it was Nikki once again. Laughing at him, licking her lips sensuously, teasing him. He didn't want her. But she was Eve again and the reality of the nightmare frightened and confused him as the taboos of his conscience tore at the fabric of his consciousness. The horror of the nightmare leaving him a shaking soundlessly screaming madman.

He woke covered in sweat, eyes wide, breathing harsh, fear and disgust shredding his soul. The familiar sight of the wooden hull glistening through the clear fibreglass sheathing was comforting, but he still wasn't sure whether it was dream or reality.

Reaching out, he touched the hull.

It was cool. Solid. And beyond the fibreglass and wood, the ocean slid past, the slight vibration detectable to the nerves on the ends of his fingers.

From somewhere on the yacht came the sound of a high-pitched woman's voice singing. The song percolating through the deck to Jake, easing the tension within him, but leaving a sense of guilt at the fact that Nikki had been so much a part of his erotic dream.

"Christ. Why can't I dream of conch."

There was a knock and he hurriedly covered himself as Nikki poked her head around the door.

"Oh. You're awake. Dinner'll be ready in half an hour."

"Dinner?"

"Sure."

'A fool indeed', he thought and swung his legs over the side of the berth, stared at the port-light with the water rushing past inches away and sank back into a reflective state as his body slowly accepted that he was awake and ready to move, the nightmare slammed back into the dark recesses of his alcoholic's mind.

*   *   *

Nikki had her share of reflection too, spending the time while Jake was asleep trying to reconcile her conflicting emotions into a rational, logical order, eventually giving up the unequal struggle and stepping sideways in her mind.

The ocean was beautiful, and the yacht a comfortable home now that she was used to the motion. She wandered the deck, freed from the cockpit as the yacht sailed herself under a full spread of sail, heading up and bearing away in the wind and the swell, finding her own route through the water better than she could steer. She didn't fully understand the mechanics that allowed this to happen, but could still appreciate the skill of the designer and the builder that resulted in the superbly balanced craft.

When Jake came into the saloon, he was greeted with a cup of coffee and a plate of hot food, served by a smiling Nikki.

"Chilli. You've got a whole store full of it."

"Oh."

"Rice."

"Ice cold beer?"

Nikki held onto her bowl as the yacht heeled sharply under a sudden gust and looked disapprovingly at Jake. "Not funny."

He shrugged and helped himself to a mouthful of chilli, noticing that his hand was steadier than it had been for days. "It's good."

"It's out of a can."

"It's still good. Can't remember the last time I really *tasted* food. Any food. Except sour conch salad."

"What?"

"I'll make you some. Raw conch. Bahamian sushi."

She pulled a face.

"It's good, you'll see. Sushi with a difference."

"I'm not into sushi."

The yacht heeled and stayed at an angle of twenty degrees under the press of wind. Jake glanced over to the barometer mounted below the clock on the forward bulkhead and frowned.

"Looks like the glass is falling. Better reef the sails after dinner."

"Does that mean we're in for rough weather?" Nikki said, watching him with a growing concern, her confidence in the vessel not yet complete after the last squall.

"We get some strong winds blowing through every now and then. Doesn't last long and the seas don't have time to build up that much, but it can get uncomfortable."

"You sound like Captain Ahab."

"Fifteen years of listening to fishermen's tales in the bar."

"I'm surprised you could remember any of it. Anyway what about hurricanes?"

"Not at this time of year," he said with a confidence he did not feel.

They talked spasmodically as they ate, always seeming to skirt what was really on their minds, but it was an unconscious act as if they had made an unspoken agreement to avoid certain subjects for the time being.

Jake helped her clear up the dishes and showed her how the saltwater foot pump worked, then how to rinse the dishes in fresh water.

"But there's a water maker. Why worry about using the fresh water?"

"Because nothing is perfect. Work on the principle of Murphy's Law, that if something can break it will. I try to keep the fresh water tank topped up just in case the water maker gives up. Only drain it when it needs cleaning."

She busied herself drying and stacking the plates back in the rack and putting the cutlery away in the drawer. There was something on her mind. Something so normal yet she didn't know how to approach the subject with him. It seemed to be so silly to be so embarrassed.

"I need to use the toilet, but..."

He glanced up and laughed suddenly at her discomfort.

"Christ. The thought never occurred to me."

"I tried to use it, but couldn't flush it. It's a mess."

Jake wiped down the sinks and the tops, then crossed to the forward head, opening the door and pulling a face. She followed close behind and leaned over his shoulder as he knelt down and opened a locker door beside the toilet bowl. Inside were two bronze seacocks. He pointed to the one on the left.

"This is the sea water inlet. Pull the handle this way." Indicated another small lever on the toilet bowl. "Turn this to 'Flush' and pump." Water flooded into the bowl. "Turn this. It's the outlet. Now pump the handle again. Water circulates. Pump until everything is gone. Now close the inlet seacock and turn the lever to 'Dry', then pump the water out. When you've done that close the outlet seacock.

And that's all there is to it."

Nikki watched incredulously.

"All that just to go to the toilet?"

"You could always just hang your butt over the lee-rail."

"Hey," she gasped indignantly.

"Anything else?"

"That'll do for now, thank you very much."

"Just one thing. No sanitary towels down the toilet. Blocks the system."

"Thanks for being so candid."

"You're on a boat. Nothing's private on a boat."

"Well while we're on the subject, I just started my period and I don't have any." She flung the ball firmly back in Jake's court, wiping the smug look off his face.

"Look under the forward berth, I think Frankie keeps some there."

While she disappeared into the cabin and shut the door, he went topsides to watch the sunset. She joined him a few minutes later.

"We'll heave-to for the night. I don't want to close the islands before daybreak."

"What does that mean?"

"I'll show you. We need harnesses and lifejackets."

Just as he spoke another gust of wind hit, heeling the yacht and sending Nikki crashing into Jake.

"That's why."

She grasped the edge of the cockpit as Jake opened the cockpit seat and took out two harnesses with built in automatically inflating lifejackets.

"Always attach the carabiner to any strong point like the base of the mast. Never onto the stanchions. There's another strong point at the forestay anchor point. If you do go over, the harness inflates when you hit the water. Takes about five seconds. There's enough buoyancy to hold your head clear. From now on, every time you come on deck, this goes on. Understood?"

"Yes Captain."

Then Jake led the way to the mast.

With her help, he dropped the main and jib, then swung the wheel so that the staysail was backed and the wheel locked to windward. The bow swung up to windward, luffed and then swung back to leeward. All the while the yacht remained stationary.

"That's hove-to. We won't make much leeway and we'll weather any strong winds that come our way."

They sat in the cockpit after their efforts and watched the last of the sunset.

Scudding clouds turned a brilliant purply red colour as the sun reached the horizon and seemed to melt and spread before disappearing. Slowly the red faded from the sky and darkness descended onto the ocean.

Jake had been confident about his position, so wasn't unduly worried about being able to get a star fix. When the last vestiges of the sun had gone, he went below and tried to calculate their drift and the position they might find themselves in the morning. He hoped fervently that by morning the sky would be clear so that he wouldn't have to 'dead reckon' the course to the Dry Tortugas.

Nikki made another cup of coffee as the yacht pitched and rolled in the increasing wind and sea, then sat down, bracing herself against the engine room bulkhead.

"Well?"

"I think we're on track. Should make landfall sometime late tomorrow morning."

They sat opposite each other. Nikki settled into her favourite corner. Curled up like a contented cat, holding the cup in her hands watching Jake as he stared around at the interior. He had seen it so many times that he'd grown blasé about the carefully crafted joinery and the many hours of labour that had gone into the building of the yacht. As he looked he began to relive the sensations and emotions he'd had when he first saw her so many years ago.

"It's funny."

"What?"

"I was thinking about the first time I saw her."

"Mom?"

He shook his head, still gazing around the saloon.

"Frankie?"

"No. The yacht. I had to have her. She summed up what I felt. A little worn. In need of repair, but still noble. Still with dignity and that's what I needed most."

Nikki studied him, puzzled. "Your dignity? I don't understand."

Gazing around the saloon, he sought to remember every part as if each had a memory of it's own to impart to him. A moment of his life held in the smoothly finished mahogany. Reflected in the high shine of the varnish. Each joint had been precision crafted, each piece of wood hand rubbed and coated meticulously with many coats so that the years of neglect and abuse it had been subjected to had not damaged the surface permanently.

"You're afraid. Something scares you." She knew, not through knowledge, but through instinct. As if being close together in the confines of the yacht had given her a perception. A telepathic link.

Jake felt her probing his mind and a part of him welcomed it, although the residual demons battled to summon the rage they knew was theirs.

He avoided her eyes.

"When you were hallucinating, you got really graphic. I mean you quoted from some really dark passages and Mom was in everything."

Frowning he bit his lip, wondering where this was leading.

"You loved her, didn't you?"

It was a statement rather than a question because she suddenly realized it was the truth.

"You really loved her. Always loved her. Isn't that right?"

At that point she wasn't thinking about Jake, but glorying in her discovery, not realizing the pain she was inflicting.

"What happened?"

He looked down at the table, rubbed his hand over the surface, speaking quietly. "Leave it alone."

"Why? What happened? Why did you leave?"

Suddenly Jake fixed her with his bleak eyes. "I didn't leave. I was thrown out by a court order. She had me removed," he whispered, his voice barely audible.

It shook her because she wasn't expecting that answer and the divisions between them were back again.

"I don't believe you."

"Of course you don't. Why should you? For fifteen years you've been force-fed what a bad man I was. Well maybe I was. I was twenty years old, horny and lonely so I fell for the first girl who opened her legs and said she loved me."

"Stop."

"Why? Don't you like the idea of your parents grunting and sweating while they fuck?" He was angry and he wanted to hurt her. To strip away the thin veneer of illusion and face her with the truth. "You don't want to know that she was pregnant with you before we married?"

Appalled, shocked and disappointed she stared at him. Silence hung between them as a solid curtain of betrayal and he wished again that he could take the words back.

"So it was because of me?"

"No," he said tiredly and lay his head back against the hull between the bookshelves. "No it wasn't you. Eve was a manic-depressive. I didn't know that when we married, only later, when she stopped taking her medication. Hell. What did I know? I thought she was taking birth control pills." He sighed deeply. "Christ. I pulled her out of more bars and jails than you can possibly imagine."

Little did he know that she knew exactly what he was talking about.

Unbidden, mental images flashed into her mind.

Eve standing at the foot of the stairs, bottle in hand, swaying and screaming at the top of her voice.

Nikki, the little girl, frightened and confused as she stared at her mother who was not her mother. Beautiful face contorted by drink and rage. Clothes in disarray. Hair disheveled. Lipstick smeared across her face in a bright red scar that made her mouth look twice the size. Nikki knew her father was there, but she couldn't see him. Later it would be different as her mother begged for her forgiveness, tears of remorse staining her cheeks. The depths of her sorrow and unhappiness reflected deep within her dark eyes.

127

She wiped the image from her mind. "I don't believe it," she said shakily without conviction, knowing that she did.

"It doesn't matter whether you do or you don't. It's the truth. Sometimes that can be hard to take. It was for me. I'm not saying it was all her fault. That's not what I'm saying at all. Hell, we weren't fit to be parents, either of us. Who is at that age?"

"It doesn't make sense. If she was the manic-depressive, then why didn't you have custody?"

They had come to the point of no return. If he carried on, then he would have to tell her everything, but that was still too painful to face.

He realized he was afraid of facing the truth he had tried so hard to bury for twenty years. "You don't need to know anymore."

Her eyes narrowed like a tiger waiting to pounce, sensing the moment was at hand. "Perhaps you are the one who doesn't want to hear it." Her new-found perception spearing home again.

Standing, he crossed to the companionway. Suddenly the atmosphere was oppressive, filling with the past like dust in a coal mine. He stopped and looked across at her. "You're right." Then turned and climbed into the cockpit.

Nikki watched him and found that her anger had lost its edge for she knew deep in her heart that he was telling the truth. There had been indications of Eve's unbalanced state-of-mind. But as a child Nikki had simply accepted *'Mom'* as *'it's just Mom, she's like that'*. Never understanding the reason behind her sudden irrational behaviour.

Now as she thought back, she remembered it was always at a time when there were new lovers about the house, with Eve behaving meanly, sometimes cruelly to her. When she grew into her teens and learned about Premenstrual Stress, she rationalized, in her juvenile naiveté that PMS was the cause and forgave Eve her behaviour.

Now she was learning that her parents were far more flawed than she had accepted and the ideals she had created were crashing around her in the chaos of pain and sickness. The knowledge was something she'd rather do without, but knew that somehow she had to reconcile the truth of the present to the illusion of the past.

EIGHT

The mainsail came down to the first reef mark and Jake secured the halyard, tied the reefing lines securely before hauling the sail up a little more to tighten the luff. Satisfied the sail was in reasonable shape, he turned his attention to the foresail. The bow fell off the wind and he hanked on a smaller jib. The wind had piped up to twenty knots and he was taking a chance that it would fall off as the day progressed, as, according to the Pilot Notes for the area, it should. Settling back onto a broad reach, the yacht headed for the Dry Tortugas while Jake set the mizzen, locked off the helm and went below to fix breakfast.

Four hours of solid sleep had left him refreshed and stronger, allowing his mind to clear of everything except the task of closing the islands and avoiding the reefs that dotted the area.

Searching through the galley locker, he had come across pancake mix, so stirred up a pint of dried milk, threw the contents of the packet into the bowl mixing the batter with an old fashioned hand mixer, winding the handle fast until he could feel the strain on his forearms.

He hummed softly to himself without realizing, enjoying being at sea and wondering why he had never done this before. Of course he knew the answer, but he asked himself just the same and while he was idly wondering, his mind turned to Frankie.

Nothing had been further from his mind for he past few days, and now that the stress had lessened, his thoughts wandered. Theirs had always been a loose relationship. Loose yet binding. A confidence in each other. Or so he liked to think, but he knew that there was more to the relationship than he was prepared to admit. There was something almost mystical about their connection and it frightened him.

He paused in his mixing to reflect on that. "Hope you're right Jake. Hope you're right." Talking to himself was an old habit. If years of loneliness had created the habit he had long since forgotten, simply considered himself an old and trusted friend who could not be lied to, but that itself was a deceit.

Shrugging away his philosophizing he searched for the pancake pan, placing it on the stovetop next to the already boiling kettle. Two cups were ready and waiting. Having stirred the coffee, he took one cup through to the forward cabin.

Nikki slept fitfully.

All night long, dreams marched through her mind and now as she bordered on consciousness, she saw herself as a little girl staring through the banisters down into the living room. She could see her mother and her father, both beautiful, both young, both standing inches apart screaming at each other. But the sound was muted as if through a heavy filter. In the far background another person stood in the room, but the shape was too unclear.

What was clear was the sound of laughter.

Gentle laughter that rose to a maniacal scream and Nikki, the little girl, descended the stairs towards the living room. Before her mother and father could turn, she reached the door.

Faces contorted in their hatred for each other. They seemed to grow larger and larger until their faces filled the room and the indecipherable screaming grew to deafening proportions as it seemed as if she was the focus of their anger and hatred.

Hands reached out to grasp her shoulder and though she tried to pull back, she was unable to do so.

She woke suddenly, jolted to full consciousness, looking up at Jake's smiling face. Shrinking back from his touch, the dream still echoing in her mind. He placed the cup on the leeward shelf and smiled at her.

"Good Morning. Sleep well?"

For a moment or two longer she tried to reconcile the dream to the reality, finally shaking away the darkness, struggling to full wakefulness.

"Yes thanks."

"Good. Pancakes in ten minutes."

Slowly she sipped the coffee, listening to the water rushing past the hull, with the occasional pounding as the bow thudded into a wave. Jake's humming a muted disharmony in the background. In spite of the dreams, she felt refreshed, without the worry of having to look after the yacht by herself, or caring for a sick patient. Indeed the patient seemed to have recovered remarkably well.

"Breakfast," he called through to her as she struggled into a pair of skin-tight short pants, slipping a loose tee shirt over the top. The sunburn had gone, but she was not taking any chances because she found that staring at the sails for any length of time dried her lips and burned her nose. So she lathered sun block on her face and used the lip balm she had found in the head. She had come to accept that most things were public domain on a yacht.

Maple syrup ran thinly from the bottle, spreading over the pancakes and pooling on the dish, ready to be mopped up with each forkful. They tasted as good as they looked and she'd finished the first two before Jake had the chance to sit down.

"There's more in the oven. Help yourself."

She did, dodging the gimballed stove, timing the roll of the yacht and bringing four more pancakes back to the table, dumping two on Jake's plate.

*   *   *

Two dolphins rode the bow pressure wave as the yacht charged onwards at six knots, heeled under a hard press of sail.

With a slight decrease in the apparent wind, Jake had decided to increase the sail area, shaking out the reefs in the mizzen and main, striking the small jib and hanking on a genoa now that the wind had veered, blowing across the starboard quarter. Nikki stood on the bowsprit and leaned over the bow pulpit, harness clipped to the outer forestay anchor point, watching the dolphins, who every now and then looked up at her, seeming to smile before streaking away effortlessly, turning a large circle before returning to ride the bow wave.

Throwing her head back, she laughed in delight, closing her eyes, letting the sun warm her face and the spray cool her body. Revelling in the sensuality of the ocean. Opening her eyes, she looked at the far horizon and noticed what appeared to be a dark bump ahead.

"Is that what I think it is?"

"Sure is. Dry Tortugas."

He felt good. The anxiety of his questionable navigation skills retreating as the islands grew bigger. Locking the wheel he went below to fetch the detailed chart and the Pilot Notes, returning to the cockpit and plotting a route leaving Hospital Key to port, heading between Garden Key and Bush Key, to the only reasonably protected anchorage.

The colour of the ocean changed from dark blue to a lighter blue, then a green-turquoise as the soundings reduced.

As Nikki continued to hang over the bow, Jake struck the spinnaker and main and continued into the Northwest Channel under staysail and mizzen. Clambering to the bow he showed Nikki how to prepare the 45lb CQR anchor by checking that the chain was fast on the windlass then releasing the securing pin on the bow roller.

"When I tell you, flip this holding catch on the windlass and let the anchor go," he instructed, showing her where the windlass release catch was before turning back to stare into the clear ocean at the abundant marine life that swarmed through the shoaling water.

Anxiety began to swell within him as he steered the yacht towards the anchorage.

Fort Jefferson on Garden Key with fifty-foot high, eight-foot thick walls imposed its presence on the anchorage, dominating the island.

In the anchorage were a couple of other yachts. A fifty foot sloop that sprouted all sorts of antennae from a stern arch and an older forty foot ketch, the crew watching as Jake steered close to the public dock where a couple of Park Service vessels were lying and then swung the bow to windward, the yacht slowing to a stop with backed staysail, before sliding astern.

"NOW. LET GO THE ANCHOR."

Nikki released the catch and watched as the anchor dropped away into the water, followed by the chain, rattling and banging as it paid out over the bow roller. Jake snubbed the anchor until it set; allowed more rode to pay out until he was satisfied there was enough, then locked off the wheel and hurried forward. The marks on the chain told him there was 150 feet paid out.

Reluctantly Nikki turned from her grandstand seat in the bow and struck the staysail, securing it while Jake dealt with the mizzen.

Once the yacht had been squared away, they sat side-by-side and stared out across the anchorage to Fort Jefferson. Jake held a book in his hand and flipped quickly through the pages.

"Okay. Here we are. Dry Tortugas. Discovered by Ponce de Leon in 1513. They lie sixty miles from Key West consisting of seven low-lying Keys. The name is derived from the turtles that inhabit the area and the fact that there is no fresh water. The construction of Fort Jefferson was begun in 1846 but never completed. It was designed to house 1500 men and 450 guns. The perimeter is one and half miles."

"This a history lesson."

"Listen. It gets more interesting," he said, pausing to run quickly through a couple of passages before resuming. "During the Civil War, it was used as a prison, one of the most famous inmates being Dr Samuel Mudd."

"Who the hell is Dr Samuel Mudd?"

"Dr Samuel Mudd, my dear, was the man who treated John Wilkes Booth after Booth shot President Lincoln."

"Dumb move."

"Maybe, but he had no idea who John Wilkes Booth was or that the President had been shot and would die. No instant news in those days."

"Bummer."

"The fort was finally abandoned by the Military and President Roosevelt named it a national monument in 1935. Now there are just a handful of Park Service Personnel here and a bunch of tourists who fly in from the Keys and the mainland."

"Thank you Professor."

"You're welcome."

It was pleasant to sit in the sunshine with a cooling breeze that took the edge off the heat and humidity, talking quietly and laughing at the occasional joke, watching the small world of the Dry Tortugas slowly unfold around them with peaceful simplicity.

Neither Jake nor Nikki realised they had reached a different level in their relationship. That they had begun to work as a team and beneath the mistrust and anger was a growing respect.

Perhaps it was the situation. Perhaps it was the atmosphere of the Dry Tortugas working magic on their souls as if some unseen hand had brought them here.

A Park Ranger motored over to them, both he and Jake recognising one another as patrons of Owen's bar. His curiosity satisfied, and with an explanation about watching for drug runners, he motored away and left them in peace.

But the peace, like one of Jake's treasured shells, was a fragile one.

Together they launched the dinghy, lowering it from the davits.

Nikki climbed aboard and Jake handed her the pump to top up the side tubes, while he checked the outboard and fuel level in the tank. He knew there was a spare tank in the aft deck locker and a full jerry can.

Happy that everything was in order, he started the engine and handed the controls to Nikki who steered them to shore, towards a small beach near the public dock, lying beneath the shadow of Fort Jefferson's red brick walls.

As they closed the shore, Nikki became aware of the mosquitoes she hadn't missed while they were at sea and again suffered the buzz and bite, reverting to the almost unconscious slapping routine that seemed so normal.

Once the hull grounded, Jake watched with pleasure as she pulled on the outboard handle, tipping it back as she'd seen him do, until the catch secured the propeller well clear of the sand. Stepping into the water as Jake pulled the dinghy up the beach she waded to the shore suddenly feeling very strange, as if the land was moving beneath her feet just as the yacht had. So she sat down and put her head between her legs, taking deep breaths.

Jake dug the small anchor into the sand and crossed to her, leaned down and helped her to her feet.

"Takes a few minutes to get used to your land legs again. It'll pass."

"That was weird."

"Come on let's walk. It'll do you good."

They passed a small camp ground, with tables; a couple of well-worn barbecue grills and clean scrubbed toilets. The ground was undisturbed except for a few footprints of boat owners who had come this way to view the fort.

Nikki smiled to herself and turned to Jake as they walked. "I always wanted to do this as a child. Walk with you I mean."

"We used to. I'd take you to the park most days. You gave those swings a work out, I'll tell you."

"I don't remember."

They were silent for a while, walking through a dusty tunnel to the centre of the Fort where scraggly grasses grew among the abandoned walls.

At the far end was a well-maintained section with a freshly painted doorway, the entrance to the Park Service offices and living quarters.

Stone steps led to the battlements where they could look out across the anchorage to the other low Keys. Some with casuarina trees and palms, others held in the grip of red mangrove.

Sooty terns wheeled in the sky over Bush Key, their nesting site. A delight for bird watchers.

"The thing I missed most was at school. It may seem silly, but I wished that you and Mom could have been together at school functions. Like concerts, plays. Things like that. Just to be able to look out and see you there. That's all. Just to see you together. Just like the other kids' parents," Nikki said quietly, watching the birds dive, jink and soar around the Key.

"Didn't Eve go?" Jake asked, matching her quiet tone, encouraging the mood.

"Sometimes. Not often. When she did, she had some guy hanging on her arm. It wasn't fun to have to explain to the other kids he was another of Mom's boyfriends. Finally I asked her not to come anymore."

"I'm sorry. It must have been very lonely. I wish...," his voice trailed off and he turned his head away, watching the terns. Free and unfettered, concerned only with feeding and mating.

"I had an abortion when I was sixteen."

It was a flat statement, without malice, without blame, just an autobiographical fact. Perhaps this statement alone struck the core of his being more than anything else. He felt something breaking inside him as when he'd first seen her cry in pain as a small child. When those big oily tears had fallen down her cheeks and the expression of hurt and bewilderment had filled her eyes. It was all he could do to stop himself from breaking down, but still tears came to his eyes.

"I didn't know. I'm sorry."

"It's okay. The whole experience was over-rated," she said with forced cheerfulness in an attempt to be flippant that didn't quite work. There was a spreading feeling of comfort within her that had grown with the days spent on the yacht.

The anchorage was beautiful. She was becoming familiar with Jake and in doing so began to feel more and more isolated in a world she did not understand. Within the confines of the yacht there was immediacy, a sense that they created their own world, but now here, on dry land, the emotion was very different. As if they were again strangers and the solidity of the ground beneath their feet confirmed the reality of the distance that still lay between them. The parameters she so longed to define in her relationship with her father kept changing.

"I didn't come down here just to see you. "

Jake had been thinking other thoughts. Lazy thoughts of fixing up the yacht and sailing full time, maybe visiting the Islands of the Caribbean, or even across to Costa Rica. He had always wanted to go there. Her voice startled him, breaking in on his idle reverie.

"Oh?"

"Mother wanted me to find you."

Jake frowned and looked at her profile, silhouetted against the sun.

"Oh." Disappointment showed in his tone as it lowered at the end of the syllable as if he were dropping some heavy weight.

"Sam didn't want me to come."

"Sam who?"

"Strauss. Sam Strauss."

It was as if a small bomb had exploded inside Jake's head. A deadly booby trap that had lain in wait for him for twenty years.

Sounds of the jungle crashed and banged around inside his skull amid fetid sweaty smells and the squelch of mud through sodden boots. Sounds of wounded and dying piercing his soul. Screams echoed into the image of Eve's bloody face and the sirens of the police cars as they arrived at the house.

Nikki turned lazily when he did not answer, noticing with shock his pale, sweat covered face and the staring half mad eyes that remembered the past with such sudden and violent clarity.

"Jake? You okay?"

He kept his eyes on her, not seeing her, seeing Eve. "How do you know him?"

"I've known him ever since I can remember. When I left school I went to work for his company." The look in his eyes warned her subconscious to say no more.

Images reverberated within Jake as a wounded animal thrashing for survival in the insanity of his youth. Slowly the sights and sounds faded and his eyes returned to normal, the mad glare diminishing with the passing of the moment, but memory remained as a constant hurt that made him crave rum and the security alcohol brought.

"You okay now? Was that some kind of relapse?"

Turning away he stared across the anchorage. It required an effort of will. A momentous effort for Jake to continue the conversation, to put the sudden urgent craving for the rum out of his mind and concentrate on Nikki.

"Sorry. Brings back memories. We were in Vietnam together, buddies from school days."

"I didn't know that. He didn't say."

"And your mother?"

Nikki looked puzzled. "What do you mean?"

"Doesn't matter."

There was silence between them. This time tinged with the sadness and tension that had existed over the last few days. Nothing they said, or did, seemed to banish the void their separate lives had created.

Nikki picked up a handful of sand and let the granules run through her fingers, waiting for Jake to speak, forcing him by her silence, to break his.

"Guess you were right when you said I was afraid of something. Guess we're all afraid of things." He paused and sighed deeply. Not so much a sigh, more a long exhale as if preparing himself. "Those were crazy days. The War. Then the Book. It was weird, some of it was fun but it didn't seem real. Now I think it was the most real thing that ever happened."

"You wrote *'Images'* then?"

"Yes. Suddenly the world was pouring gold at my feet and I let them spin my mind into a notion that I was the greatest writer that ever lived. Conceit and arrogance can do that you know." There was a slight reprimanding tone in his voice but no barb to the comment. As if he was trying to impart a small lesson to her.

A warning perhaps.

And she took it as such, watching the sand dribble through her fingers onto the small pile between her feet.

"I don't understand why you left."

It was the question, the statement, the charge he had been running from for twenty years and he knew that, this time, there was no escape. The demons mocked him from their vantage point, pricking his conscience with their barbed pikes and dancing with glee at his discomfort and fear.

Picking up another handful of sand Nikki let the fine granules, eroded from the living coral, slip through her fingers again.

"I didn't want to. You were my life." He paused again and Nikki glanced up at him, but he didn't see her. Instead he saw the jungle, the aircraft, helicopters, smoke and bodies.

Most of all he saw bodies.

Young bodies blown apart.

Perfect bodies that had been trained to sculptured physical perfection.

Then mutilated and tossed aside like so much offal.

Sacrificial lambs, slaughtered for some insanely immature political muscle and a misunderstood global fear.

"When I came back I was angry. Not bitter. Angry. It was the lies, the deceit and the misunderstandings that were here at home, where people had made careers of protest for protest's sake." Remembering painfully.

Even the demons were quiet.

Nikki watched and waited for him to continue.

"Oh there were some who had true belief, who were like the soldiers who fought and died. Who had true morals and values and understood the pain and confusion. But most found it an excuse for the sixties. The age of irresponsibility. Free drugs. Free sex. 'Drop out, tune in, turn on'. Mock everything that was beyond their experience. But it was a lie. The dropouts and protesters made millionaires of their idols and couldn't see that they had bought into the same system of self-deception. That's what I felt. So I wrote 'Images'."

"But my teacher said it was one of *the* books of nineteen sixties protest against the war."

"That's the problem with writing a self-revealing book. It gets distorted by how it is promoted. Publishers and the critics saw it as a vehicle for their own thoughts and beliefs. Not mine." Again he paused and sighed deeply. "Hell I didn't argue. It made me a fortune. A millionaire overnight. But when I tried to write a novel. A serious book about relationships, they turned their backs. I was yesterday's news. They didn't want that. They wanted more of the same. But there wasn't more of the same. I was the darling of the literary set. The hero to all the concave chested, wispy beard hippies and their vacant eyed longhaired girlfriends. The problem was I believed what they'd said about me, and then when they disowned me I had nowhere to go."

"What has all this to do with me?"

Ignoring her question, he held his hand up in a silent plea for her to wait, to hear him out. So she waited and scooped up another handful of sand. The pile between her feet grew then the sides slipped and the base spread until it began to cover her feet. It was pleasant, a warm tickling sensation.

"The system beat me. I tried to deliver what they wanted but it didn't work. Nobody wanted Jake Kimble's new novel. Even my publisher said I was worth more dead than alive with the first book. I just didn't understand what they wanted."

Floodgates of memory opened and he was back there, feeling the emotionally charged atmosphere, pain of rejection and the futility of continuing.

"You were my lifesaver. Eve was getting worse. She'd taken to the bottle and refused her medication. I think now, that my success and the roller coaster we'd been on were too much for her. I couldn't write anymore and she spent most of the time visiting one bar after another, sleeping with everyone she could find. For me, there was only you. I fed you. Clothed you. Rocked you to sleep. Read you stories. Played games. And when you were hurt, I held you in my arms until the pain went away. If you had nightmares, I soothed them away, making up stories until you fell asleep."

He grew silent, throat tightening with emotion.

Again unbidden mental pictures flashed into Nikki's mind.

A park.

The swings.

Laughter and the smiling young face of Jake that suddenly became Monroe's. She dropped the handful of sand with a start, shocked and surprised by the clarity and force of the images.

"I think I remember. It's vague, but I do remember. I just could never put a face to that person. I thought it was one of my dolls." She touched his arm gently and he started as if woken from a dream. "Go on."

"After a year, I started to drink. I'd put you to bed and then hit the bottle, but of course I denied the fact that I was fast becoming an alcoholic. I was turning into the person I despised most of all, a coward. I was running away. Not from you. From myself. From my failures. I'd come back from the war despised. Become a literary hero and then forgotten. All before I was twenty-four years old. I couldn't control anything, least of all my marriage."

"Why didn't you leave? Put mom in a sanatorium?"

He shook his head. "I don't know. I guess I was too immersed in my own misery to know what to do. Maybe because I still loved her, no matter what she did."

As he talked he found that the demons, instead of growing were shrinking and he found strength in facing them at last. Seeing for the first time that they were shadows made substance by ignorance, fear and cowardice.

"Then why did you leave?"

Again the question. This time there was no avoiding it.

"You know. You were there."

Nikki looked at him, frowning, her mind a blank. "No I don't know. Why would I be here if I knew? Why would I ask?"

Jake squirmed, he knew what was coming and it had the inevitability of the bullet that had torn into his leg in the jungle. Before him, dancing across the waves, he could see Sam's terrified screaming face as he cowered in the foxhole refusing to fight.

"I didn't really understand how far things had gone until that last night. I was very drunk. You were asleep upstairs and she came back with a man. She taunted me with him, telling me how good he was in bed and how bad I was. Obscene details until I couldn't stand it anymore."

Breaking off again he stood and walked away a little before turning to look at her. He remembered the expression on the face of his old school friend, Barney, who snapped the handcuffs on him that night, of his eyes that echoed the sadness and betrayal he felt.

Jake would never forget those eyes.

"The man was Sam Strauss. He and your mother were lovers. When I came back that night they were thrashing about on the floor in the living room."

"NO." The cry was wrenched from Nikki's very soul. "YOU'RE LYING."

Jake turned. Surprised at the intensity of her emotion as she stood and faced him. Face screwed up in anger.

"You're lying."

"No I'm not. You were there. You saw it all. I nearly killed them both. You saw it happen."

Nikki felt the shock hit her as a physical blow and put out her hand to steady herself as the screams of that night echoed through her nightmares and sounded in her conscious mind.

Images flashed in front of her eyes.

Lights.

Sirens.

Men in uniform.

Well meaning people, softly spoken in cold sparsely furnished rooms. "Oh God."

He walked towards her and reached out, but she shrank back.

"No. He was *my* lover. He loved me. We loved each other. You're lying."

Blood drained from Jake's face and he felt lightheaded. The beach, anchorage and the fort faded into nothing as he looked at Nikki. His daughter, his wife, the image of her mother, the beautiful girl and all the images and thoughts teemed together until he could no longer separate them.

"No."

"Yes. He made me feel loved," she lied, knowing the truth but not wanting to give him an excuse for his actions.

"No," Jake said, speaking quietly holding Nikki eyes. "No. You were there. You saw what happened. You know. How could you have forgotten?"

For an instant Nikki saw the scene, but only for the merest instant.

Then banished it from her mind, refusing to let the fragment of a childhood memory destroy the illusions she had created.

Jake leaned forward and grasped her arms suddenly. "How could you sleep with that son-of-a-bitch? How could you?"

"Because I needed someone and he was there for me." Words tumbled out, a subconscious admitting of guilt that confused and upset her. So she turned and ran just as she had run from the mansion on the Narragansett Bay.

Jake watched her go and sat down staring numbly after her and he wondered how the horrors of the past could have followed him for so long, to deliver a final blow.

It was as if Eve was mocking him from the grave.

Nikki ran stumbling across the sand until she reached the mangroves and clambered over and through them without realising, unaware of the mosquitoes that swarmed around her and feasted on her young flesh.

While she ran, quick pictures of that night flashed across the canvas of her mind, but too fast for her to hold onto until at last she stopped and lifting her head, screamed up into the beautiful clear blue sky.

For an hour or more she sat alone in the mangroves, until the mosquito bites drove her back to the beach, where she lay in the warm water, soothing the bites and trying to sort everything out in her head.

It had seemed so simple.

So straight forward.

Now she was being told something else. Something she could not and did not want to remember. Rationalising to herself that if she could not remember the incident Jake had said happened, then it had never happened. But she knew it had happened. She knew who and what Sam was but she did not want Jake to be like her and run from that coward.

She had a deep sense of misgiving. Of foreboding.

The parameters of her own responsibility crumbled as a seemingly logical explanation for the grief she had suffered became apparent and made sense of her pain and anger.

But it was all painstakingly illogical.

There was so much she needed to know that was more important than whether or not she had slept with Sam.

There was a whole lifetime.

An ancestry she did not know and a family comprising simply of her mother and a father that had existed only in fiction. Weren't these more important than what had happened that night? Did it matter that she either could not remember or that Jake was lying as a way to escape his own guilt?

Where was the sense in all of this?

She walked slowly back along the beach to where Jake was still sitting, staring out across the anchorage.

He looked up as she sat down four feet away from him, avoiding his eyes.

"Nikki..."

"I don't want to talk about it." Watching Jake carefully, she remained cool and distant.

There was nothing more he could say, but she had changed for him and he saw her as a woman now. A woman who had been violated by his school friend. A man who could have been her father.

Appalled at the thought, he looked at her again.

They were so different. She had her mother's dark hair, and Jake had light brown hair in those days. Only their eyes seemed the same. Blue. But then Sam had blue eyes too.

He tried to wipe the thought from his mind, but it was persistent, the demons finding something else to play with, bringing back the craving for a bottle of rum.

Jake shuddered suddenly from the horror of the thoughts that teemed. Could she be Sam's daughter? Was that possible?

She had skin like Eve.

A body like Eve.

Thoughts of Eve naked before him played across the dancing sunlight on the waves as they lapped up the beach. He wanted the thoughts to stop but some part of him wanted to continue to remember her as she was before the insanity began. To remember the first flush of parenthood.

"Guess we better get back to the yacht," he said gruffly.

She nodded and they stood, hardly daring to look at each other as they walked back to the dinghy.

"Where is he now?" Jake wanted to know, perhaps he still wanted to hurt Sam, perhaps he still wanted to hurt Eve, but these were irrational thoughts.

Nikki loosened the anchor, folded it, stowed it in the bow of the dinghy as she had seen Jake do before.

"I don't know," she lied again.

Jake watched her as they pushed the dinghy out, climbed aboard, started the engine and headed back towards the yacht. The gulf between them seemed bigger than it had ever been before, a chasm that seemed impossible to bridge.

"I don't believe you were lovers."

The pain she saw in his eyes was real. A deep sadness that she could not bear to see and she turned away, watching the sooty terns head towards Loggerhead Key.

"Yes. We were," she continued to lie, wanting to hurt him as he had hurt her. She could see the pain in his eyes and rejoiced in an adolescent revenge to account for the missing years.

"You in trouble?"

"What makes you say that?"

Jake shrugged and looked away. "Sam was always in trouble."

Anger stirred again. "He saved your life, why are you so ungrateful?"

"He told you that? I guess he would. He was a liar too. Asshole nearly got half the platoon wiped out." He stuck his leg out for her to see the ugly purple scar where the bullet had torn away the flesh and muscle. "Got this trying to drag his ass out of a hole in ground."

"I don't believe you," Nikki felt her control slipping.

Anger burst like a fountain from Jake as if Sam was here and he was unloading the pent up emotion on him personally. "I don't give a shit what you believe. He was the cause of everything bad that ever happened to me. My leg, my wife, my child, my whole existence changed because of what your lover did to me." Again he held up his hand as she tried to interrupt him. "Don't say a word. Not a word. You want to know the truth, I'll tell you the truth. When I got back that night they were fucking on the living room floor and they laughed, shit how they laughed. Thought it was a huge joke. You choose not to remember what happened, and I can understand that. But it happened and they made me leave. Didn't press charges so long as I promised never to try and contact you or her ever again. Ever. So I didn't. So don't try and tell me your asshole lover is a saint. He isn't."

He found that he was standing in the dinghy shouting at her and sat back feeling deflated, unhappy and a little foolish.

"I'm sorry, but that's the truth. I never wanted to leave you. You were my life, my sanity."

Like a marble sculpture, her face was almost devoid of all expression as if she didn't believe a word he said and he turned away.

"Ah what the hell. You've been fed all sorts of crap for years, why should you believe me."

But Nikki wasn't listening; she was seeing some of the scenes from that night a little more clearly. She could see Jake hitting Eve and a man in the background, but she could not make out the man's features.

It was too confusing, too hazy, too terrifying and it was not a place she wanted to revisit.

"I just don't know anymore." Her trembling voice sounding like a little girl and for a moment she was, but there was an uncertainty in her conviction.

The Woman was replaced by the fragility, innocence and fear of the Child and he remembered how she looked when he held her close in his arms on that night. How her little body was so rigid and the blank expression on her face so devoid of life. How she had not reacted when the Child Welfare Officers had taken her away and Jake felt his heart crumble again as it had twenty years ago.

NINE

Frankie had spent the past four days in suspenseful anticipation. Her entire perception of her own personality and place in the scheme of things had changed dramatically.

The past was an illusion.

A long-term hallucination from which she had been suddenly propelled.

The surroundings were the same. Friends and acquaintances the same but she saw them differently, more as they saw *her* rather than how she saw herself. It was uncomfortable, leaving a knot in her stomach as the future appeared as an unknown dark seascape stretching to a limitless horizon.

Even Jake had assumed the mythical proportions of a tragic stranger whom she knew and yet did not know and now the need to learn about him and his background was of paramount importance.

So she spent the days in the local library searching through old newspaper articles until she had pieced together a somewhat obtuse view of the man she had viewed as her lover, confidante and friend for all these years. And for all these years, both of them had remained isolated in their secrets, in the delusion that it secured their relationship.

Having exhausted the newspapers, she turned to the shelves and found two well-thumbed copies of his novels, settling down in the twilight as the tourists began to disperse from their nightly ritual, she turned to the first page of the novel, *'Images from a Locked Mind'.*

To her the language was obscure and a little fanciful. Not the pragmatic linear style of the thrillers she was used to reading, but she stayed with it and gradually became immersed in the story of Monroe and his descent into depression and near suicide, until his final salvation.

As she read she began to realise the extent of her ignorance about Jake, and he began to appear more and more a complete stranger.

Finally at three o'clock in the morning, she could bear it no longer. Physical and mental exhaustion causing her to break down in tears and cry herself to sleep as the ghosts of her own paternal past entwined with the horrors that infested Jake's novels.

When she woke, it was with a throbbing headache that four Tylenol did little to suppress, and a resolve to discover the truth one way or another.

The Coast Guard reported nothing amiss.

No wrecks.

No distress calls.

Then she remembered that Jake had stripped all the electronics from the yacht to have them repaired, but never put them back.

Later they called again to tell her that Jake and Nikki were anchored in the Dry Tortugas. Both were fine and would be returning to Key West within a few days.

During the day she prowled the restaurant, scowling at the customers. Retreating to her apartment at night, to stare at the anchorage and read the novels.

There had never before been any threat to her relationship with Jake.

Rum had taken care of that.

Now, when she looked back, she realised that she had allowed him to drink because it kept him to herself. Jealousy, anger and stupidity, a volatile mixture of juvenile emotions that embarrassed her in a way she had not felt since Grade School, surged through her soul.

Mary watched and wondered and finally could stand it no longer.

"Listen girl. You better get yourself out there. You're drivin' the customers and me outta our minds. For the sake of my half of the business, go. And fast. And there's some guy downstairs wants to talk to you."

Mary had lapsed into an exaggerated Louisiana drawl in an effort to be both comical and serious. She had known both Frankie and Jake for years and felt as if it was *her* family that was being torn apart.

"Who is it?"

"No idea. Says he's looking for Nikki Kimble."

"I don't want to see anyone right now. Tell him I'm out of town."

Mary shrugged and, shaking her head, turned to leave the room as Frankie reached for the telephone. "Wait. Tell him I'll be down in a minute," she said and then spoke into the handset. "Alvin. It's Frankie."

"Hi Frankie. What's it gonna be?"

"I need to get to the Dry Tortugas. Today."

"Sorry hon. Don't have a full load. 'Specting some people in tomorrow."

"I'll pay double."

"Sorry Frankie."

"Listen Alvin, don't screw with me. Jake's out there on the yacht, so you get me there or Martha's not gonna like what I have to tell her."

"Shit, Frankie. When you got a hold of some guy's balls, you don't let go do you?"

"Well?"

"Okay. Okay."

"I'll be down in an hour."

Alvin was the local floatplane pilot, who sometimes gave lessons, especially when the students were pretty and rich. His wife knew that he had wandering eyes and kept a close watch on him to his complete ignorance, and Frankie used that ignorance to her advantage.

There were many times when she and Martha had chuckled softly at Alvin's minuscule indiscretions that amounted to no more than a pathetically lustful yearning. But he was a good pilot and knew his business well enough to stay solvent and reasonably lucrative when others floundered in the hostile waters of the late eighties economic depression.

So Martha put up with his fantasising and led her own comfortable life supplying a plethora of 'arty' trinkets for gullible tourists.

*   *   *

Sam Strauss waited patiently in the restaurant; sipping a whisky sour and watching the young bikini clad girls flaunt themselves in the sunshine. In another time and another place he would probably have made a move on them, but his mind was on other matters right now, and the girls were an annoying distraction.

For several days he had considered whether it was worth the trip and finally decided that he could not let Jake spoil it for him. He had worked too long and too hard to see his future disappear. Exactly what course of action he was going to take was uncertain.

"I was told you wanted to see me," Frankie spoke quietly but firmly, appearing as if from nowhere, startling Sam. She was not as he expected and for a moment he was lost for words, but of one thing he thought he was certain, she would have no idea of his identity.

"Sam Strauss," he said easily, standing and offering his hand, which she took uncertainly.

Something about him set the hairs on the back of her neck on end. "I'm Frankie. How may I help you?"

"Well I am one of the trustees of the late Mrs Eve Kimble's estate. Her daughter, Nikki Kimble, is, I believe, visiting her father and I need to find her." He paused to look out across the harbour. "However I am told that neither of them are here and that you may know exactly where they are."

It was the smile that unnerved her most. It spread across his face like a wound, not touching his eyes. Those remained cold and watchful.

"It is very important that I find her, there are some matters concerning the estate that must be dealt with immediately."

"You a lawyer?"

"In a way."

"In a way?"

"I no longer practice. I simply manage the estate as one of the Trustees."

"Really. Well they're not here."

A look of irritation flickered across his face and then the smile was back again. "Is there anyway of knowing where they might be?"

Frankie shrugged and walked to the door to stare out across the ocean. "Anywhere between here and Panama."

"You mean..."

"They're out there."

150

His eyes followed the line of her arm pointing out to sea, then swivelled back to stare at her as she walked away towards the back of the restaurant. She knew where they were, he was sure of it, but for some reason did not want to share the knowledge with him.

A coldness swept through him. An overwhelming feeling of hatred, sudden and strong.

The look in Frankie's eyes was the same he had encountered before.

From Jake in the jungles of Vietnam.

From the police on that fateful night.

From Nikki when she knew he was lying and that Jake was not dead.

But if they were out on the ocean, there was nothing he could do. He was impotent and knew it was a waste of time sitting in Key West waiting, not knowing when they would return.

*　　*　　*

As far as Frankie was concerned, the Cessna 182 floatplane could not fly fast enough to cover the short air distance between Key West and the Dry Tortugas.

Alvin grumbled all the way. "If there's even the slightest hint of a chop or swell, I ain't putting' her down."

A fifty-year-old veteran of the Vietnam War, he complained constantly and yet always carried out whatever mission he began with safety and skill.

She ignored his continuous grumbling and strained her eyes to see the islands she knew were just ahead.

As they drew closer, Alvin became more melancholic and reflective. It was as if the islands were exerting their magic as the distance shortened.

"Guess I could visit with Stan. Sure plays a mean game of cribbage. Hell, might stay over couple of days myself. Maybe catch me some dolphin." The 'dolphin' he was referring to were not mammals, but dolphin-fish, or Mahi-Mahi that could be found offshore with the blue marlin and swordfish. Strange looking with large heads and colourful bodies that dulled when they died lying on the deck of the fishing boats. The dark flesh was rich and delicious when cooked over an open fire and served with a spicy sauce.

On occasion, he would go out with his Coast Guard friends from Key West but those trips were getting fewer and farther between.

The appearance of the floatplane was, in this off-season, a novelty for the few visitors and resident Park Rangers of the Dry Tortugas. All turned out to watch the Cessna pass low overhead, bank and land on the calm waters of the anchorage.

Alvin steered the plane towards the dock, where his friend Stan was waiting.

Frankie spotted Jake's yacht as they banked and turned in her seat to see both him and Nikki standing on deck, watching.

Jake knew it was Frankie as soon as he saw the aircraft. It was a gut feeling and he risked a glance at Nikki, wondering if she also knew.

She caught his eye, confirming his fears, withdrawing from him as she looked quickly away. They had spoken little since they had returned to the yacht.

"I'll go alone. Okay?"

Nodding, she turned away, stepped down into the cockpit and vanished below. As he watched Nikki, he cursed Frankie, crossed the deck to the stern and lowered the dinghy. By the time he started the engine and motored the short distance to the dock, Alvin had shut down the Cessna's engine and let it drift, stepping onto the float to pass a line to Stan the Park Ranger who stood waiting.

Impatiently, Frankie jumped across the gap onto the dock and walked to the end, watching Jake guide the dinghy towards her. She was shocked by how different he looked.

Thinner. Somehow healthier and as he looked up at her, she saw his eyes were clear and bright, instead of the dull bloodshot orbs to which she'd grown so used.

Here was Monroe.

Here was the character of the novel, and in that moment she could see who he so longed to be and she was cast back into a state of near hallucination. Confusion of that which she knew, juxtaposed with that which she didn't know, creating a fertile arena for her doubts to grow stronger.

"Hi," she said with brightness she did not feel and smiling took the painter, securing it to a dock ring with a bowline knot.

"What the hell are you doing here?"

She had not been prepared for the hostility in his voice and suddenly felt an intruder in a strange world.

An outsider.

"Thanks for the warm welcome. Where's Nikki?"

"On board."

She moved towards the dinghy, but Jake climbed onto the dock instead.

"Let's walk."

Falling into step beside him, she noticed the fluid way he moved, a memory of the old Jake. The Jake she first met so many years ago.

"What's going on?"

"Why did you come? The message I sent said we'd be back in a couple of days."

"I was worried," she snapped, bristling with anger. "Why the hostility?"

Stepping down onto the beach, he turned to face her. "I'm sorry. This isn't good timing. Not now."

"That's it? I'm not welcome?"

Looking into her eyes, he was determined not to be emotionally blackmailed. Convinced he was doing the right thing. That was always his mistake, believing what he was doing was always right, refusing to see all sides of the situation. Stubborn intractability may have been a laudable quality in some instances, but this was not one of those times.

"That's right."

It was a like slap in the face. A physical blow. A shock like a douse of ice cold water and she could see her world beginning to crumble and fall apart. Turning away she walked towards the water's edge, not seeing the beauty of the Islands or the anchorage, but instead feeling naked under the scrutiny of a judge and jury that had brought in a guilty verdict.

Why guilty?

Because she knew that she'd used Jake over the years to hide her own insecurities. He had been a lover she could control and not worry about unduly. A child she could mother. A financial safety net if all else failed.

But was it true?

All these thoughts teemed through her head, not new, but suddenly all brought together. Crystallizing as she turned and looked back at him seeing a steady, poised man. Showing a confidence she had not been aware of before.

Then she realized. "You've stopped drinking."

He nodded.

"She do that?"

"Threw the booze out. Boat's dry."

It shouldn't have been a disappointment to her, but it was. She should have been glad, but wasn't. It was as if some vital part had been torn away from her and she was in free fall.

Her subconscious fears were now a reality.

"Owen's gonna been pissed." Her flippant remark a way of maintaining control, but it was starting to fracture and disintegrate. "Is this it then?"

He frowned. "What do you mean?"

"You know what I mean."

"No I don't." He was annoyed. Irritated. "Tell me."

"You want me to go?"

"I need to spend more time with her. I owe her that much."

"What about me?"

"What about you?"

"I feel you're pushing me away. That you don't want me."

"Don't make as big thing out of this, Frankie. I need to spend time with my daughter. That's all."

"And you've stopped loving me?"

Then he began to understand and laughed, a sound like a deflating balloon. "For God's sake. You're jealous. Jesus Christ."

She stiffened. "I don't find this funny."

"It's ridiculous." He threw up his hands in exasperation. "What the hell's the matter with everyone. I just want to spend time alone with my daughter. Shit. I haven't seen her in twenty years."

Exploding in anger, she rounded on him, her voice turning the heads of Alvin and Stan who were deep in conversation. "I was worried, you ungrateful son-of-a-bitch."

"If you were so worried, why didn't you call out the Coast Guard?"

There was no answer to that. The void between them was suddenly as wide as the ocean. She wondered whether they had ever really had anything in common after all, apart from loneliness. And now it seemed he was lonely no longer. If Nikki had been another lover, she knew she could fight and win.

But this was entirely different.

This was Blood.

This was Family.

Something bigger than anything she had ever encountered.

Perhaps the memory of her childhood made it impossible for her to accept Nikki's claim, yet perhaps the memory of her own father and how she had felt, the confusion between hatred and loyalty, made it clear to her the bond that existed between Nikki and Jake.

Ever since Nikki had arrived, nothing had been the same and nothing would ever be the same again. Jake realized that as he looked at Frankie, seeing the fear, disappointment and haunting loneliness in her face.

Moving towards her, reaching out, but she pulled back, shrinking from his touch as if he were somehow repulsive to her now.

"You're right. I shouldn't have come. This isn't going to work is it?"

Again he moved towards her, but she turned and stepped away, hoping tears would not betray her.

"Frankie. Come on. Be reasonable. I need this time. It's important. I love you. Nothing will change that."

This time when he approached, she let him take her in his arms and pull her close to his chest. Instead of the soft flesh she'd been used to, she felt his muscles firm beneath the shirt.

"I'll go back with Alvin tomorrow, if that's okay?" she said softly as the tears started to flow.

"Thank you."

*   *   *

A five-foot barracuda swam closer, its long slim mouth open slightly with a row of razor sharp teeth waiting in anticipation. The gunmetal and silver body changing shades as the sunlight glinted and refracted through the wavelets on the surface. Nikki was too intent upon watching the snapper, yellowtail, parrotfish and angelfish swim around the coral to notice.

Occasionally she caught sight of a bright red squirrel fish as she dived down and peered under the coral ledges, with their huge eyes watching her and then darting back out of sight. Nor did she take notice of the sound of the outboard as the dinghy passed her and continued to the yacht.

The barracuda wasn't intent on causing harm, merely curious. Fascinated. Intrigued by this creature flapping its extremities in a seemingly useless fashion. If there happened to be a meal here, then that was a bonus and bonuses were always worth checking out.

A lobster scuttled across an exposed area of reef, drawing a squeal of delight from Nikki as she peered through the mask and kicked her unflippered feet in an effort to keep close. The movement and splashing startled the barracuda, which backed off a little way before having its curiosity strengthened by the appearance of another of his kind.

Together they drifted closer to Nikki as she floated, watching the lobster back itself into a hole, waving its antennae at her. These were not the clawed lobster of New England, for these creatures lacked those enormous 'claws', instead they were equipped with long antennae. They were valued for the meat in their tails. The heads used to make delicious lobster bisque.

Beneath her, under a ledge and out of sight, a nurse shark lay facing the current that washed through the tunnel under the reef, sleeping, waiting for summer and the time to breed. If Nikki had been aware, she would have been out of the water in a flash, not knowing that the shark was no threat to her, simply a victim of bad press.

A hammerhead, or mako would have been a different story, but they tended to stay away from the shallows.

Yellowtail, parrotfish and angelfish swam in and around the coral, darting in perfect precision, 'flying' through the clear water.

The pair of barracuda slid quietly closer, following Nikki as she paddled around to a shallower part, only five feet deep, keeping a small grouper in sight, who had wandered into the area absentmindedly and, spotting the barracuda following Nikki, suddenly dived down and into a seemingly impossibly small opening in the coral.

Then in a small area of sea grass, she spotted a conch shell. Diving down to retrieve it from the bottom, turning it over and seeing that it was empty. A perfect shell without blemish about twelve inches long, its mouth curved and rolled like a discarded piece of pink and cream tissue paper that had been frozen into shape.

Breaking the surface, she turned and head up, paddled back to the yacht, surprising the barracuda as she unexpectedly swam towards them.

Discretion being the better part of valour, they drifted out of her way, to resume following at a safe distance.

Barracuda are always in the habit of attacking their prey from behind, especially if it was this big, but something about this creature confused them and they kept a respectful distance until Nikki disappeared up the swim ladder and onto the yacht clutching her prize. Disappointed but not dispirited, the barracuda swam slowly away in search of a more amenable meal.

"That looks a good size. Is it whole?"

She turned at the sound of Jake's voice, smile dying on her lips as she saw Frankie sitting in the cockpit. Dropping the conch into Jake's outstretched hand, she watched as he studied it carefully.

"It's beautiful." Looking up, he smiled, aware of the tension and trying to ignore it. "Did you see the barracuda?"

"The barra what?"

"Barracuda."

"What's that?" Stepping down into the cockpit, she picked up a towel and dried her hair.

"Oh it's a fish about five feet long, could take off your leg with a single bite. Likes young soft flesh, especially women."

"What?"

Jake pointed down into the clear water where the barracuda could still be seen, swimming lazily beside the yacht.

"Those fish. There."

Nikki looked down and recoiled with surprise. "Shit."

"Don't worry. They rarely attack humans and if they do it's usually just a nasty bite. They don't come back for more."

"That's a comforting thought, after the event."

Frankie sat uncomfortably, as if she was not a part of the conversation, wishing she was back in Key West, cursing Mary for pushing her, yet wanting to stay close to Jake.

"We kill a lot more of them than they do of us," she volunteered nervously, eliciting a quick look and half smile from Nikki, who turned back to Jake, taking the conch from his hand, looking at it and then at him.

"Where can I put this?"

"Leave it on deck until it's dried out. We'll see if there's any conch left inside before we bring it in, otherwise it'll stink the boat out."

Leaving the conch on the cockpit seat she went below.

A tangible feeling of discontent drifted with the afternoon breeze eddying around the cockpit, enveloping Jake and Frankie.

As before, a sense of desperate frustration that none of the occupants could disperse, beset the yacht, turning the brilliant blue of the sky reflected in the turquoise waters, into a pale shadow.

Nikki lay on her berth and cried quietly, as loneliness again swept over her. She heard the conversation between Frankie and Jake as a low murmur, one word indistinguishable from another, but she thought she knew that they were talking about her by the rise and fall in the rhythm of their voices.

A part of her wanted to sneak into the saloon to listen, to hear what they had to say, yet the rational part kept her in her berth.

If she had heard, she would have been disappointed. For it was not, as she believed, a conversation about her, but a cat-and-mouse game around every topic Frankie and Jake could think of, to avoid creating a confrontation.

Neither wanted the other to be forced to choose.

Dinner centred on the fresh grouper Jake had caught late that afternoon and Frankie had prepared with a ginger, tamari, orange juice and green onion sauce. It was a delicious delicate taste, the fish melting like butter in their mouths and even Nikki appreciated Frankie's culinary skill.

"This is terrific. Best fish I've ever tasted."

"Thanks. Fresh fish is always best."

Frankie walked carefully, as if on egg shells, knowing that any comment could be taken the wrong way, feeling the strain as an unwanted itch she couldn't scratch.

Neither of them had approached the topic of the last time they had seen each other, Frankie sensing that now was not a good time, and Nikki simply hoping the subject would remain dormant. Nerves were stretched to guitar tension as Jake, the centre piece of the drama, eyed both with a degree of mistrust, wondering whether or not accusation and counter accusation would again erupt and he would be forced to choose a side.

*   *   *

Jake had discovered a box of mosquito coils in the bottom of the port cockpit locker. In their plastic bags, they were dry and once lit and placed in the four corners of the cockpit, they were able to eat free from the interminable buzz and constant need to slap or scratch. One or two got through the net, but not enough to spoil eating outside.

After the dishes had been cleared, washed and put away, they sat in the cockpit drinking coffee and watching as the setting sun painted vivid colours in broad strokes that slashed across the sky, changing with each minute, until at last the fire burned itself out, leaving a pastel glow that faded as night settled over the Dry Tortugas and the moon rose to throw a silvery path across the anchorage.

The fifty-foot sloop weighed anchor and slid out into the darkness, her running lights gradually fading as she rounded the far headland and disappeared into the night.

Frankie retired early. The unspoken truce had taken its emotional toll, leaving her limp and lightheaded with exhaustion. The incident with Sam had drifted from her mind.

For a while, Jake and Nikki talked of seashells, barracuda, shark and the dolphins that all shared the watery environment.

On occasion, Frankie could hear a gentle laugh, until footsteps on the companionway and in the saloon, told her that at last the day was coming to a close and soon Jake would be lying beside her. His body next to hers. To hold and to comfort her. But she fell asleep before he peeked in to see if she was still awake.

Too hyped to sleep, he considered sitting down to write again as he lay on the foredeck watching the shooting stars, listening to the gentle sounds of wavelets against the hull and the low hum of wind in the rigging.

The thought of writing again was a surprise, but not an unpleasant one as the sensation of putting down groups of words and phrases on paper to create a time and an atmosphere once more began to flow through him.

TEN

Small whirlpools swirled and eddied behind the floats, spreading out and vanishing in the wavelets, the back draft from the propeller flattening the water as the plane moved forward, gathering speed, sending sprays either side until it gradually lifted onto the step, freed itself from the surface and rose up into the blue late morning sky.

Frankie looked down as Alvin banked over the anchorage, the yachts below moving in a slow circle as if the Cessna was stationary and the earth moving.

Jake stood on the quay, raised his hand and waved slowly. She responded, feeling the bond between them snap and the safety net fall away, leaving her out-of-breath, heart pounding. A wave of dizziness swept over her and for a moment she felt nauseous.

Alvin throttled back and coarsened the pitch, changing the engine sound, quieting it, then levelled out and set the autopilot for Key West.

Frankie sat beside him silently, and he knew enough to keep his questions to himself, knowing that the Golden Rule was never get involved in domestic disputes. She would volunteer if she wanted to talk.

He had never seen Frankie or Jake have even the slightest hint of a public argument until now, but then he had never seen Jake anything less than drunk before. As a couple they were the talk of Key West amongst the long time residents who were usually so reticent about discussing other people's business. And he knew that as soon as he got back, the silent stares would eventually force him to divulge what had gone on, against his better judgment.

As the plane flew overhead, Nikki looked up, felt a brief pang of remorse at having behaved so coldly and then went back to reading the manuscript she was holding in her hand.

The sun was hot on her shoulders through the tee shirt, but she was too engrossed to notice.

On the cover was the title.

'Exile in Paradise'
A Novel
by
JAKE KIMBLE

She flipped back to the page she was reading the night before, settled herself comfortably and read.

> *He found the innocence he was seeking amid the gnarled roots of the mangrove. The spirit of the ancient trees voiced in the incessant sound of mosquitoes, made physical by the tiny bites of no-see-ums. And because the irritations were constant and undiminished by light or darkness, he ignored their presence. Rather his attention was focused on the abundance of life that teemed in the shallow quiet waters.*
>
> *As a metaphor for his miserable condition, beneath the tranquillity, death stalked unhindered, announced only by the swift attack, a momentary useless struggle and then peace returning as if nothing had occurred. The memory of horror and violence cut mercifully short by the need for survival. But the guilt of the past lay like the oppressive tropical heat on his soul.*

The clatter of an outboard disturbed her concentration and she looked up to see Jake pulling away from the dock and heading back to the yacht.

Somehow, as she looked at Jake and remembered the words of the novel, she found it difficult to reconcile the two. She knew it was him she was reading about, yet there seemed such an anomaly with the real man.

The sound of his voice. The way he moved. They didn't seem to fit the picture she was creating in her own mind and yet somehow they did.

She could see and understand Monroe clearly in the novel and yet not see or understand Jake clearly as a person.

Which was he?

He was both the fact and the fiction. The man in the mirror. The man seen through the eyes of another. And the man inside. He was whatever she wanted him to be. Whatever she felt he should be, whatever would fit her mood and needs at any time.

But was he the man she *needed* him to be?

In his novels, he existed and she knew that he was in reality the same man, but the difference remained and she wondered whether that was simply her perception of reality, juxtaposed with her perception of her own demands.

Where did one stop and the other begin? And perhaps the most important question of all. Did it matter? It sounded flippant, but she really did wonder, coming to the conclusion that it must.

The dinghy drew closer. Nikki laid down the manuscript and helped attach the davit blocks and lift it clear of the water, watching as sparkling crystal drops fell like a shower of diamonds from the rigid fibreglass hull back into the water. She looked up slowly and saw Jake silhouetted, his body etched against the sun, features unrecognisable and she could paint in the character from the novel. Making him younger, more dashing, by somehow changing his age and features, creating a father she could forgive.

He moved and the sun blinded her momentarily.

Jake opened one of the aft deck lockers and drew out diving gear that Nikki had somehow missed. For a moment she wondered whether there was some booze she'd missed too, but dismissed the thought quickly. He tossed her a pair of flippers, a mask and a snorkel.

"Let's go diving."

"What about barracuda?"

He grinned. "Maybe they've already eaten."

*   *   *

Shadows of small waves danced across the sand and sea grass as she dived and swam close to the bottom, swirling the sand behind her with the flippers, hands before her acting as elevators to make her rise, dive and turn like a submarine. The ocean had become her element, blotting out the cruel world above, enveloping her with calm beauty with just the sound of blood pounding in her ears for company.

Slowly she rose to the surface in a cloud of bubbles, experienced enough now not to panic as her air ran out, but remain calm and in control as Jake had taught her.

He watched from the surface as she ascended, streamlined, beautiful and relaxed, letting the tension of the last twenty-four hours seep from his body into the surrounding water, allowing the gentle waves to massage his muscles.

From a hole in the reef a large grouper eyed them curiously, its huge head and down-turned mouth making him look like a grumpy old clown.

As they approached slowly, the fish turned sideways, keeping them in view and just out of reach, trusting enough to allow them within six feet, but no further.

It was a Nassau Grouper, with alternating bands of wide light and dark grey stripes running vertically up its body, much like the one Jake had caught the day before, but this one was not going to be dinner, and having seen enough of Jake and Nikki, it swam easily away, vanishing into a hole in the reef where it could watch them safely.

Nikki turned and swam away from the reef toward a patch of sea grass, looking for another conch to add to her singular collection. She searched with a growing sense of disappointment until she spotted what looked to be a small rock moving along the bottom. Once she had seen the first, the others became clear.

There were at least thirty of them dotted amongst the sea grass and sandy patches, moving slowly. She dived down equalising the pressure in her ears and swam close to one. The top was rounded in shape, looking like an encrusted cannonball with protuberances like blunted spikes randomly sticking out from the surface, sitting on a triangular base. The surface was covered with algae and grassy growths.

Tempted to pick it up she hesitated, reaching out and then withdrawing her hand. A movement beside her caught her eye and Jake swam into view. He nodded and grinned, his mouth taking on a strange shape as the rubber mouthpiece of the snorkel contorted his features.

Her hand closed around the rough surface and she plucked the shell from the bottom. If it had not been for the blunt spike, she would never have been able to grasp it, as the round top was six inches in diameter. Her air was running out, so she floated up to the surface, feeling her ears pop with the decrease in pressure.

They broke the surface together. Treading water, she turned over the shell, seeing the utter contrast of the underside to the dull top. The mouth was a horizontal slash across one side of the triangle, with ribs like the frames of a boat leading down inside where the black foot of the animal that lived there could be seen. It was coloured light cream on the edge gradually getting darker, turning to stripes of dark brown closer to the ribs, which were a mixture of both colours.

Jake popped out his mouthpiece. "Queen's Helmet. Weird isn't it?"

She nodded.

"Want to keep it?"

She nodded again and they swam slowly back to the yacht.

As she watched Jake pull the foot of the conch from the shell and loop a thin line around the horny claw, she wondered whether she wanted the shell after all. This particular conch was inedible and it was simply her desire to own something so beautifully ugly that was slowly killing this creature.

"The best way to ensure that the whole creature is out of the shell is to let the weight of the shell pull it out," he explained as he tied off the loop and strung the shell from the mizzen boom. "Too heavy a weight and the animal will be torn in half. Makes a real stink when it dries out. This way all of it will come out. I mean, you try hanging onto a bar with a fifty pound weight strung around your ankles."

"I'd rather not know," she said and he looked away, trying to ignore the procedure.

"If you're going to collect, you should learn the unpleasant side too."

It wasn't a challenge, just a statement. But to her it was a glove that had been thrown down. She turned, took the line and the conch from

Jake and finished tying it to the mizzen boom before looking back disdainfully at him, waiting for a comment.

He smiled and shook his head. "When the animal's out, I'll show you how to clean the shell with bleach and scrubbing brush. If you look in that locker next to you, you'll find a canvas bag."

Delving into the locker she pulled out a blue canvas bag, laying it on the cockpit sole.

"Should have done this before."

"What is it?"

"Bimini top. Well sunshade really. Don't have a proper Bimini so I use this."

Together they laid out the canvas, Jake showing Nikki how to lay it over the mizzen boom and string out the corners to the shrouds, giving enough height for them to stand beneath.

As she tied off one corner, she glanced across at him, looking away before he could catch her eye.

"I have a confession to make."

"Oh?"

A rush of adrenaline coursed through her, leaving her lightheaded as the critical point arrived. But at the last minute, her reticence pulled her back. "I found one of your manuscripts. I guess I should have asked first."

Initially Jake felt a sense of annoyance, but he shrugged as the feeling passed. What did it matter anyway?

"So how is it?"

"Okay."

He nodded, concentrating on tying the line to the forward mizzen shroud.

"Why haven't you had it published?"

"Pull that tighter."

"It's autobiographical isn't it?"

The sunshade threw a shadow across the cockpit and he could see her clearly, her big blue eyes staring frankly at him.

"What I choose to do with my work is my own business." He returned to tying the knot. "Besides, you ask too many questions."

166

AFN Clarke

"Sorry."

"Anyway, it's my turn now."

"What is?"

"Questions. My turn."

They finished tying off the makeshift Bimini and she turned to look at the Queen's Helmet shell, seeing the conch beginning to be pulled from its home.

"You finish your education?"

"Yes."

"And?"

"I majored in business studies. I have a degree."

"So what did you do after that?"

He knew this was treading on dangerous ground, but he wanted to probe, to find out more about her and her motives for becoming involved with Sam Strauss.

"Sam owned a brokerage house. I was his assistant." Was. Used to be. No longer. "I have an apartment in New York. The office is on Wall Street."

"Sounds good."

"It is. Look do we have to do this right now?"

"Why? Find it uncomfortable? You been doing it to me for days."

Suddenly he laughed. It seemed so absurd to be worried about what had happened in the past. She was here. Now. Surely that was all that mattered.

It was infectious and soon she was laughing too, more from relief that the tension had been broken than at anything funny.

The sound echoed out across the water in the silence.

*   *   *

While laughter drifted softly across the anchorage of the Dry Tortugas, Frankie made her way slowly along the darkening streets to the restaurant and her apartment. The moment she had landed in Key West, she had driven straight to Jake's beach out of some subconscious need to maintain a connection with him, spending the afternoon and

167

early evening in quiet contemplation.

The property was not easy to reach by road and having parked the car she struggled along the overgrown path, hidden to anyone but Jake and herself, until she arrived. Stripping naked she plunged into the clear water, salt stinging the tiny cuts and scratches on her arms and legs from the mangrove roots, drifting on her back and slowly letting the tension drift from her body.

Much later, she sat back in the shade of a palm tree, watching as the occasional yacht sailed past some distance offshore, the crew unaware of her existence.

There were no answers here.

Nothing except for the beauty of the curving beach, the soft sound of the wind in the trees and the constant lap of the waves on the sand. But time passed as if in a blur, and the sight of the sun lying low on the horizon shook her from the trance-like state she had descended into and moved her away from the beach back to the mundane predictable murmur of Key West and the restaurant.

Mary noticed her entering through the back door, making her way upstairs to the apartment. Quickly taking a lunch order from the little old ladies who seemed to have found a second home at the restaurant, she followed Frankie up to the apartment and knocked on the door.

"Not now Mary. Deal with it yourself." Came the tired reply.

Frankie was standing at the balcony, glass of very dry vodka martini in hand, staring out across the quiet harbour as Mary entered. She stared disapprovingly at the glass, watching as Frankie drained the glass in one swallow, refilling it from a jug on the table.

"That booze ain't gonna help one bit. You know that."

Frankie shrugged and stared down into the street as the tourists ambled by and a couple of bikini clad young girls rolled gracefully past on their blades, Sony Walkman earphones clamped firmly to their blonde heads. At the end of the day, they, like the others, would parade on the waterfront to watch the sun sink into the ocean, then eye the crowds for suitable lovers to while away the night hours.

"You want to talk to me or just drown in that stuff?"

"It's over Mary. I can't compete with his daughter."

A spark of anger jumped into Mary's eyes and she grasped Frankie's chin roughly, pulling it around to face her.

"What you saying? What the matter with you? Compete? You're out of your tiny mind? There's no competition. Never was. If you don't realize that then you just plain dumb."

She relaxed her grip and turned away disgustedly.

"Ahve never seen such chillen in mah life." Putting on a high-pitched whiny schoolgirl accent, again laying on the exaggerated Southern drawl to mock Frankie. "*'He don want me Mary'.*" She was in full flood now, letting out her anger and concern no matter what the consequences. "What do you 'spect the daughter to say? *Oh my Frankie, how I love you. You're the mamma I never had.*"

Frankie stared in disbelief.

Mary reached out and gently took her hand.

"Slow girl. Slow. She's his daughter, not his lover. He needs you to be here. Maybe she too. You think about that next time, before your heart makes your mouth do things it ain't oughta."

Pent-up emotion spilled from Frankie, running down her cheeks in tears that washed away the loneliness and she clung to Mary, who held her tightly, stroked her hair and made soft cooing sounds of comfort.

Gradually the outpouring of emotion eased and she pulled away from Mary, looking into her closest friend's gentle face and smiling.

"Thank you. It's good to know I have a friend that cares."

Mary took a small embroidered handkerchief from the pocket of her skirt and dabbed the tears away from Frankie's cheeks.

"Now, in case it escaped your attention, we've got a business to run."

Frankie laughed and kissed her on the cheek. "You're wiser by far than I."

There was a twinkle in Mary's eyes. "Ah ain't as dumb as ah sounds. Comes from listenin' to mah mamma and pappa talking wid mah elder sisters. Where you come from don' make no difference when it comes to fambly 'fairs. An ah betta be careful what ah says, 'cause ah'll be back in the bayou 'fore ah knows it." She laughed, dropping the fake heavy accent. "Come on. He'll be back."

Frankie watched her walk towards the door and disappear down the stairs and once more she thanked whoever was responsible for putting them together. But she couldn't resist another glance across the bay on the off chance that by some minor miracle, Jake's yacht was sailing into the harbour.

She loved him deeply. With a certainty she never had before and that made the ache in her heart all the more painful.

Then the pain eased and it was as if the laughter from the yacht moored in the Dry Tortugas had crossed the ocean and permeated the atmosphere of the apartment, working its magic on Frankie, who felt free and relaxed. As if an invisible hand had wiped a cool damp towel across her forehead and taken away the worries and fears, leaving only a pleasant exhaustion behind.

Curling up on the settee, she drifted off to sleep, to float in erotic dreams of Jake and herself on a desert island, waking aroused. Then she slept a little more and woke in the early evening refreshed and ready to resume work.

*   *   *

While Frankie dreamed, Jake sat on the foredeck splicing an eye into a sixteen plait sheath and laid core line, working slowly with a book open in front of him, using the marlin spike, concentrating on not losing the individual strands of the outer sheath as he weaved them into the core.

It seemed simple enough in the photographs, but the written text was unsatisfactory. He had pulled the core out through a hole in the sheath into a loop and having unlayed a length of the sheath above the loop, separated the exposed core into three strands that he wove into the loop.

That was the easy part.

Nikki looked up from the manuscript watching him with the handful of strands and unravelled plaiting, wondering if he knew what he was doing. It seemed a mess to her. She watched him pull the core back in through the hole he'd previously made, forming a loop with a tangle of threads hanging from it. He then made three more staggered holes along the body of the line and pulled through three batches of the loose

170

threads.

As if by magic, it suddenly appeared that he had a neat eye in the end of the line and having cut off the loose ends, it seemed impossible to see the join.

Jake sat back admiring his handiwork with pride. The seemingly impossible task had proved to be manageable after all and he flipped through the book to find more challenging splices to perform.

"What's it for?"

So engrossed in his work, he had forgotten she was sitting only a few feet away, manuscript on her lap.

"Oh, a painter for the dinghy. I can attach it to a shackle with this eye."

"Uh huh."

"It's fun."

"I guess."

"You mean for an old man."

"Not the old man in this book."

"He could never live in the real world. It's easy when somebody else is making the decisions."

"Some racy stuff."

"Fantasy."

She laughed awkwardly, knowing they were approaching a difficult subject. Jake watched her smiling slightly, wondering if she would follow the thought, or shy away.

"I wonder." Jake laughed.

"What?"

"You'd love to know wouldn't you? I mean, secretly you'd love to know?"

"Know what?"

"Whether it's based on experience or not."

"What for?"

"Because you're insatiably curious. Because you wonder whether this old man and Miss Cellulite 1950 are the models. Right?"

"No. Not at all. Why should I care?"

Jake grinned at her discomfort, not unkindly, but with a joy in what he thought was her innocent curiosity.

He leaned forward conspiratorially. "What if I told you it gets better with age."

"Jake."

He howled at her shocked expression. "Your face."

She watched him with a mixture of both disdain and enjoyment as he laughed and laughed, eventually joining in, knowing that this was the father she had wanted to know. He wasn't the image she had created, that was fading now, and she was beginning to like this crazy flawed person who created such incredible worlds within the pages of his novels. Worlds that existed half in fact and half in fantasy. Her difficulty had been sorting the one from the other.

"I'm sorry. But your face was a picture."

"I've never heard you laugh like that."

"Not a pretty sight eh?"

"Not a pretty noise."

"Well beats the hell out of crying now doesn't it?"

As always when the laughter ended, there was an awkward silence, broken when Nikki volunteered to make a jug of iced coffee and carrying the manuscript went below, leaving Jake to stare after her, taking a deep breath and letting it out in a long exhale.

Lying back on the teak deck watching the cumulus clouds drift by as another long day wandered to a sleepy conclusion, he let his mind drift.

Simple thoughts.

Inconsequential thoughts.

Thoughts without responsibility.

She was back on deck within minutes carrying two glasses of iced coffee, handing one to Jake and sitting down beside him.

Frigate birds swooped low over the yacht just in case there were any titbits and finding none, jinked disgustedly away, heading towards Bush Key.

"Can we go over there?" She pointed to the Key where frigate birds had settled on the root of a red mangrove, eyeing the sooty terns close by.

"No. It's the nesting season for the terns. However we can take the dinghy out to one of the wrecks."

Her eyes sparkled with romantic images of pirate sailing ships, with Errol Flynn and Maureen O'Hara blazing a trail across the oceans. A love of old swashbuckling movies and the musicals of Fred Astaire and Ginger Rogers were perhaps the only things she and her mother had in common. Many nights, she had curled up beside her and watched the American Movie Classics channel until she had fallen asleep halfway through one epic or another.

That had been in another life. A life she could look back on as if it were a dream. A classic movie of its own.

*   *   *

Jake stopped at the Park Ranger's office and checked the weather forecast before they set off across the one and a half miles of channel separating Garden Key and Loggerhead Key. There was a front moving in but wouldn't hit for another thirty-six hours. So calm sea conditions would prevail for at least the next twelve.

Jake had not wanted to take the yacht across, and the sea was calm enough for the dinghy loaded with their diving gear and a picnic lunch. It was almost a flat calm, with slight swell, but nothing to worry about and the dinghy flew across the channel between the Keys quickly and easily, Nikki handling the tiller like a seasoned mariner as Jake pointed the way.

In the waters close to the Key was the wreck of an old sailing vessel, which, according to the cruising guide, provided excellent and exciting diving. The Coast Guard had warned that there might be nurse sharks and tarpon in the area, but apart from that, just to watch for squalls. Local weather could sometimes make nonsense of the area forecast.

Jake had stowed extra line on board for the anchor and chose a spot near the wreck where the nylon rode wouldn't catch on any coral heads. Without tanks, it was too deep to reach the wreck itself, but they enjoyed swimming amongst the coral heads, the wreck clearly visible beneath them some sixty feet down.

Nikki tried diving down as far as she could before the water pressure on her ears got the better of her, and colder water forced her back to the surface again.

Drifting up, head back so she could see the surface that looked so far away, with Jake paddling along as if floating on a mottled thin film of plastic that divided the ocean from the sky. Once she reached the surface, she floated looking down noticing in alarm as three nurse sharks drift slowly by beneath.

Panic set in as she watched the sleek gunmetal grey bodies wriggle through the water and images of Jaws the movie flashed across her mind followed by the sounds of the sinister music in her ears. Then to her horror, Jake dived down towards them, getting as close as fifteen feet before they accelerated away, far into the distance.

He surfaced grinning at her, spitting out the mouthpiece.

"Don't worry about them. They're friendly. It's the Tiger sharks and Hammerheads you want to worry about. They'll take a piece out of you just for the hell of it."

The sight of the smooth muscular bodies gliding through the water unnerved her and the dive ceased to be much fun after that, no matter what Jake said about the nurse sharks' hospitable nature. They didn't return, but Nikki kept a look out for them just the same, ignoring the other wonders that teemed around her.

After an hour swimming and diving, Jake tapped her on the shoulder, nearly scaring her to death. "There's a squall on the horizon. Better get going. Don't want to get caught out here when it hits."

They headed back to the dinghy and ate a hurried lunch before weighing anchor and heading back across the channel. The swell was bigger, but long, so they could still make good time and Jake felt a sense of relief when they slipped back inside the safety of the anchorage and security of the yacht.

Looking back over his shoulder he saw that the squall was closing fast. It seemed to be small and would probably pass them by, but Jake felt satisfied he had made a prudent move. Indeed, Nikki heaved a sigh of relief when they clambered aboard, washed down the diving gear, stowed it and hauled the dinghy up onto the davits.

She scrubbed away the image of the sharks in a hot shower and rubbed her body down with moisturising cream, noticing the stark contrast between her white breasts and buttocks and the deep tan of the rest of her body. She looked into the mirror and a stranger stared back. Not the pale uncertain woman of a couple of weeks ago, but a bright and clear-eyed beauty. Skin and hair shining with health, her body with the puppy fat of adolescence now trimmed into a slim, flat-stomached shapely woman.

It shocked her and pleased her at the same time and she wondered if this was how Eve had looked at her age and then she felt the guilt. Instead of being happy, she felt she should be showing remorse at the death of her mother, but that seemed so far away now.

So very far away.

Images from the novel wandered back into her mind.

Of Monroe and the world he inhabited and it seemed not so far distant from this world. And the warm water, gentle rocking of the yacht and the sound of Jake whistling softly on deck brought the submerged emotions to the surface. Leaning back against the hull she cried as the water ran down over her body in soft caresses as if trying to alleviate her suffering.

Turning the water off, her sobs eased and that empty feeling of loneliness she knew so well, stole into her, staying as she dried herself. She knew that it would not go away, even with the answers to all her questions. As she looked at herself in the mirror, she decided that she finally had to find out what happened that night so long ago.

It seemed that the time she had spent on the yacht had strengthened her. Had turned her fears and confusion into a self-confidence she had never known before. She was sure that somehow in the past week, both she and Jake had taken the first uncertain steps towards a lasting relationship.

Confusion she felt about his alter ego were relegated to the closet of uncomfortable guilt. What she saw as a clear road ahead, the cynicism and hindsight of her old age would show as yet another youthful whim. But without those whims, youth itself would be a rapid transition to old age. And in her old age, she would smile and colour the events with a soft focus that allowed the indiscretions of the past a forgiving place in her life.

When she appeared in the saloon, she found Jake had come below and was sitting at the navigation table, chart spread out in front of him, plotting a course for Key West.

He looked up as she entered. "Hi. What do you fancy for dinner?"

"I don't know. I think there's only chilli left."

Groaning he closed his eyes in mock agony. "Oh no. Please. Not chilli. Not again."

"I'll see if there's anything else." She crossed to the galley then noticed a pan on the stovetop. In it were two medium-sized lobster tails.

"Stan brought them over. Good eh? We'll broil them in butter and black pepper."

ELEVEN

Jake rose early, rubbed the sleep from his eyes as he set a coffee percolator half full of water on the stove, poured ground coffee into the basket, popped on the lid and having lit the gas, climbed the companion way steps, slid open the hatch and blinked as the rising sun bade him welcome to a new day.

There was another yacht in the anchorage. More precisely, a luxury fifty-foot Viking motor yacht. A sleek white craft with covered aft deck, flying bridge and sporty arch supporting a radome and antennae.

It must have slipped in early in the morning, just as dawn had stolen across the sky and Jake was struggling awake, and was moored less than one hundred feet from Jake's yacht.

A crew member, a young man with a shock of blonde curly hair, deeply tanned and dressed in sparkling white tee-shirt and long white cotton pants was just securing the windlass. He walked quickly back along the side deck, slid open the saloon door and disappeared inside.

Except for his annoyance at the yacht being here and so close, Jake had to admire the way they had negotiated the channel at dawn. He mused that they must have sophisticated electronic gear on board and itched to see what it was like. And that annoyed him.

He went below to check on the percolator, satisfied the coffee was the right colour, turned it off and poured a cup with sugar and milk.

When he returned to the cockpit, he glanced over to the Viking. The young blonde woman, dressed in a black thong bikini, stepped out onto the aft deck and stood for a moment, stretching before sitting down at cockpit table that had been laid for breakfast. The woman waved to Jake, who suddenly felt guilty for his animosity towards the motor yacht and waved back. A few moments later, the woman was joined by the man, his body lean, muscled and tanned. A thick growth of hair on his chest looking as if it had been stuck there. He too waved and grinned at Jake showing a mouthful of very white teeth.

When he spoke it was with a slight accent that Jake could not place.

"Good morning. I apologize. We seemed to have moored a little too closely. I confess to being asleep when we arrived."

Jake sort of waved and sort of shook his head, accepting the apology that made him feel uneasy.

"Perhaps you would care to join us for breakfast?" The offer came out of the blue. An odd gesture. "As a token of my apology. I'm sure we must have woken you."

Jake shook his head. "Thank you, no. We'll be leaving soon. Things to do."

"Of course." The man waved and the blonde woman stood and stepped down onto the swim platform and dived neatly into the clear water. The man followed and they both swam with powerful strokes towards the shore.

"Hey. What the hell," Jake muttered and then cursed as he burned his lips on the hot coffee.

Nikki had woken with the low hum of the motor yacht's diesels and the rattle of the chain as the anchor splashed into the water.

She had lain dozing and waking. Lying in a half sleep, half dream state as the morning sun gradually spread light into the cabin. And then she listened as Jake rose, crashed about in the galley and clambered topsides. She heard a short conversation, muted as it reached her and something nagged at the back of her mind as she yawned and wriggled comfortably in the berth.

It was quiet except for the call of the birds and the sound of Jake's footsteps on deck and low muttering, and she felt a pang of regret knowing that this couldn't last and that 'civilisation' beckoned, stretching its long tentacles out here to this small part of paradise.

A cold shower washed off the sticky sweat from the humid night and she struggled into a pair of short pants and the familiar tee shirt, then slowly walked through the saloon and up the companionway steps.

Jake was sitting in the cockpit staring at the Viking with his second cup of coffee, as Nikki climbed the steps.

"Morning Jake."

"Hi. Coffee's in the pot and it's hot," he said and nodded towards the motor yacht. "We've got company. Goddam stinkpot. Still they did invite us to breakfast."

"Breakfast?"

"Yup. As an apology for waking us up and mooring so close."

"And you accepted?"

"Nope."

Nikki heard the sound of laughter from the beach and looked over, seeing the couple sitting on the sand. They were too far away to see clearly, but she caught the soft laughter of the woman and could see her blonde hair in the sunlight.

They stood, walked to the water's edge and swam with slow strokes back to the yacht as Nikki went below to pour herself a cup of coffee.

When she returned to the cockpit, the couple had already climbed onto the swim platform and disappeared inside the Viking's saloon. Jake was watching them and she wondered what he was thinking.

Whether he was considering them for characters in the next novel.

Whether Monroe was inexplicably ensnared in a network of deceit and deception and her mind began to play with the scenario.

> 'She was being followed; no matter how carefully she covered her tracks they were right behind like the ghosts that inhabited her nightmares. Always smiling always courteous and always deadly. Theirs was but one purpose. To see her die. Slowly. Tortuously. Monroe could not help, or would not help, or perhaps he was simply biding his time waiting for the opportunity to present itself. Sometimes his cool exterior was too much to bear, but she knew that he would always come through in the end. Just in time. To save her from the brink of disaster. But how could events have descended to this level? How could she have allowed this to happen? Why had she not met Monroe before?'

"Interesting couple."

Jake echoed her thoughts sounding like Monroe, and for a moment she was trapped in the illusion of her imagination and the glare of the real world. He was silhouetted against the skyline with the sun back-lighting him so that she could not see him in detail and for a few moments more her imagination continued to play with reality until he moved and came into sharp focus. And he was no longer Monroe.

"I guess."

"Take a look."

She turned and stared at the yacht. A beautifully made monstrosity, with its brutal power and tacky ostentation. It seemed to her that she had seen hundreds like it in the Narragansett Bay every week-end, with the owners sporting white pants and blue blazers, wearing yachting caps with brims full of gold perched jauntily on their heads in a purposefully casual manner.

Quite suddenly she realized she had become a sailor and could now understand why motor yachts were so despised by the sailing community.

She felt as if her body was here yet she was somewhere else, looking at the two of them standing in the cockpit. It was an odd feeling, as if they had stepped into another dimension.

"You're the novelist."

"Really. Thank you for that. I had forgotten," he turned away from her to stare at the Viking and its occupants who were now back on deck. The man in cut off jeans and a tee shirt and the girl in a different coloured bikini.

"But if you look, you'll see that they really do not belong on that yacht."

She turned listlessly to stare at the Viking and gradually she too began to see through his eyes. She looked beyond the apparent and saw the reality.

He was right, they did not belong.

'It was not their yacht. Monroe had known from the start and knew when...'

Her mind jumped back into the reality of the present with a suddenness that startled her, making her jerk in an involuntary spasm and she glanced at Jake but he was still looking at the couple on the Viking and had not noticed.

"I see what you mean."

"Interesting isn't it, how our perceptions are so easily led astray by what we expect to see, against what is actually there. My guess is that they are delivering the yacht to some owner in Costa Rica or Panama and because they are ahead of schedule, decided to stop here for a day's relaxation."

Slowly she was beginning to warm to the game and echoes of the past began to play at the corners of her memory imparting an atmosphere, a familiar texture to the space that surrounded them.

"How about their relationship?"

"What do you think?"

There was a calm about the day that made entering the game easy.

Sooty terns swooped overhead flying backwards and forwards from the islands. And the breeze across the anchorage and through the yacht's rigging was a soft lullaby.

"She's the skipper. That's easy to see. There is a natural authority about her and he's the hired help."

"So the owner hired her and she hired him?"

"Correct. But something interesting happened. They fell in love. No, not in love. There is a mutual attraction between them. Maybe they knew each other before. That would account for the friendliness between them. They decided to leave early and stop here because it gave them a change to get to know one another better."

As they watched, the man leaned forward and kissed the woman lightly on her lips and sat back smiling, oblivious to the fact that they were being observed.

"What does that tell you?" Jake studied Nikki as she lay back, watching the couple intently as if they were specimens in a laboratory jar.

"Kinda sinks my last theory. That was a husband kissing a wife."

"Oh?"

"It's obviously not a lover's kiss. It's kinda friendly yet intimate."

"Good observation. But they could be lovers?"

"Definitely not lovers. Not passionate enough. Besides he's too relaxed."

Spontaneous laughter burst from Jake and echoed across the anchorage making the couple turn and look in their direction, the man waved briefly when he saw Jake, who responded lazily.

Nikki stared at him, a look of petulant annoyance clouding her expression. He caught the look and lapsed into silence not being able to suppress the twinkle in his eyes and smile on his lips.

"Sorry. You're well informed for an unmarried, unattached young woman."

"I never said I was unattached."

"Oh?"

"I'm not." Not wanting the game to end, she turned her attention back to the couple.

Jake watched her, studying the determined set of her jaw and the slightly narrowed eyes, looking so much like her mother that he was taken aback by the sudden surge of emotion that rushed through him like the first flush of some exotic drug, leaving him a little lightheaded.

"What about the owner? What's he like?"

"Could be a she."

"Could be."

"It isn't though."

"Why?"

"Too pretentious. Look at all that stuff on the roof. All those poles and antennas and other stuff. I bet the inside is like some space ship. Only a man would have that many toys to play with."

"Ouch. Doesn't say much for our state of evolution does it?"

Glancing sideways she saw him smiling wryly and she suddenly grinned, relaxed again.

"Tell me it's not true."

"I can't, but I can say there are woman out there who like gadgets too."

"Maybe, but I bet they know when to stop. We're a much more practical creature than you men."

"Where's the romance."

"Kept in between the pages of cheap supermarket paperbacks where it belongs."

"Remind me to make sure none of my books ever end up on supermarket racks."

The image she had painted burned brightly in his artistic soul for longer than he cared and struck a deep-seated fear that maybe that was where his works were eventually destined to reside. Fingered by the false nails of bored suburban housewives looking for a quick escape from the mundane predictability of their lives. Allowing their eyes to wander over the garish book covers and their imaginations to sweep their beautiful bodies into the arms of the painted, over muscled, chisel jawed heroes that infested the pages.

He could never see Monroe as over muscled or even chisel jawed.

"They won't," Nikki said confidently.

"That good huh?"

Again she looked at him quickly to see if he was making fun, but there was earnestness, a childlike pleading behind his eyes that belied the smile.

"I'm no critic," she said softly.

"Everyone's a critic. Every time you open the pages of a book and read, you're a critic."

The atmosphere had suddenly and subtly changed back to the prior guarded hostility, the couple on the Viking forgotten.

"I'd like to know what you think. It would be nice to think I had some support."

It was a vain selfish comment.

He felt foolish and immature, knowing that he would not have a suitable and effective reply when her answer came and any answer he gave would only serve to make him more foolish and more isolated.

"Isn't that what Frankie's for?"

He looked at her and saw Eve.

"You never give an inch, do you? You want me to pay, don't you? Well I won't give you the satisfaction."

And the words were like a fanfare from the past, heralding the deluge of images and emotions that he never wanted to feel again.

He could see Eve's face contorted in hate, her voice mocking him, her beauty a weapon that slashed and stabbed his soul and the images of the past were here before him.

For a surreal moment he thought it was the nightmare revisited, that somehow she had come back to haunt him. That the hallucinations had not ended and that maybe he would never wake from the nightmare.

Nikki turned to look at the Viking. Her nightmare became reality as Sam stepped onto the side deck and stared across the short distance between the two yachts.

"We need to talk Nikki," Sam shouted across the short distance between the yachts.

She could not speak. Her throat was dry, body shaking suddenly as if a cold wind had sprung from nowhere.

Jake looked at her with concern.

Slowly the image of Sam disappeared as she stared across the water. She shivered, closing her eyes for a second to shake the hallucination free.

"You okay? You look as if you've just seen a ghost."

She grinned suddenly and smiled. "No, just burying a few."

Jake watched Nikki's face. Saw the confusion written in the sadness of her eyes. He made no attempt to stop her as she walked along the side deck to the bow and sat looking out towards the Fort.

The anchorage echoed to the dull boom of a small cannon.

Jake poked his head out of the companionway and squinted in the glare of the sun, looking towards the Fort where a puff of smoke was rising.

A square red flag with a small black square in the centre was being raised on the flagpole.

"What's that?"

Nikki returned to the cockpit and stood, hand shading her eyes.

"Storm warning. Time to go."

"Go? Why don't we stay until it's passed?" The thought of another knockdown scared her and she did not want to repeat the experience.

And she did not want to leave the comfort of the Dry Tortugas. There was a peace here. It was here that she was finally finding both herself and her father. She did not want to go back to the real world.

"It's better to be in deep water. These anchorages are not really suitable for riding out a storm, besides we better be getting back. And I don't have a storm anchor."

Leaving the anchorage without the use of an engine meant Jake studying the wind direction and shifts for a short while before deciding just how to accomplish the task.

Nikki stood poised on the bow, waiting for the order to weigh the anchor. Feeling the scrutiny from the Viking across the water, she avoided looking in their direction. Suddenly as anxious as Jake to be away from here. Yet at the same time she felt angry at being forced to leave the quiet of the anchorage and the barren beauty of the islands.

Jake hoisted the mizzen, then trimmed the staysail and Nikki felt the tug of the wind on the yacht. "Okay. Bring it up."

Grasping the windlass handle she bent to the task, winding the anchor up, making sure the chain slid easily into the locker. There was a certain sense of relief and release as the chain clanked and the anchor broke free.

Jake held the yacht against the wind with backed staysail, until Nikki signalled that the anchor was clear of the water, then he released the staysail sheet and the yacht moved off the wind heading out of the anchorage down the channel, past Iowa rock and through to the open ocean beyond.

Once out of the protection of the anchorage, the wind picked up to twenty knots on the beam, the effects of the approaching front clearly seen in the building seas as the waves rolled steadily towards them. Occasionally the crests would break in crashing white caps that slapped at the side of the yacht, sending spray over the deck.

Jake was keen to put as much distance between them and the Dry Tortugas as quickly as possible. Setting full sail, the yacht heeled with the rail almost under water, careening along at the hull speed of eight knots.

Nikki scrambled back to the cockpit as soon as they were clear of the channel and in open water and sat looking over the stern at the fast disappearing low lying islands.

"Better get the harnesses out. It's going to be a rough passage."

He had been strangely quiet, only talking to her to issue commands. Passing him a harness, she watched as he put it on. Wondering what he was thinking. They clipped the carabiners onto the hooks at the base of the steering pedestal.

"How long's it going to take?"

"Depends whether we stop at Marquesas Keys or not." Pausing, he reflected on the options open to him. "I don't think we will."

"Why not?"

"We'd have to anchor outside the anchorage and I don't think the wind will let us do that. The front will be through before we get there and looks like it's gonna be a rough one." Again he paused, calculating the time. "Probably take us ten hours. If we get headed, it'll take longer."

"Then we won't get there till about midnight?"

"If we're lucky."

Jake spun the wheel to starboard as a wave crest broke and raced towards the yacht. The bow dropped off the wind, heading down the wave, the breaking crest catching the stern and trying to throw the yacht sideways into a broach.

For several gut-wrenching seconds, it hung at forty-five degrees of heel and then rolled back as the wave passed and they slid down the back into the trough.

The seas were getting steeper and more aggressive than he had seen before. Instead of the gentle long swells, these were shorter, angled, some with triangular peaks as the current and the wind tried to move in different directions, with the waves objecting violently.

Inside the pit of his stomach was an unsettling feeling that he had not experienced since night patrols in Vietnam. It was a sense of foreboding about the immediate future.

His sixth sense.

His instinct.

And beneath his feet the forces of nature were again at work, but now with a renewed energy as the waves surged against the yacht, straining the keel and the garboard planking and the cracks opened a little wider, increasing the flow just the tiniest bit, but as each hour passed the cracks would widen more and more.

Nikki kept her face turned away from him and a question jumped unbidden into her mind.

"How long had you known Sam?" There was a burning curiosity that would not lie dormant coupled with a morbid fascination to discuss, against her will, everything. To open up the wounds, for she thought that finally she had found a way to reach him, to hurt him, to repay the pain and loneliness of her own youth.

Her voice penetrated through his thoughts snapping both into the present and the past at the same time and he glanced over to her. She was staring down at the water rushing past.

"We grew up together."

She was silent for a moment, still staring at the passing water. "I didn't know. He didn't say."

Jake didn't volunteer any more information, concentrating instead on steering the yacht down the steepening seas. For twenty years Sam and Eve had been forgotten, drowned in rum and sun as he lived in constant denial.

Now this girl, his daughter, had exposed his life as a lie and with it his relationship with Frankie. For she too would have been an unwitting part of that lie.

As the wind rose, they put two reefs in the main and replaced the No.1 jib with the No.3, a smaller sail area and the yacht felt less out of control although the speed was only a knot lower.

Every now and then a cross wave broke against the stern quarter and tossed water across the deck, but it stayed out of the cockpit. The yacht slewed and bounced on the waves, sometimes slamming down with a jarring thud as it fell off a wave and pounded into the flat water in the trough. The sea was a wall of grey marching towards them until the wave itself became the horizon and they tore up the slope and slid down the other side.

Jake watched the approaching walls of water, sensing the cross patterns and steering the yacht between the swells and the wind waves, easing the pounding. He was new to this, operating by instinct without time to think, trusting in his ability to be at one with the forces of nature and not fight them.

Nikki disappeared below for an hour, returning to bring Jake a cup of coffee, still fighting the creeping feeling of seasickness.

He had been thinking of Frankie, suddenly needing her beside him, needing to rest on her shoulder and ask her help, for he felt Nikki slipping away from him again. He wanted to tell her that their life together had not been a lie, that he loved her deeply and truthfully and he thought of the first day they met at her restaurant.

They were both new in town. Both wounded. Both lonely. She was struggling to get her business off the ground with Mary and he sat down at one of the patio tables, staring at the yacht in the harbour.

As she walked towards him across the sparsely occupied restaurant, he noticed the small things. Her eyes; wide; direct; with a hint of sadness rather like a scared rabbit.

Her breasts as they moved beneath the tee shirt. The curving sweep of her hips, and the almost translucent texture of her brown skin.

But his gaze came back to her eyes and somehow he knew he was about to meet someone who, although she knew all about pain and suffering, also knew how to disguise that pain. She stood out from the crowd and when their eyes met, there was an instant rapport.

Falling in love was not something that either of them planned, so when their relationship grew to encompass sex, it was more to satisfy their bodily needs within the security of a deep friendship for each other, than a true deep love.

Love was taboo.

Both had tried it and both had failed and they tacitly agreed never to fall victim to its constraints again.

From that first day when he had asked her who owned the yacht, it had been a slow friendship. They had grown used to each other and when Jake had not come into the restaurant for a few days for his usual rum and conversation, she had grown worried. She found him sick with a recurrence of malaria he had contracted in the Far East and had nursed him back to health. That had marked the turning point and she had stayed on the yacht, keeping her apartment above the restaurant, but spending more time with Jake, until that too became routine.

Now he knew they had lived a lie, for he loved her with a depth and clarity that had been buried beneath his own selfishness and fear, drowned in rotgut rum.

"Why don't you say something?" Nikki's voice snapped him back again and he saw the fear and anger in her eyes.

"What do you want me to say?" Jake said, confused at her sudden mood change.

"Shout at me. Do something. I can't stand your silence."

"What can I tell you? What can I say? What the hell do you want from me?"

She looked away suddenly, guiltily. Thoughts were becoming more and more confusing. Emotions piled one upon the other. Hate, love, fear, desperation, the terror of being alone again and the surging confusion of the emotions she had for Jake, that ebbed and flowed, see-sawing backwards and forwards.

"Why didn't you tell me about Sam before?"

"Would you have listened?"

"Of course I would have. You're my daughter," he said, and for a moment he wondered whether that was true.

The wind had risen and the clouds were gathering and pushing closer. On the horizon Jake could see the rain moving towards them.

"We have to strike the main and jib."

He locked the wheel and they crawled along the side deck. Nikki staying at the mast while Jake went forward and pulled down the jib as she released the halyard. Once it was secured, he returned to the mast and together they hauled down the main and lashed it to the boom.

The speed dropped off the yacht and she became more upright, taking the waves with a steadier motion than before.

He watched her climb back to the cockpit and secure her carabiner to the eye at the base of the mast. Then he joined her.

With the sails reduced the seas did not seem so bad and the wind, although still a growing moan in the rigging, not so threatening. The sun was still visible so Jake took a position sight, waited another hour and took another before the clouds started to encroach.

Leaving Nikki at the wheel he went below to plot their position, returning half an hour later to adjust their course five degrees.

With the current sea state and wind direction, he knew they would have to run off as the storm grew, so until it hit them he decided to head up a little and make as much ground to windward as possible.

They were just keeping pace with the drift and if he had been a better sailor he would have increased the sail area to drive the yacht harder to windward.

Nikki sat huddled in a foul weather jacket against the increasing cold.

The air temperature had dropped twenty degrees with combination of the approaching front and wind chill.

"Jake," her voice was barely audible. Childlike.

"Yes."

"I'm sorry. I didn't mean to get you into this mess."

He relaxed his shoulders and smiled at her. "It's okay. Hey it's an adventure. I haven't had one for a long time." There was an awkward silence as he searched for something to talk about. "How did you get the job with Sam?"

Nikki stirred from her thoughts. "Mother. Now I guess it makes sense."

Jake held his silence.

"It was the first real job I've ever had."

"I know this isn't easy," he offered.

"I just don't know what the truth is anymore," she said quietly, her words whipped away in the wind. She seemed so small and frail, pale face peeking out from beneath the foul weather jacket hood.

"Go below. Get some hot food inside yourself and sleep. I'll wake you in a few hours."

Leaning down she unclipped the carabiner, then slid open the hatch and disappeared below, sliding the hatch back in place.

Jake heaved a deep sigh and tried to straighten the events out in his mind. He gave up and concentrated on steering the yacht as the afternoon drew onwards into evening.

The berth felt snug and secure even with the rolling of the yacht and the sound of the water rushing past the hull had a calming effect. Nikki reached out and took the small pendant from the bag, held it tightly in her hand for a moment, then slipped it over her head, tucking it inside her tee-shirt.

The metal felt cold against her skin.

Cold but comforting.

Again she saw Sam giving it to her, but it seemed strange, as if there was something hidden. Something not real and for a brief moment she saw the little girl that was her, standing alone, tears falling down her cheeks as she held the pendant and she didn't know why the little girl was crying.

Gradually a dreamless sleep banished the troubled thoughts and allowed her to rest as the wind grew and the yacht charged across the ocean, happy to be sailing.

TWELVE

It was the low moan that rose and fell, accompanied by a high pitched whistling and the slapping of the staysail sheets that woke him. An eerie sound as if the ghosts of long dead mariners had risen to envelop the yacht in the darkness.

He had fallen asleep at the chart table, wedged in against the roll of the yacht. For a moment he thought he had just nodded off, but a look at the chronometer showed he had slept for nearly three hours, which was not a good sign, because as they sailed closer to Key West there were shoals, low lying uninhabited Keys and an oil platform to deal with. He moved and winced in pain from a stiff neck, his right arm numb where he had been leaning.

Nikki was nowhere in sight until he glanced through the forward cabin door and saw her stretched out on the berth.

The lazy routine of the past few days had carried forward to the voyage, when it should have been left with the slow lap of the waves against the beach.

Jake only stepped below to work up the log and complete his Dead Reckoning calculations, but had drifted off to sleep. Looking up and listening to the sound of the gathering storm, his heart began to pound a little faster, the yacht's motion becoming more violent as the front began to move through.

Then he heard the rain on the coachroof.

It had been raining for some time, continuous background rhythm to the rising wind, but it was only now that he heard it like ten thousand pine needles clattering on the teak deck.

For a few minutes he sat listening to the rising sounds as if in a strange world that was devoid of all other human beings.

It seemed that he and Nikki were the only people left in the world.

And the elements were the only friends and the only enemies they had.

It was a world defined entirely by the size of the yacht, for in a storm at night, the sea and the sky ceased to exist and the only extension to their world was lit by the over spill of light from the spreader lamps and the intermittent flashes of lightning that, for an instant, showed him the entire panorama of the boiling sea and the angry scudding clouds.

"Nikki," he shook her shoulder gently.

She started and her eyes blinked open, instantly awake, all the sounds and the sight of Jake clambering up the companionway ladder immediate in their clarity. Her sub-conscious remained aware of the growing storm and enabled her to move into action without any further words from him.

By the time she reached the cockpit, he had fitted his harness and was behind the wheel, steering the yacht down the waves that appeared suddenly out of the darkness and swept past the yacht with an eerie roaring, crashing sound, a bass counterpoint to the howling wind in the rigging.

"Take the wheel. I'm going forward to reduce the staysail."

Struggling into her own harness, clipping the carabiner onto the pedestal anchor point, she slipped behind the wheel.

"Keep her at this angle to the waves. Don't let her head up or she'll broach."

Acknowledging him with a nod, she watched as he climbed from the cockpit and on all fours, crawled along the pitching side deck to the mast.

Clipping the safety line onto the anchor point at the base of the mast he released the staysail halyard a couple of feet before crawling forward and pulling it down to the reefing points and tying off the sail.

Then he clambered back to the cockpit and reduced the mizzen.

Immediately the yacht slowed a little, but still surfed at high speed as the wave crests carried her forward on a sudden acceleration.

Jake tapped Nikki on the shoulder and grinned encouragement.

"You're doing fine. Just fine. I'm going to rig up a warp to tow astern. It'll slow us down a little more."

As Jake worked, rigging the warp, Nikki gripped the wheel until her knuckles showed white, her face pale in the beam from the spreader lights.

Every now and then she glanced behind to see another breaker rearing up, white crest racing towards them, threatening to swamp them. But every time the stern rose in the nick-of-time and the wave rushed beneath the yacht, which rolled and yawed, threatening to broach before it responded to the rudder and turned back on course.

Nikki could feel the strain across her shoulders and in her legs with the struggle to maintain balance as the yacht rolled from side-to-side corkscrewing down the waves.

Jake leaned over and hauled the wheel to port a little more.

"Don't steer straight down. Angle off, like this."

She did as she was told as he secured one end of the thick rope warp to the starboard sheet winch and the other to the port stern cleat, then threw it over the stern after first ensuring that it passed beneath the dinghy davits.

The warp streamed out behind the yacht two hundred feet and the speed slowed to a steady five knots, making it easier to steer and allowing the waves to pass beneath without the yacht surfing. They were not yet large enough to roll over the stern and swamp the cockpit, but for two novice sailors, the sights and the sounds were unnerving.

Nikki peeked behind again and saw the face of a wave reaching up nearly twenty feet, the crest breaking as it caught the bight of the warp and the boiling foam sweeping beneath the yacht as it rushed on its way.

They were in control again, barely, and Jake sighed in relief. He was hoping the front would move through quickly before they lost too much distance downwind.

He took the wheel from Nikki.

"Can you make us some hot instant soup? We'll need it before the night is out."

She nodded and struggled below, closing the hatch.

The rain had eased a little, but the wind kept up its force, driving the rain and the spray against Jake's back as he steered the yacht down the waves.

It seemed to him they were in the middle of a maelstrom, a boiling cauldron of water and wind more fierce than he had ever experienced, but it was only a Force Seven with occasional gusts to Force Eight.

That put the maximum sustained wind at about 33 knots and the gusts at about 40 knots. Not a life threatening situation for an experienced mariner, but for Jake and Nikki more than they had ever seen before and would ever wish to see again.

Cups refused to stay still. They slid from the galley counter and but for the fact that they were enamel with cane handles, would have smashed on the cabin sole.

She solved the problem by wetting a paper towel to stand the cups on, then she wedged herself into the corner opposite the stove and waited for the kettle to boil, all the time praying that the yacht wouldn't roll and fill with water while she was below.

An irrational fear she knew, because she had learned to trust the yacht and Jake, but this was not the same feeling, the same motion that she had experienced before and there seemed no end.

Claustrophobia began to creep around the corners of her mind, raising her heartbeat and breathing, requiring an enormous effort to control.

The motion would have been bad enough in the daylight, but darkness seemed to make matters worse. Disorienting, so that she didn't know which way was up, only the stove on its gimbals telling her when the yacht was upright and not heeled to sixty degrees.

Everything that was not secured properly in a locker was thrown about the saloon as the yacht rolled violently from one side to the other.

Ignorance, fear and inexperience made a nightmare from an uncomfortable but controllable situation.

Seasickness rose again and looking out of the port-light at the rushing waves did little to calm her stomach. She poured the boiling water into the cups and stirred the instant soup, carrying one cup at a time into the cockpit, closing the hatch and securing her harness.

Sitting down on the cockpit sole, her back to the companionway doors out of the wind, she was thankful to be outside and not trapped below like a rat, should the yacht fill with water.

Finally she relaxed a little, watching Jake steer the yacht safely down the waves. They hadn't grown any bigger and the rain had dropped off to an annoying drizzle that seemed to seep into her clothing through the foul weather suit.

Then she saw the lights.

Only for a few moments, but like Jake, she blinked and they were gone, vanished behind a wave.

Staring at the same place for a couple of minutes, she saw the lights again. A red light and a green light both fairly close together.

"JAKE," she shouted as loud as she could, to be heard above the clamour of the wind and waves.

He glanced down at her, seeing her pointing. Turned, following the line of her pointing finger but saw nothing. "What?"

"Lights."

"I don't see anything."

"They were there. Two. A Red and a Green. And maybe a white one. I couldn't be sure."

Again Jake felt the warning signs. The hairs on the back of his neck rose, stomach tightening into a hard knot as adrenaline began to course through his body. Straining to see through the darkness to where Nikki was pointing he too saw the lights.

Less than a mile away he saw a tramp steamer, and from the angles of the lights, it was headed in their direction.

"What the hell are they doing?" Nikki crouched on the cockpit sole shivering, half in fear and half with cold as the wind and rain found their way through her clothing.

"Here, take the wheel."

Waiting until she had a firm grip on the wheel before turning his attention to the winch to haul in the warp. It came in slowly foot-by-foot until he nearly had it all on deck, then fate dealt another low card. A following sea broke on the stern, catching the warp and driving it under the yacht where it fouled the rudder.

Panic gripped Nikki as the wheel froze solid in her hand. "Jake. It won't steer."

He turned and fell back into the cockpit wrenching at the wheel, but it wouldn't move. "Shit, that's really annoying."

"ANNOYING?" Nikki yelled in panic as she glanced astern to see the ship moving closer and closer.

But they had no means by which to steer from its path.

The yacht picked up speed again, but the wind strength had lessened and she was not surfing on the waves as she had been before, although the motion was still unbearably uncomfortable, the rolling, corkscrewing action making both Jake and Nikki feel seasick.

"I'm going to set the small jib and reefed main, it'll give us more speed. Then I'm going to cut the warp. Be ready and keep her at an angle to the waves when we have steerage."

Not trusting her voice she nodded, wishing she was back in her warm bed in Rhode Island and that none of this had ever happened.

That Eve had not died.

And that Jake had never left home.

But the wishes of the child were empty wishes and the realities of the adult were oppressive and frightening.

Jake struggled forward towards the foredeck, unclipping and re-clipping his safety harness whenever he reached the end of the nylon strop.

Looking back he saw that the tramp steamer was closer, bow rising on the waves charging towards them. Jake knew they could not risk too much speed and he wondered why they had not seen the ketch. Someone must on be on the bridge and must be able to see the yacht's navigation lights.

Releasing the jib, he crawled back to the mast, secured himself firmly, hauled on the halyard, then winched the luff tight.

Moving to the mainsail, again making sure the luff was as tight as the third reef would allow. He could flatten the sail by keeping tension on the kicking strap and tightening the main sheet.

Taking a knife from the lazarette, he struggled to the stern and hacked away at the warp.

Finally free, it slipped into the ocean and vanished.

Nikki found that there was a little movement in the wheel and each time she wrenched, it gave a little more. But beneath her feet, the rusty steering cable was stretching with each jerk. Suddenly it gave way and the wheel spun uselessly in her hand, knocking her onto the cockpit coaming. And the ship inexorably continued to head in their direction.

"JAKE," she screamed in panic.

He had just begun to make his way back to the cockpit when the yacht broached and he was flung across the deck, smashing into the port stanchion, the strop of his harness preventing him from going over the side.

The blow caught him on the left side of his chest and he heard three ribs snap like dry twigs and a searing pain jump through his body as if someone had lanced him with a red-hot knife.

His body was suddenly on fire.

Every breath, every movement, a torture.

Nikki saw him fly across the deck as if he were a rag doll and hang for a moment on the lifelines, the ocean covering him as the yacht stayed heeled over for ten seconds before righting, and he slumped to the side deck his face screwed up in pain.

Her first thought was to run to his assistance and she unclipped her safety line, but he screamed at her. "STAY THERE. STEER THE BOAT. STEER," and moaned as the pain shot through him again. Coughing blood. Only a little, but enough to tell him that he had been badly hurt.

Shouting had cost him dearly and, doubled up in pain, he crawled foot-by-foot back to the safety of the cockpit.

"I can't steer. It's broken. Are you okay?" Nikki whimpered in terror.

"Broke a couple of ribs. I'll be okay in a few minutes." Steeling himself, he looked over the stern.

It was strange to be watching the lights, the enormous bow of the ship rushing towards them and the phosphorescence in the surging surf from breaking waves in the dark of the night.

It appeared like a scene from *Lord Jim* in the crashing roar of the surf, the pounding rain and screeching wind.

He looked at Nikki and saw she was crying with fear.

Then he looked at the ship and knew there was nothing they could do.

The pain in his chest made every movement an agony, but he had to put his own pain aside as he joined her at the wheel and put his arm around her, not noticing that her harness carabiner was unfastened.

"HOLD ON GIRL. HOLD ON. WE'LL BE OKAY. TRUST ME."

Looking into his eyes seeing them steady and calm, strong and purposeful, she took hope and courage from him.

Ripping open the lazarette he found the emergency tiller and struggled to the stern deck, tearing open the deck plate and jamming the tiller onto the top of the rudderstock. It took all his strength to pull on the tiller screaming in pain. Not twenty yards off the stern, the tramp steamer rose on a wave and charged down upon them.

Watching the ship, he experienced a strange feeling of deja vu and for a moment he was back in the jungle as the rain beat down, the wind howled through the trees, and the lightning flashed showing the fleeting shadows of the NVA creeping towards his position.

And like that time, he felt a calm descend over him, even though the pain from his wounds threatened to take consciousness from him before he could complete his mission.

He had survived that time in the jungle, when his training and his own need to survive had coolly enabled him to outwit the enemy.

A sense of the same time and place took hold of him now, peeling back the years until he was that young man, bleeding and afraid in the jungle watching his death approach through the dripping bending trees, back lit between the flashes of lightning.

He was unaware of the pain in his throbbing chest, as the ends of the bones grated together. And yet he was aware of everything else that was happening, such was his heightened sense of reality, and yet this was not reality, this was a surreal moment from which he thought he would soon wake.

Suspended time collapsed as the ship's bow rammed the stern of the ketch, sending the yacht into another wild broach. Throwing Nikki out of the cockpit into the ocean.

He saw her fall.

Saw the rusty sides of the ship throw the yacht away.

Saw Nikki bob astern of the ship, tossed in the wake of the propeller.

Suddenly the surreal world folded into the reality of Nikki falling to her possible death.

"NIKKI," he screamed at the top of his voice, panic seizing him before he struggled to the Man Overboard Pod and threw it into the water where he could see her head bobbing as her lifejacket inflated.

The Pod burst open, releasing the marker pole. A rescue light blinked on and before the yacht surged away down a big wave he saw the small life raft bobbing on the surface within thirty feet of Nikki.

And then she was gone, hidden behind the black oily waves covering her like a blanket.

And the ship sailed on into the darkness unaware it had hit anything.

Again his training, remembered from all those years ago came to his aid and took over.

Struggling to the wheel, he checked the course, then took out a hand-bearing compass from the seat locker and snapped a bearing on the pole light before it disappeared from view.

The pain in his chest made every movement an agony and every second an eternity. Grasping the tiller, he hauled with all his might and felt the warp finally let go of the rudder and the yacht respond, coming about until she was heading back on a reciprocal course. But the speed had dropped off and she was ploughing forward against the breaking wave crests, throwing sheets of green water back over the deck towards the cockpit. They seemed to be barely making progress and Jake had to bear off the wind a little to make headway.

Before the incident they had been heading almost dead down wind and he would have to make a series of accurate tacks to get anywhere near the area where Nikki went overboard.

Each time he wanted to adjust the sails, he had to tie off the tiller and then haul himself out of the cockpit, make the changes and then struggle back.

Once the sails were set the yacht settled and began moving at a reasonable speed, bounding over waves, smaller than they had been at the height of the gale.

And all the while the pain in his chest fought for his consciousness, and every cough brought blood to his lips, but his will overcame the pain and forced him onwards.

His will to save his daughter whatever the cost to himself.

The Man Overboard Pole was nowhere in sight, but Jake refused to let despair settle over him as his eyes swept the dark waters for any signs of the light.

After five minutes he tacked, but the yacht seemed sluggish and unwilling to turn, the water in the bilge adding to the weight and sloshing around at will as the cracks in the garboard widened until now the drip was a trickle. And soon the trickle would be a stream as the forces of the ocean worked maniacally at the fragile art of man.

Gradually the bow came around and the yacht headed reluctantly back towards the imaginary line he had drawn in the water that was the centre line of his track.

He could not lose control.

He had to concentrate.

Blot out the pain.

Become cold and calculating.

It was the only way.

Nikki had glimpsed the bow of the ship out of the corner of her eye, then there was a loud crashing sound and suddenly the yacht slewed sideways and rolled, pitching her out, her head hitting the boom as she went, knocking her senseless.

As she hit the water, the lifejacket inflated automatically and the shoulder light came on, but not before she had swallowed a lungful of seawater.

The ocean boiled white around her and the thrashing propeller passed inches from her head and then she was bobbing in the wake, feeling that she was floating in a warm bath.

Every now and then, a wave crest would break over her and she would cough and splutter. Drifting in a timeless place, devoid of all feeling and yet she knew what was going on around her. She could see the waves, the life raft and pole close by, the breaking white foaming crests that would race towards her and smother her and she could feel the loneliness of the ocean.

There was no fear.

It was strange.

Not unpleasant.

As if she was observing the scene as part of an audience, yet she knew she was a participant but the outcome did not seem to matter.

She was detached and unemotional, even as she coughed and retched.

Her body was simply another piece of flotsam flung upon the ocean to be pushed slowly and relentlessly towards a distant shore and the curious stare of a solitary beachcomber who might happen by in the early morning of a strange and foreign land.

She wanted to laugh at the thought and imagined that she had, yet the face she was looking at, her face, was pale and expressionless. Eyes closed as if asleep. Even the coughing had ceased now and the seawater washed in and out of her open mouth at will. But it did not matter. It was interesting to watch with such detachment.

There was still a connection she felt for this person that was her. Then suddenly there was an emotion. It was anger that flared quickly. Anger at the injustice of it all. This was not right. This was not fair.

And the body she saw before her seemed to fade as her conscious thought lurched suddenly into a world of buzzing noises and faint light.

Behind a grey curtain, fear, desolation and loneliness swept back, replacing the pleasant floating timeless sensation. Her brain didn't seem to want to function. There were no thoughts. She knew she existed, but there were no images that she could conjure up in her mind. No words she could see or understand. Simply a knowledge of existence. A world without vision, without form, without senses, without thought. A dark black world, filled with a feeling of absolute terror.

Then a vision appeared.

A bright vision, as clear as if she was there in the house. A little child, opening the door of her bedroom, woken by sounds of laughter and cries of abandon, and she walked down the landing to the head of the stairs where she could look down through the open door of the living room.

It was strange.

She could see her mother, naked, lying on the rug in front of the fire and a man on top of her.

To her young mind they seemed to be wrestling, naked, enjoying themselves.

The man moved, jerking his body and she saw, as he rose, that his penis was big and stiff and seemed to be thrusting into her mother. And she was appalled and shocked and feared that her mother was being hurt. But her mother's face was smiling and she was laughing.

Then the front door opened and she saw her father enter the house.

He looked tired and stopped when he heard the sounds from the living room.

Then he quickly crossed the hallway and stood in the doorway staring at her mother and the man.

Nikki saw her mother turn and begin to laugh. Then the man turned and she could see that it was Sam Strauss. He quickly rolled away and scrabbled for his pants as her father strode into the room and began to hit him, beating him senseless before he turned his attention to her mother, and beat her too.

Blood burst from her mother's nose as it split like a ripe peach and screams filled the house. Echoing through the rooms, becoming the only sound that existed, as if it were some strange light melody playing in the horror of a Hieronymus Bosch painting.

Finally Nikki could stand no more.

Covering her ears, shutting her eyes she screamed and screamed and screamed, until her screams blended with her mother's screams in an unnatural harmony of sound.

Watching the scene from a separated viewpoint. She saw Jake run up the stairs and take the little girl in his arms. The little girl that was her. The little girl that stared expressionlessly, limp in his arms, the shock of the beating having traumatised her so much that she was almost catatonic.

And she knew the truth. The truth of the guilt he had carried for all these years and slowly the vision faded and she could neither see nor feel.

As Nikki was slowly drowning, Jake searched the wind swept ocean.

It was no longer a threatening fearful place for him. Anger and resolve had overcome fear and driven him onwards. His own strength and power of will rising above his pain and the forces of nature, in the desperate search for his daughter.

There was nothing else that existed.

For him, death would be an inconvenience not a disaster and he knew that if she died, he would also die.

Nothing else mattered now. Only Nikki.

Tying off the tiller, he struggled painfully below to fetch the high-powered searchlight he knew to be beneath the forward berth. It was still there in its original packaging.

There was a watertight twelve-volt socket in the cockpit near the binnacle pedestal. Having closed the hatch, he sat for a short time until the pain eased, before setting up the light on a coachroof bracket and switching on the powerful beam.

Bright light jumped out across the water and shimmered on the rolling waves, oily and evil looking in the unwelcome darkness, reminding him of the jungle as the flares popped and splashed brightly, hissing, spluttering through the rain, flickering across the green jungle canopy.

> *'And there was silence in the jungle, as the waiting soldiers on both sides lay low and watched, waiting for someone to move. Exhaustion and pain scrambled their senses and played with reality until it didn't matter anymore.'*

Glancing at his watch he saw it was time to tack again and set the yacht on its new course. He reset the jib and main, all the while his eyes searching the ocean for any signs of the pole light.

Waves appeared black and monstrous in the night, seeming to take the beam of light and bend it to its own shape, hiding its back behind peaks that changed shape suddenly, either falling over in spray or flattening as if they had never been there.

But he was not concerned with the awesome sight of the angry ocean.

Every fibre of his being concentrated into spotting the bobbing head, the light on her harness or the Man Overboard Pole. He switched off the searchlight to see better and at times thought he spotted her and his heart leapt, only to be disappointed as the illusory ocean fooled him again.

Then he saw the pole.

By accident as he turned to check the compass.

On the port side, hidden every now and then behind a wave.

He stared and saw it again, remembering to look slightly to one side of the object, so that his eye could better focus the light in the darkness.

Another useful trick learned from the military.

Saw it a third time before he was convinced that it was indeed the pole light.

Spinning the wheel he headed for it, to arrive just upwind. If he went downwind, she would be thrown against the yacht.

Painfully slowly the gap closed and he searched the surrounding sea for signs of Nikki.

Was she close?

How long had it taken him to throw the Man Overboard Pod into the water?

Would she be upwind or downwind?

Questions without answers rebounded through his head.

As the pole came abeam the cockpit, he leaned over, grunting in pain and hauled in aboard, followed by the small sea anchor and life raft to which it was attached.

It was empty.

Again he scanned the ocean.

Fifty yards away to port he thought he saw another light.

Looked again but saw nothing.

Looked again and thought he saw it.

Then reached for the searchlight, snapped it on, swinging the beam across the water, forcing himself to move it slowly so as not to miss anything.

Then he saw her rise on a crest, caught for an instant in the bright glare of the powerful searchlight, about fifty yards away and although he tried to keep the beam on her, it was impossible to steer the yacht and focus the beam at the same time.

Switching off the searchlight he watched for the small harness light.

Sure that the yacht was on the right course, he struggled forward to the mast, dropped the staysail and, sitting on the deck, slowly and painfully hauled in the sail, then tied it down to the inner-forestay anchor point.

Turning he searched the sea for Nikki and saw her rise on a crest, the small harness light shining more brightly as the distance between them closed.

Back in the cockpit he rested until a sudden violent coughing fit eased and the painful throbbing faded a little, then he checked the mizzen sail.

The ship had torn away part of the davits, with the dinghy stern partly trailing in the water in danger of being swept away by the next wave. The mizzen boom had snapped and half the sail was ripped away. He would deal with the mess of the stern later.

There were spare blocks in the cockpit seat lockers and as the yacht slowly closed the gap, he rigged a block and tackle to the end of the main boom.

Every stretching action grinding the edges of the broken ribs together so that he thought he would pass out with the pain. But he couldn't afford to succumb to unconsciousness, forcing himself to work through a red mist of pain, holding the image of the little girl in his mind as she looked at him with those dead eyes, traumatised into catatonic shock. This time he vowed to give his life for her, to make amends for the past.

Gradually the gap between the yacht and Nikki closed.

At times she was clearly visible.

At other times, lost amongst the white caps.

Steering so that when he came alongside, he could heave-to just downwind. Bringing the yacht up, tacking, back winding the jib, heaving to with Nikki's limp form just abeam the cockpit.

As he leaned over with the boathook a wave rolled the yacht, banging Nikki against the topsides with a sickening thud. But it enabled him to grasp her lifejacket. Hold her there, while he waited for the next wave to pass.

Securing his own harness, he took a line tying it to the harness shackle, bringing the end up through the block he'd attached to the end of the main boom. Then he began to haul her up out of the water.

With the first pull on the line he thought his ribs would burst through his chest wall, but slowly, inch by inch as the waves tried to snatch her away from him, he hoisted her out of the water and swung her into the cockpit.

As he caught hold of her, he failed to see the small silver Buddha on the chain around her neck as it wrenched off, falling, washing into the corner of the cockpit.

Her face was deathly pale.

No movement in her chest.

And then there was nothing else.

The wind ceased to exist.

Waves ceased to exist.

The pain in his chest ceased to exist.

It seemed to take hours for him to carry her down through the hatch into the saloon and lay her gently on the cabin sole that was now almost awash with bilge water. Neither the state of the yacht nor the foul smell of the bilge made any difference to him. Stripping off the harness, foul weather suit and her sodden clothing, he wrapped her in a sleeping bag.

Then he saw her face. Pale. Eyelids slightly open. Peacefully serene and he knew she was dead.

That's what logic told him. But emotion told him she was alive.

The logical part of him screamed in anguish at her death, but the other part set to work, tilting her head back and putting his mouth over hers.

A vision appeared in her mind. Strong and bright, viewed as if she was separate from the action.

The little girl that was her, standing in the hallway, Jake kneeling in front of her. Crying. Tears falling down his cheeks as he reached into his pocket, pulling out a small object, holding it up for her to see.

It spun in the light as she reached up and took the object.

It was a small, exquisitely made silver Buddha on a silver chain.

For a moment the blank expression on the little girl's face seemed to flicker with life as she looked at the pendant.

Jake wrapped her in his arms, whispering into her ear, the words clear.

"Remember that I will always love you. Wherever I am, I will always love you."

Then he was gone and the little girl stood in the hallway looking at the little silver Buddha.

When she looked up again, Sam Strauss was standing in the doorway.

Gradually the image faded.

Nikki found herself looking down at Jake kneeling over her body on the cabin sole, breathing into her mouth as the yacht surged on the waves.

And she felt a strong and sudden urge for life that seemed to rush towards her lying on the floor and darkness swept over her, wrapping her in its warm arms.

For five minutes he worked, stopping every now and then to push hard down on her chest with the base of his hand, forcing the heart to start again.

She was his only daughter.

He had found her and wasn't going to let her go again.

For another five minutes he worked and thought he saw a faint movement and bent down, listening to her heart.

It was there.

A faint beat growing stronger and he breathed into her mouth willing her back to life with renewed energy.

From somewhere in her consciousness, the grey veil began to lift.

Images began to form again. Words appear. Sounds heard.

Instead of it being soft and comfortable, she was aware of pain, cold and nausea.

She vomited.

Coughed.

Vomited again and opened her eyes.

Jake knelt above her, tears pouring down his face as he looked at her, sobs coming in huge painful gasps, wrenched from his body in emotions long since buried.

Nikki felt as if her entire body had been put through a meat grinder.

Chest hurting. Throat raw. Head pounding.

Jake took her in his arms and held her while she retched again, then lay her head against his chest.

"What happened?" she said, her voice weak and trembling.

"You went overboard," he said, his voice cracked as he gently brushed the hair away from her forehead. "You're safe now. Safe. I've got you."

Exhaustion swept over her and she closed her eyes. "Want to sleep."

He carried her to the forward cabin and laid her on the berth, wrapped the sleeping bag around her and covered her with a comforter.

She was asleep before he had finished.

Jake tore himself away from her and returned to the cockpit. Now that the immediate danger was over, pain hit him with the force of a giant hand clutching him and squeezing him tight, wanting to crush the life from him.

Sitting down, holding his chest, he waited for the searing pain to ease before he began slowly clearing the mess from the stern. The dinghy still hung drunkenly on the remaining davit.

For the next two hours Jake slowly, piece-by-piece, straightened out the damaged stern.

The aft pulpit had been partly torn away and there was a gouge in the topsides where the ship had struck but no hole and miraculously the rudder was undamaged.

Where the davit had been ripped out, the aft deck had not fared so well.

Teak decking torn open during the collision had exposed the locker beneath. Jake fixed a canvas patch over it to stop any more water from getting in then hauled the stern of the dinghy on board, lashing it down to the bent pulpit.

Loosening the mizzen halyard, he removed the scrap of sail that was left. The splintered boom needed removing also, so he returned to the saloon and dragged out the toolbox.

By the time the work was done, sails struck and the yacht lying a-hull in the still angry waves, he felt as if his chest and lungs were damaged beyond repair and prayed he hadn't punctured a lung with his exertions.

His breathing was shallow and painful. Every cough brought fresh blood bubbling on his lips. He wondered how long he could continue to function before death, the phantom that had been chasing him since the jungles of South East Asia, finally caught up with him.

Every roll of the yacht was a nightmare of pain as he braced himself and moved back into the saloon, closing the hatch, securing it, shutting out the world.

Nikki had not moved from the position he had laid her as he leaned down fearfully to check her breathing just as he did when she was a baby. Relief flooding through him when he felt her soft breath on his cheek.

It had taken this to make him see what his life had become and as he stared at her and gently stroked her arm, he remembered the baby.

> *"Hush-a-bye, don't you cry,*
> *Go to sleep little baby.*
> *When you wake, you shall take*
> *All the pretty little horses*
> *Pintos and bays, dapples and greys*
> *Coach and six little horses*
> *Hush-a-bye don't you cry*
> *Go to sleep little baby."*

Jake's soft singing transformed the pitching berth back to the small nursery when Nikki was a baby lying looking up at him with eyes that gradually closed, although she fought so hard to keep them open, as she drifted off to sleep.

If he moved too soon, she would wake again, so he sang and waited while his arm grew numb, but he dared not move until he was sure.

Then slowly and carefully he would remove his arm and she would stir, roll over onto her side and clutching her favourite rag doll, would go to that place where adults were not allowed. And he would smile down at her and feel the lump rise in his throat as he looked at her and wonder how such a perfect creature could have been created by two such imperfect people.

The tragedy of the past caught up with him and he wept tears of self-pity and sorrow, wishing he could have undone the errors of the past and given his daughter the life she should have had.

Then he too slept, sitting with his back to the hull beside his daughter.

Waking every time she moved. Waiting until she was settled again, before drifting off himself.

The pain from his ribs was intolerable, but he considered it just punishment.

THIRTEEN

While they slept, the wind and the sea paid homage to their courage, leaving them in peace and taking instead the souls of the demons that had come to claim them.

It was as if the spirits of the earth, the sky and the sea had tested their resolve and love. And having seen the Truth, harnessed the devil winds and waves, driving them from the yacht. Leaving the dawn to rise on a smooth sea with the ketch riding sluggishly to a long swell.

When he awoke, he was greeted with two inches of water covering the cockpit sole and the foul putrid stench of the bilge and the contents of the ruptured holding tank. Slowly, clutching his chest, he knelt down, pulled up the bilge covers and stared down into the water. It was too dirty to see anything and he gagged at the smell, struggled to his feet and staggered up the companionway steps to vomit over the side.

He grabbed the manual bilge pump handle from the cockpit locker, attached it to the pump socket and began to move it backwards and forwards with a steady rhythm, as much as the pain in his ribs would allow.

The specifications said the pump would move eight gallons a minute and there was a swelling relief within him as he saw the water begin to gush from the outlet.

As he pumped, his mind began wandering as a way to combat the pain. Here in the expanse of the ocean, there were no limits to where his imagination might fly. Before him the horizon stretched infinitely in every direction he cared to look. Above only soft, billowy, high-pressure cumulus clouds kept him company as they moved slowly across the sky, while below his daughter slept.

Perhaps God was speaking to him in a thunderous voice he could not hear. Speaking to him through a convergence of circumstances that had arrived at this time and this small spot in the Gulf of Mexico, that may well have been in the middle of the Atlantic Ocean instead of forty miles from Key West.

Civilisation all around, just over the horizon. Safety and comfort a few hours sail away.

Solitude closed around him like an early morning fog.

After half an hour pumping, he stopped and went below to check on the bilge. The cabin sole was clear with six inches of water still in the bilge but no sign of where the leak might be.

Unseen, dark water seeped back into the boat, insidiously insistent without the pump to keep it at bay. Jake fetched a cloth and spent the next fifteen minutes cleaning the sole of the mess, opening all the hatches and port-lights to rid the interior of the smell. He checked in on Nikki to see that she was still soundlessly, deeply asleep and went back to the bilge pump.

Another half hour would empty it so that he could find the leak.

Back into the rhythm of the pumping, letting his thoughts wander again without purpose as the pain in his chest rose and fell with the pump handle and the pulsing gush of the water from the outlet into the ocean. He pumped until the outlet ceased to gush, until there was nothing more than a dirty grey dribble. Then sat down grey with pain and fatigue, only for a moment, enough to catch his breath before clambering down the steps to check the bilge.

It was virtually dry and stretching down, ignoring the almost intolerable pain, he wiped away the sludge from the bottom of the bilge until he could see where the water trickled in through the cracks in the garboard.

It was an unexpected shock.

A violation.

And for an instant, panic seized him until reason and pragmatism took over and he rolled over, lying on the cabin sole, breathing shallowly thinking hard, remembering that there was a locker beside the engine room where the previous owner had stored tools and hull repair items.

Jake had not looked in the locker for years. Slowly he crawled across the cabin sole, down the short passage towards the aft cabin. Inside, the locker was full of tins of paint, sealants, brushes, packages of fibreglass, tools and other paraphernalia.

Searching carefully through the locker, pulling out all the contents until he found an emergency epoxy repair kit that worked underwater. Armed with the can, a putty knife and roll of thin canvas, he went back to the bilge. Looking down he could see that there was already two inches of water in the bottom. It meant another laborious trip into the cockpit and more pumping until most of the water was out before settling down to patch the cracks.

There was no way of telling whether or not the epoxy would be any good as he ripped the cover off the stick. He scraped away the paint from around the garboard where he could see the water trickling in, wiping up as much as he could before working the epoxy stick to mix the resin and hardener together, then slapping the filler into the groove he had created.

He had to work it well into the wood until the leak eased to a trickle.

He sat back and watched. The trickle stopped.

Cutting the canvas into a strip, he laid it over the filler and using a short block of wood and the handle of a cut down broom, wedged the block hard against the canvas to apply pressure to the patch.

For fifteen minutes he stared at the temporary repair, watching to see if the water started to trickle back in again. It didn't and he rolled onto his back, grinning up at the ceiling with relief.

Even the pain seemed less.

What he failed to realise was that because the sea was calm and the yacht wasn't sailing, there was no pressure on the keel to work against the garboard and so the patch was just an illusion. It would work perfectly until the yacht began sailing, and only then would the ocean try to claim another victim.

Nikki was still sleeping deeply as he checked her pulse and pulled the blanket up a little further. For a while he sat with her, watching her face, seeing the little girl he had forgotten for so long, then went slowly back into the saloon, swallowed several Tylenol and checked the bilge again.

It still held and was dry.

Jake stood on deck, naked, letting the early morning sun cleanse his soul. At last allowing body and spirit to join in long overdue communion. And in his nakedness, he felt his rebirth ending as physical pain flared, a constant memory, a friend of his future forged in the past and he came to terms with the real possibility of his own death with the bubbling blood on his lips.

But he knew with certainty, that no growth is instant. And even as he thought of his death, he also thought of his rebirth, and knew that it would have to be nurtured with love and patience until he could respect himself. But the path was strewn with pitfalls yet unseen and he wondered if he would be allowed to start down that path and grow into the future alongside his daughter.

For an hour he stood, watching the sun rise and the warmth begin to flood through his veins and calm his soul. Then dressed and went below to check on Nikki.

She lay as he had left her. On her side, her arm beneath her head, expression peaceful, the bruise on the side of her temple, purple and swollen where the boom hit her.

Satisfied she was in a stable condition, he touched his finger tips to her lips, the lightest of touches and went back to the saloon where he rescued an old typewriter from the locker beside the navigation table and a ream of paper, carrying both into the cockpit.

He fed a sheet of paper into the machine with a long forgotten familiarity, turned the knurled knob, rolling the sheet until it was halfway before centring the carriage.

There was a sudden and urgent need to write.

To put down his thoughts and emotions onto the virgin page.

A need he hadn't felt for so long, made all the more crucial by the shadow of death sitting close by, hovering, patiently waiting.

He typed slowly, with two fingers.

The long since forgotten skill would soon return, but as he began, he felt a sense of fear at the unknown as the words began to appear on the blank white sheet.

THE CONCH COLLECTOR
by
JAKE KIMBLE

Removing the sheet, he placed it carefully face down beside him held down by a winch handle and fed a fresh sheet into the typewriter.

FOR MY DAUGHTER

Again he removed the sheet, placing it face down on top of the title page before inserting a third sheet into the machine.

Pausing to look up at the sun sparkling across the flat water, to where three dolphins quietly broke the surface fifty yards away and as if they were aware of his need for solitude, nodded in his direction and diving, swam away.

He looked back at the page and let the story begin to take hold of his mind and guide his fingers.

CHAPTER ONE

Monroe steered the twenty-eight foot flat-bottomed Sharpie through the shallows as if in his sleep. His mind following the usual pattern of lost thoughts that began every new day. The wooden boat seemed to have a mind of its own, following the narrow shallow channels unerringly, homing in on his favourite conch beds. Once there, he would begin the daily ritual by furling the sails and dropping anchor, letting the boat swing and drift until it held and settled in the quiet morning.

He liked it here, where mangroves curled gnarled roots into the sand beneath the water, thrusting fat boughs upwards in short stumpy arms, motionless while mosquitoes buzzed a constantly moving cape over them.

Monroe stretched, picked up the flask and uncorked it, tipping it up to his mouth, gratefully tasting the liquor as a gift from the Gods to the start of his new day. Then he slept for an hour or two in undisturbed peace, away from the clamour of the town and the constant gossiping tongues and staring eyes that accused him in silence without once charging him with anything.

If he were guilty of a crime, then it would have been wishing for solitude. He was guilty of desiring his own peace and he found it in his secret conch beds.

Jake continued to work gradually allowing Monroe to become him and he to become Monroe. Blending fact and fiction so the edges blurred and it was impossible to tell where one began and the other ended.

There was no beginning and no end. For he knew now that Monroe and he were the same. The fictional character carrying his dreams and expectations as well as his flaws and fears.

The work was satisfying, the atmosphere created in the world of the novel one that he wanted to inhabit, but then the character would take off on his own as he became more real and rounded. Sometimes it was gratifying, at others supremely annoying.

He spotted a sail entering the channel and suddenly the day became bleak as anger rose in him like a dark cloud across the sun. From the cut and colour of the sail, he knew it was Sigourney who had followed him out here, and anger died as quickly as it had risen.

For weeks she had been badgering him, her Cajun twang cutting through the quiet conversation at the bar as her Zideco band belted out offbeat, out-of-tune music. Then he saw that her boat was stuck fast on a sand bar, unable to negotiate the shallows and he smiled and lay back, pulling the straw hat over his eyes until he heard the distant splash and looking up saw her wading through the waters of the channel towards him.

At that moment he knew that his world was changing forever, and the peace of his escape was now a prison.

He worked for hours, pages building to a small neat pile beneath the winch handle as the yacht lay still on the ocean. The elements allowing him to begin his life again with each word he lay down on the pristine white paper.

And for the first time in years he felt the deep contentment that came from creation.

Nikki heard the clatter of the typewriter as if from a distance. A sound that gradually came closer until she opened her eyes and stared at the side of the hull where the wood could clearly be seen beneath the epoxy fibreglass coating.

For a moment she had no thought, just a pounding in her head that slowly spread to the rest of her body and died away to a dull ache.

Only the clatter of the typewriter remained.

Then she knew she was alive. That she had dreamed a nightmare where she had seen the 'Other Side' and returned, but she did not know to what extent reality and fantasy mingled.

She was tired and hungry. Her throat hurt and her mouth was dry and as she sat up, the thudding increased in her head. Reaching up she touched the lump on her temple and winced.

Slowly she stepped off the berth and stood naked in the cabin, before reaching for her clothes, dressed and then walked unsteadily into the saloon. Weak from her ordeal. Lightheaded to the point where she almost passed out, steadied herself against the saloon table until the moment passed and the blackness on the edges of her vision receded.

The clatter of the typewriter continued unabated from the cockpit and she looked up to see Jake bent over the machine, concentrating deeply.

"Jake," her voice a whisper not loud enough to be heard over the typewriter so she forced herself to shout. "Jake."

This time he heard and the keys stopped slapping the page. There was a shuffle and he peered down at her.

"Hey. What are you doing out of bed?" He climbed down into the saloon as she sat on the settee, lightheaded and dizzy.

"What happened?" she whispered.

Sitting down beside her, he placed his hand against her forehead, then took her pulse.

"You went overboard last night." He felt he could not broach the events of the previous night in detail. His instinct warning him to let the horror simply be a distant memory that would fade in time.

She looked at him uncomprehendingly, a vague memory stirring at the back of her mind just out of reach. "I don't remember anything."

"Don't worry about it."

"I remember floating. I think. It was like a dream. Like watching myself. From a distance," she closed her eyes leaning back. "It was not unpleasant. Just strange." Then she started to cry, unashamedly, letting the emotion pour from her as her father held her close to him.

When at last she stopped, he laid her down on the settee, propped a pillow beneath her head and smiled.

Then the memory of her vision came back to her and she looked at Jake's face as if for the first time.

"I know the truth, now. I was there. I saw what happened."

"It doesn't matter anymore. It's in the past," he said, reaching out brushing her hair away from her forehead.

"It matters to me. Could you bring my bag from the cabin?"

Jake reached into the forward cabin, picked up her bag and placed it beside her on the settee, watching as she rummaged quickly through looking for the silver Buddha and then remembered she had put it around her neck, reaching up but it was gone.

"This what you're looking for?" It spun in the light as it had the day he gave it to her.

Reaching up she took the pendant from him, holding it tightly, eyes filling with tears again.

"You gave it to me. I thought it was from Sam, but I know you gave it to me. You told me to remember that you would always love me. That I was not to forget that. Why did I forget?"

"Trauma. It was part of an incident you just didn't want to remember."

"How do you know?"

Reaching down, he picked up a book, holding it in his hand.

Both spoke at the same time.

"Books."

They laughed and the horror fell away as Jake hugged her to him. Pain savaged his body and he coughed, wiping the blood away from the corner of his mouth.

"You okay, Jake?"

"Yeah. Little painful," he closed his eyes for a second. Opening them again, he grinned. "Hungry?"

"Starving."

"Can't promise anything spectacular. But it won't be chilli."

It brought a smile to her pale face.

While he prepared the meal, he talked almost non-stop about every subject he could think of without referring to the events of the previous night. And while he talked she dozed, woke, and dozed a little more until the meal was ready.

There were chicken pieces already defrosted in the broken freezer along with a sauce Frankie must have prepared. While they waited for the chicken to cook, he mixed up a cup of mushroom soup. It was a strange combination for a hot day, but as Nikki drank the soup she began to feel human again as it warmed her chilled body.

As she sat hunched over sipping her soup, Jake showed her his shell collection and explained each of them, making her smile and at times laugh. Nikki didn't tell him she had discovered the collection when he was in the throes of his alcoholic delirium. Instead she enjoyed his boyish enthusiasm.

Then he cleared away the dishes, washed up and when he turned back to her she was lying on the settee fast asleep. He took her pulse and temperature again, then satisfied that she was in surprisingly good shape after her ordeal, left her and returned to the cockpit.

He sat nursing his broken ribs and trying not to move too suddenly.

Occasionally he coughed and small amounts of blood sprayed up from his lungs. He knew that one of them might have a tiny tear from the broken rib. He was not in immediate danger, but any sudden movement could cause a serious wound.

Having eaten the chicken and put some aside for Nikki, he went back into the cockpit and sat as evening stole over the ocean and the swell increased with the breeze blowing in from the Atlantic. He shivered and pulled his sweater out from the seat locker, slipping it gingerly over his head. It took a few minutes, some gentle deep breaths and an extra degree of pain, but finally he sat back and gently massaged his chest.

The yacht rocked gently with the ocean swells. Halyards rattling in rhythm to the wind blowing steadily across the now darkened ocean. Slipping over and around the yacht. Feeling its way over the contours as if testing for strength and vulnerability.

It felt good on Jake's face as he stared sightlessly out over the void, feeling himself leaving his body, floating over the ocean a free and separate spirit. It was an illusion, for when he lay back, the pain in his chest forced the spirit back to its cage and he saw the oily surface of the waves and the phosphorescence trailing in the wake as the yacht moved sideways, pushed by the swell.

"Can't just sit here Jake. Can't just wait for land to appear. Got to move your ass." But he just sat there, staring at the deck, the masts, and the sails lying secure but untidily. "Guess it can wait until morning. Get your rest Jake." He shook his head. "Can't rest. Got to stay on watch."

Sometime in the middle of the night, he thought he heard a loon calling, the sound echoing across the water, but he knew it was a dream and yet it was so real. He sat up, looking from the window across the lake, watching as the storm approached.

Black clouds hurrying towards the lakeside cabin like a cloaked messenger. Forked lightning throwing trees into stark relief, frozen for an instant like an Ansel Adams photograph and he watched in awe as it swept across the lake. The mournful ghostly sound of the loon drowned by a crash of thunder and sheeting rain that hurried across the water, the preceding wind churning the flat surface into angry wavelets that protested the onslaught. And then it was gone and the lake became the ocean and the sounds were the creaking of the yacht and chattering of the halyards. He fell asleep again as if he had never been awake, and the dream was a hazy memory that faded in the remains of the night.

"Where are we?" Nikki said, a gleam back in her eyes and colour in her cheeks.

Jake finished shooting the sun and climbed gingerly down beside her, wrote down the figures and the time in the little notebook, then put the sextant carefully back in the box. "About fifty miles from Key West."

She sat down turning her face to the sun, letting it warm her and heaved a sigh, feeling the tension flow from her. "I remember someone singing a lullaby. Maybe I was just remembering when I was a baby," she said, smiling at the memory, not noticing Jake's unease. "You used to sing to me, didn't you?"

"Yes."

"Mom never did." She was silent for a moment or two. "What happened to your parents? I know Mom's died when I was eleven."

"Mine died before you were born, in a car wreck."

"Oh. Wonder if they would have liked me?"

"I'm sure they would."

"Would I have liked them?"

"I think you would have. They were good people. Nothing fancy, just good honest folk. Dad liked to go to baseball on Monday night and sit between third base and home plate hoping that he'd catch a foul ball. He never did but he always took his glove and I always took mine, just in case."

"And your Mom?"

"She couldn't understand why grown men should throw a leather covered ball at each other. She liked to write poetry and paint."

"Was she pretty?"

"Wait here."

He went below, returning a few minutes later with a worn, leather-covered pocket photograph holder. Opening it and flipping through photographs of Nikki as a baby, of Frankie, stopping at a photograph of a middle-aged couple.

Nikki took the holder and stared at her grandparents, strangers with pleasant smiles, the man slightly taller than the woman. "She was pretty."

"You can bet she was stunning when she was your age."

"You look like her."

Handing back the holder to Jake she watched as he stared at the photograph for a few moments trying to remember them. It was difficult. So long ago that it seemed like another life.

They had died before he went to Vietnam, and twenty-five years had dulled his memory. There were vaguely remembered incidents, but to recollect their faces without the aid of the photograph was impossible.

"You were writing."

Her voice shook him out of his reverie and he shut the photograph holder. "Rewriting."

"Oh?"

"Thought I'd have another shot at *'Exile'*. Get it right this time. But I think I'll change the title."

"I thought it was good."

"Pity you're not my editor."

She closed her eyes again as a wave of exhaustion seeped slowly over her body, mind drowning out the sounds of the ocean, reducing Jake's voice to a soft murmur.

"I could be a writer," she said as she lay in a twilight world, hovering between sleep and wakefulness. "Just never got around to putting the words on the page. Every time I would start it looked so foolish, so childlike. None of it made any sense, as if I knew what I wanted to say in my head but it never came out that way on the page."

"It happens."

"Not for you."

"Yes for me. It's been years. Each time I tried nothing happened. It was if I'd run out of things to say and ways to say what I thought I wanted to say."

It was comfortable for her in this state. Eyes closed. Mind drifting with no sense of ultimate destination. Allowing the conversation to flow with her thoughts. *"'Guilt was as much a barrier as passionate love. Each overpowering emotion consuming the unfortunate soul with a doubt as solid as a medieval castle wall, and just as impenetrable. And in Monroe, both emotions vied for prominence.'* You wrote that. I always remembered that passage."

"Why?"

She was silent for a moment, quietly considering the answer, remembering the time and place where she'd first read the book.

Bought it with her saved pocket money, and kept it secreted away from her mother's prying eyes, in a box hidden in a hollow tree down by the shore of the Bay where only she knew. And she would sit there alone as her mother drank herself into oblivion, and read. A chapter at a time, sometimes two and she imagined her father as Monroe.

"Because I could feel those emotions."

"How old were you?"

"Sixteen."

"So young." He tried to imagine her at that age and couldn't. All he could see was the woman before him and the child of his memory; the two images a stark reminder of his own folly.

"Are you Monroe?"

"Maybe. Some parts of me. But he is whatever he is. A fiction. It's not me. Perhaps I'd like to be like him, perhaps that's why I like to write about him, but...," he let the sentence trail off. And in the silence Nikki drifted off to sleep.

Jake went on deck and looked at the horizon before retiring below to rest himself, tired from his exertion. The pain from his ribs beating at his resolve.

It had been years since he'd thought of his parents. Sometimes in the past there had been fleeting images before alcohol dulled his senses and he floated in the rum filled cocoon of the present. It had always been painful and he could see now how Nikki would have felt. To have this constant loss in her life. This sense of betrayal. He *had* betrayed her and wondered if that sense of betrayal would ever leave her.

He found to his surprise that he could remember parts of his life with his parents.

Father's raucous uninhibited laughter.

Mother's gentle touch and deep mysterious eyes that always gave him the feeling that she knew everything that was happening in his life, and everything he was thinking and it was disconcerting. He found he could not lie to her. It was an impossibility and he would always give himself away and then, break down and cry at the wretchedness of his deceit. As an adult he found no need to lie until that fateful day, and then alcohol had given him the illusion of strength that was in reality

224

simply self-deception and then lying came easily, especially when it concerned his daughter.

He saw fragments of his adolescence. Heard the laughter and caught the sweet smell of freshly cut grass, of pine needles, of the rotting seaweed on the shores of Long Island Sound and the trip back to Ireland to the land of his Mother's birth. And he could see reflected in the eyes of the natives that which he saw in his mother's every day.

Images began to tumble and jumble in his mind.

A frothing pint of Guinness. Folk songs. Spectacular scenery and old men sitting easily in front of turf fires, talking in soft lilting tones as one story after another ran from their memories like lively streams down the forlorn and desolate mountains of Eire.

These were the memories he should have been able to give his daughter, instead of the horror of a dimly remembered incident that had haunted her life, compounded by the sorrow of a father who was not there for her at any time.

Self-recrimination could not solve the problems. Love and understanding could, but they were alien words to him and he did not know how to tell her that he could not change the past, but could only affect the future and somehow be the father she had always wanted.

But that in itself was a riddle, for who was that person? Was it Monroe? Was it Jake Kimble the novelist? Or could she settle for the shadow of the man he once was, because the man who had existed, before fame fortune and alcohol destroyed him, was dead.

"Jesus Christ. You're a pathetic cliché of a man," he mumbled as he struggled to his feet. "Sitting around like some dumb ass wimp who left his balls in the locker room. Fuck you Jake. Fuck you asshole."

He clambered up the companionway steps into the cockpit.

"You made your own choices. Ran. Ran. Still running. Fuck you Jake," he continued to berate himself as he sat down on the port cockpit seat and looked at the mess on the decks. Then started to laugh quietly. "Lighten up Jake. Lighten up for Christ's sake."

Beside him, in a small stowage compartment was the winch handle and grasping it, he made his way slowly across the deck to the mast and began to winch up the staysail until it was flapping busily and the yacht lay bow to wind. The mizzen sail came up easily and he settled down by the wheel, drew in the sheets until the yacht heeled under the moderate press of sail, and began to move on track towards Key West.

The choice of sail configuration was deliberate, because he didn't want to put too much pressure on the keel until he knew how the temporary repairs coped with the constant side force and the buffeting as the yacht ploughed into the waves, beating slowly upwind towards its destination.

Two sun sights he had taken had determined their position some fifty-five miles south east of Key West and he knew it would be a hard slog upwind to reach land and home.

Home.

The word sounded strange. A word that almost everyone took for granted and he wondered where his home really was; whether it was really in Key West, or that the town in the Keys was really a transitional point, a metaphorical motel in his lonely journey through life. He thought of Frankie and that altered his view and he saw the beach, the hut and envisioned the ketch on the mooring and he knew that indeed Key West was his home. Certainty solidified by his sudden, urgent feelings for Frankie.

He loved her.

Loved her with a depth he thought he had lost forever. A depth his daughter had uncovered and explored. A depth he had been avoiding all these years and began to cry as he felt the grief and sorrow that had been his life.

And as the yacht plunged onwards, stricken, a dying creature on the sea, he felt so very alone.

A loneliness almost too much to bear, and his mortality hovered on the edge of decision. It would be so easy to end it all, here and now, to slip overboard, let the sea take him so that he need never feel the grief and the sense of loss that penetrated his soul with a surgeon's precision. Just as Nikki had felt nearly two weeks ago.

That's what the alcohol had been for, to bury the past, to obliterate the pain and the grief, but deep within him, a consciousness told him that he must walk side-by-side with the grief and let the experience strengthen him and the tears were not tears of surrender, but a manifestation of his courage to face the depths of his pain and survive.

He cried uncontrollably, a part of himself detached, watching with interest as the psyche that was Jake Kimble continued his rebirth.

When it ended, exhaustion as a fresh breeze blew through his mind, disentangling a myriad disconnected emotions, solidifying his resolve and purpose. Finally the man that had fought many physical battles with courage and endurance was returning.

FOURTEEN

There was a swirling darkness. A black viscous liquid that bore a resemblance to oil but more fluid.

Every now and then bubbles boiled from the centre of the darkness.

Bright energetic bubbles that carried Life. When they burst, a scream filled the air like the hellish torture of a thousand souls stranded in eternal darkness. And still the bubbles came and with them the screams until they became one, and the sound wailed without pause.

She knew they were dying.

Although she could not see them, she could sense their presence.

Gradually the darkness eased and the black oily liquid turned a turgid green colour that slid in serpentine waves around and about her. She could feel the cold fingers seizing her skin, insistently pulling and pushing.

Sky appeared brilliantly, vividly blue with a crackling sun that burned across her eyes temporarily blinding, until she reached up her arm, shielded her face and then it was gone as if it had never existed.

Clouds boiled angrily, rolling across the surface of the fluid as if both were in alliance against her. Then she saw the yacht, masts pointing accusingly skyward, bowsprit carried as a lance speared forward until suddenly it rose upwards and with a terrible sound of smashing timbers, sank from sight.

Trapped within the shrill scream a cracking snapping sound grew like thunder, joining with the wailing into a cacophony of noise that pounded at the core of her soul, bursting from her mouth as she sat up in bed, bathed in sweat.

The room was, as always, sparse and quiet, with the dull echo of all-night dance clubs in the distance, muted between the distant rolling of surf on the beach.

For an instant, as Frankie stared out of the open window across the harbour, she saw Jake's face, eyes closed, skin pale, only the faintest sign of breath from his lips; and on the breeze was the sound of his voice,

228

whispering forlornly, *'Frankie. Frankie'*, dying in the room.

"Oh no. Jake. Oh no."

Sobs competed with the lasts echoes of the nightmare as she staggered from the bed and stumbled into the living room to the telephone.

"Art? It's Frankie."

"Hey Frankie, what you doing up this time of night?"

"Listen. It's Jake. He's in trouble. I know he's in trouble."

"Last I heard they'd left the Dry Tortugas, should be back by morning. Don't worry, Stan told me the yacht was fine, called me the moment they left."

"There was a storm."

Art laughed gently. "They'll be fine."

"Art, listen. I had a dream."

"Go back to sleep Frankie."

"LISTEN TO ME DAMN YOU," she shouted, her voice rising to fever pitch.

"Okay, okay. I'm listening."

"I know they're in trouble. You have to send help. You have to send help now."

"Frankie, it's not possible in the middle of the night. We have to get a plane up first and they just can't see at night. Not well enough to find anyone. We have to wait until the morning. Then if they haven't arrived I'll start a search pattern."

The logic of his argument and the calm tone of his voice told her that he was right. He knew his job and if he said there was nothing they could do right now, there was nothing.

"I'll have a crew standing by at first light. Okay?"

"Okay."

But she could not shake the vivid reality of the nightmare.

Every now and then Jake's face would shimmer in her mind so clearly, that even closing her eyes could not shake the vision. And the dormant mysteries of her ancestry began to assert themselves in her soul.

She crossed to the window as if in a trance, to stand staring out across the ocean. Then slowly she sat down in the wicker butterfly chair, crossed her legs and let her body relax and her mind empty.

Slowly her mind became separate from her body until it freed itself, seeming to hover close by so that she could see herself in the room sitting in the chair. It was difficult to maintain the concentration and suddenly with a rush she was back in her body again with a jolt that made her jerk violently and gasp in pain.

It had been so long. The little girl that her grandmother had taught the mystery of out-of-body experiences, and how to accomplish the seemingly impossible, was here in this room now. She had regressed and those memories that had been so long repressed by choice began to flow.

Maturity and cynicism had consigned the skill to an elaborate party trick, but deep within her she knew that existence was not merely physical and there was a plane upon which she could travel that existed beyond her body.

Whether it was a reality or a hope, or some trance-like state that bordered on the paranormal, she couldn't care less. Now, at this moment, belief was more important than scientific fact, and ancient mysticisms more effective than the inadequacies of modern day technology, so she relaxed.

Eyes closed again, she concentrated. Focusing her energy into the expanse of the unknown. Letting her mind move out across the water, across the ocean, away from her body, from her existence in the present and the place that was Key West.

This time she held the state for five minutes, entering an existence that was both conscious and yet not, before 'returning' to her body. Realizing normal physical consciousness again with a jolt that was almost painful. For the slightest of moments, doubt crept into her mind, but her need to help Jake was stronger than her modern cynicism.

Somewhere in the background, she heard her grandmother's voice speaking softly. "Relax chile. Yo jus take it slow. Empty yo mind an let yo body go. Slow chile. Slow."

And the memory of the rhythm of her voice covered her fears and smoothed away her doubts.

*   *   *

Jake felt the garboard crack before he heard the tearing sound as a breaking wave crashed against the topsides.

It wasn't an enormous wave and ordinarily would not have been serious to any other yacht, but the jolt put too much pressure on the keel joint and the garboard split under the strain. Under normal circumstances, with a healthy and capable crew this would certainly have been a crisis, but a manageable one.

But these were not normal circumstances and the crew was neither healthy nor capable.

Pain was forgotten in the urgency of the moment as he rushed down the companionway steps, and ripped up the bilge cover. He could see from the light in the saloon, that the trickle was now a gushing stream and already half the bilge was full and he knew with a horrific certainty that the yacht was sinking without hope of recovery.

Nikki struggled awake as Jake let the bilge covers down with a crash and stared at him uncomprehendingly for several moments.

"Get the lifejackets and follow me on deck. Hurry." His urgent tone propelled her from the settee without question, following, dragging the lifejackets from the locker beside the companionway.

Jake was already in the cockpit with the starboard seat lifted. He pulled out a medium sized valise, which he hauled to the rail and tipped over the side into the ocean.

The valise hit the water and the life raft inflated as he turned to help Nikki up the companionway steps into the cockpit. Glancing into the saloon he saw that the water was already covering the cabin sole.

"GET IN. NOW."

Again, she did as she was told without question, still in a state of confusion and half sleep. Jake pulled the life raft closer to the yacht as Nikki rolled into it, and lay looking up at him.

He was staring back into the saloon, the water was now a couple of feet deep, the yacht wallowing, mortally wounded and it dawned on him that this was his home that was sinking out of sight.

Manuscripts, documents, passport, ID card, everything that gave him an existence in society would be gone and there would only be his fragile life and the memory sitting on dusty bookshelves to show that he had ever existed.

With the sadness and desperation of immediate danger, there was also a sense of rising elation.

Even in the darkness of the night, everything took on a new perspective. A new colour. A new rhythm.

There was a stunning clarity of detail in the light from the spreader lamps.

Peeling varnish on the coachroof grab rail.

Patterns in the crazing of the Plexiglas hatch.

Lines lying against winches and the sound of the sails flapping without direction.

Wheel spinning forlornly from side to side with no effect.

The damage to the stern, where splintered wood poked through shattered fibreglass like tiny daggers and he could see how new and clean the wood looked as if it had been freshly cut.

He felt the yacht was speaking to him in a language that was no language.

With words that were not words, but an unspoken understanding that required nothing more than an acknowledgment of its existence and its fleeting importance in his life.

He felt its need for recognition and silently acknowledged the ketch before turning to jump up into the life raft as the water cascaded through the hatch into the cockpit.

And at that moment he felt the tear in his lung rip and the excruciating pain as it collapsed. But he did not cry out because he didn't want Nikki to fear anymore than she did already. He needed to be heroic for her, to save her.

As he lay in the life raft, watching the yacht through a red mist of pain he felt as he had never felt before, so close to the yacht and in that bizarre moment realized that she did not even have a name.

They watched in silence as the yacht disappeared into the dark waters, swallowed up with the lights blinking for a few moments under water, creating a surreal illusion of a city below the waves. Blinked for the last time and then there was no sign at all of where she had been.

It had happened so quickly that for fully five minutes neither of them spoke.

Perhaps their subconscious had been expecting such an occurrence, but it did not diminish the shock.

Neither wanted to admit that they were alone on the ocean without power, without food, without water. There had been no time, but Jake knew that was an excuse.

Lack of preparation and inexperience had landed them in this situation.

And no matter what the events that had led up to this moment, it would have happened some time and in some way or other.

Nikki lay on the other side of the tiny life raft, pale, eyes slightly unfocused, shivering suddenly as the breeze blew across the open life raft. Every now and then a larger wave would roll beneath them and the life raft would ride up the face, heeled over before teetering on the top of the wave, sliding backwards into the trough while the next wave built up and came rushing towards them.

The sound was louder than she had been aware of in the yacht and instead of looking down at the waves, or at least on the same level, she found herself looking up as the next breaking crest tumbled down towards them, occasionally sending water into the life raft.

Jake connected the small manual bailing pump that was part of the kit and found the waterproof flashlight. It gave a weak light that he knew would not last long, but was enough to see that the inlet and outlet hoses were secured before he started pumping.

"What happens now?" Nikki's voice was quiet, almost a whisper as if she dared not ask.

"We'll be okay. Don't worry," he whispered hoarsely through his pain, putting a sense of levity and confidence in his tone that he did not feel. "The Coastguard will be out in the morning."

"How did this happen?"

To that question he had no answer and was silent for a moment. "It doesn't matter how. We're here and we'll be fine," he paused for breath. "Tell me about school. Your friends. What you did every day."

She was silent for a long time, and Jake did not interrupt, learning finally that there were times just to wait and not push.

He watched her carefully.

Images came into her mind that were at first confusing, interrelated with the constant sound of the waves that rolled continuously beneath the life raft, until she became used to the rhythm and her mind drifted with the flow of the images.

Sounds of laughter, girlish laughter echoing in the hallways of the school and in the dormitory late at night.

She could see Jennifer Sturges lying on her side, propped up on one elbow in the bed next to hers, moonlight streaming through the crack in the drapes to highlight her slightly rounded body. As always she was talking about boys, never anything of substance, boring Nikki so she turned over, let the whispered sound of Jennifer's voice become part of the background that lulled her to sleep. It was always like that and morning would dawn and Jennifer would be the last one to get up and drag herself to the bathroom barely speaking to anyone.

Her only true friend was Odessa, a tall slim distant girl, with a personality that exuded quiet rebellion. Uncontrollable most of the time and yet had an unnerving ability to maintain straight A's in her academic work. It was a mystery to the teachers and a source of constant speculation amongst her peers, except Nikki. She didn't care how Odessa maintained her average, just that they were friends who found in each other areas of common ground and the enjoyment of spreading mischief and dissension wherever and whenever they could.

"I'm surprised they didn't throw you both out of school."

"They weren't really smart enough to know and we both managed to keep up our grades." She grinned but Jake could not see her face as the moon darted behind a racing cumulus cloud.

She and Odessa had discovered boys together and on many occasions had been close to expulsion when they'd had parties in the dorms late at night, the boys creeping in up the fire escape.

And they had also discovered that Jennifer was all talk and no action as she hovered in the corner away from the whispering, giggling and awkward fumblings that were going on around her.

Even Nikki had been shocked by the lengths to which Odessa would go to enhance her reputation and it was the reporting of Odessa's sexual activities and Nikki's involvement that had led to lengthy questioning by the school authorities. The two friends stood stoically by each other and again escaped, but they felt the leash tightening and it made them bolder and less caring.

"It was fun. We didn't hurt anyone. Besides, the faculty were so stuck up and anal retentive," she paused, smiling. "I wonder what Odessa's doing now?"

"Probably married with two point five kids and regularly attends local council meetings and church on Sundays," Jake whispered.

"Hardly."

"It would surprise you just what happens to people once they leave school. Even the most rebellious become model citizens."

"A gross generalisation. Look at me."

Laughter forced a coughing fit and the broken ends of his ribs rubbed together agonisingly. She could not see the pain etched into his face.

"Really. She's probably in jail or running for Congress."

"And running for Congress is rebelling?"

"Not rebelling but it's full of crooks and liars. Seems to me she's well suited to that kind of life."

Nikki suddenly saw Odessa, dressed in black wool skirt and jacket, carrying a briefcase, able to be completely amoral and detached, simply enjoying the game without having to become emotionally involved.

When Odessa had spent the summer with Nikki, they had gotten themselves into a lot of trouble.

That had been the summer she took to riding in the Ferrari while her mother was passed out in her favourite position on the cane settee in the conservatory. Only the silence of the mechanic and the local policeman, who had stopped them one day, saved her from continuous recriminations.

Odessa simply breezed through every incident and ignored Eve when she became obnoxious, never questioning or commenting about her to Nikki, as if she didn't even exist. It was an easy, simple, non-threatening, free from responsibilities relationship. Neither owed anything to the other, so were free to enjoy each other's company and the pranks they pulled together.

And Odessa had been the only one of her friends that she had confided in about Jake. Had shown her the hiding place where she kept the books and press clippings away from her mother's eyes, and again, Odessa had neither condemned nor approved, simply accepted the status quo and listened, then read Jake's book.

Another wave swamped the life raft, shaking her back to the present, away from the warm summer sun and days spent with Odessa on the shores of the Narragansett Bay.

Jake began pumping again but he knew his strength was fading fast.

"Go on. Don't stop. I'd like to know."

It was cold and she shivered again, looking out across the black ocean to the light glimmering on the horizon.

*   *   *

Frankie sat motionless in the chair. Eyes closed. Barely breathing. Just the faintest of movements of her chest confirming that she was still alive.

Images in her mind were confused, swirling patterns.

Strange cloud formations and the vast expanse of empty ocean, dark and menacing beneath her, as she seemed to fly over its surface.

She knew there was a spiritual beacon out there, that somehow she would see it and it would be Jake, forcing herself to believe that he would somehow be aware of her presence and allow her to connect with him.

They had never talked of out-of-body experiences, had never even mentioned each other's pasts except in a brief and perfunctory way that left out all the relevant details. They had an unexplainable passion for each other that was frightening. But alcohol had dulled fear so thought was banished to the subconscious and they simply reacted to each other's bodily needs and the habit of being together.

Had she felt that she could not share the depths of her true personality with him because he might not understand and spoil it for her? Or was she somehow ashamed and if she was, why?

But none of this mattered, for there was a Truth. And the Truth was an undeniable spiritual bond between them that was stronger than sex and more frightening. It affected the depths of their souls and all the demons that where hidden there. All the baggage they brought to their relationship. All the negative influences. And in order for their relationship to survive and grow, they had to acknowledge the depths of their love and involvement, and allow that love to protect and inspire them.

As the sun rose and bathed the harbour in a warm glow, the town awoke slowly to its normal ritual as the two old men ambled up to their favourite place on the wall and sat down with their coffee mugs. They stared out across the water and talked sporadically, enjoying the security of each other's company and the beauty of the early morning, blissfully unaware of the drama that was playing out beyond their sight and their comprehension.

Frankie's spiritual entity continued to roam the ocean, searching, feeling for Jake and for Nikki and just when she thought she could feel their presence, her own began to flicker as the demands of her earthly body brought her suddenly back into the room and the sunlight lancing in through the window.

Exhaustion filled every part of body and soul and she shook violently, the spasm lasting several seconds before it left her body limp and unable to move.

There was a knock at the door and Mary came in quietly, crossing the floor to stand next to Frankie.

"You look terrible. What have you been up to?"

Frankie stared out across the harbour. "Trying to find him."

Mary's eyes narrowed for a moment before she understood.

"Come on. That's nothing but old women talking. You know that."

"I was there. I was close."

"I tell you you're dreaming. It's not possible, just a bunch of ancient mumbo jumbo voodoo crap."

Frankie turned to her slowly. "Do you believe that you can tell when people that are close to you are in trouble?"

237

Mary paused, sighed deeply, resignedly. "Okay, I'll buy that one."

"How do you think that happens?"

"I have a feeling you're going to tell me."

Frankie turned away and reached for the telephone. "Art. It's Frankie."

"I alerted the air patrol five minutes ago Frankie. They'll be airborne in thirty minutes. "

"I appreciate it Art."

"No problem. I'll keep you informed."

She replaced the receiver. "I know I can find him, Mary. Whether you believe it or not makes no difference."

"Well we've still got a business to run, so don't be flying around on that astral plane too long or I'll be calling the controller to get you back on the ground." Turning, she stalked from the room.

Frankie had forgotten Mary had been in the room before she had even left. Once more she settled down, relaxed, and emptied her mind as a prelude to departing from her body again.

*   *   *

At first as the sun rose, Nikki was grateful for the warmth as her clothes partially dried out and she stopped shivering. It was becoming uncomfortably warm and the salt on her face dried her skin. The seas were still big, waves relentlessly pushing the fragile raft about at will. Jake had settled into a rhythm on the pump and there was just a quarter inch of water in the bottom. The pain all but consumed him and he started to ramble.

"I can't change what happened Nikki. I wish I could but I can't. I'm so sorry I was so weak when I should have been strong. But I'm here now. I *am* your father and I love you."

The words seemed to come from someone else. Jake knew it was him, but they seemed so alien and yet at the same time fitting and true.

"I'd like a chance to be your father if you'll let me."

The words, she knew, could have sounded trite, but there was a simple honesty in his tone and expression. Pain and exhaustion had given him a skeletal look, eyes sunken and wide, cheekbones prominent and she could see dried salt embedded in the lines on his face. And she felt the last of the strands of the cobweb that had been holding her back slip away.

Nothing mattered anymore.

Whether they lived or died was immaterial, because now she had her father for the rest of her life. The thought made her smile.

"I hope we'll get the chance," she said, pointedly staring at the life raft, the ocean, and the empty sky with the sun blazing down upon them. "*'...she lay in the bottom of the Sharpie staring at Monroe, her eyes following his every movement and it disturbed him that he felt so uncomfortable as if he could not escape. For a moment he thought he might throw her back as he might have done with an undersized fish and then he felt ashamed.'* I never understood why Monroe should have felt so uncomfortable with that woman in the boat. It was never explained."

Jake sat back against the side of the raft and closed his eyes, still feeling the sun burning through his eyelids.

"He never wanted any responsibility. Never wanted to feel that he was responsible for anyone's physical or emotional well being. He was trying to follow the principle of everyone being responsible for their own emotions, feelings and physical well-being. Not having to care about anyone else. He was wrong and he knew it, which was why he felt ashamed and then angry."

"Why anger?"

"We're back to guilt again. Nobody likes to be made to feel guilty, even if they have fouled up. Taking responsibility for your actions and the emotions you create in people that care about you is important. It's what makes us worthy as human beings. I knew that, but I never lived it. Never took responsibility for anyone else's emotions and feelings. Always felt it was their problem. It's not. We are responsible."

Nikki watched him for a moment. "You love her don't you?"

Jake sighed deeply, but did not open his eyes. For a moment he saw Frankie in his mind, sitting in the wicker chair facing out across the ocean.

Then the image changed.

He saw her naked, dancing hypnotically on the deck of the ketch in the moonlight.

"Yes. I do. I love her very much. The pity is she doesn't know that."

"Does she love you?"

"I hope so."

"I'm sorry for what I did to her. It was a pretty mean stunt."

"Yes it was. You can tell her when you see her."

Again she looked at him, but his eyes were still closed. "We're going to die out here." The words were softly spoken, barely audible above another breaking wave crest that sped beneath the raft, causing it to surf down the wave before settling back into the trough, waiting for the next.

Jake opened his eyes and leaned forward, beginning to pump again.

"We'll come through this. You have to believe. You have to."

There was a ferocious intensity in his eyes as he stared at her, then it was gone and the gentleness was back.

"We will make it because we have to. I'll bet they're out searching for us right now. Tell me more about your friends."

"Tell me about yours."

He smiled softly. "Not much to tell. I don't make friends easily. Just Owen at the bar. Guess you'd call him a friend. We play chess together most nights. I always win. He's a really bad player but refuses to admit it."

"Why don't you make friends?"

Why didn't he? Was that really a question he could answer?

"Maybe it's fear. I know I never used to be such a hermit. Your mother and I...," voice tailing off as the memories flooded back again. Unwanted, half-forgotten memories. He could see her there, laughing, turning to him and smiling and the love in her eyes was undeniable.

"Go on."

There had been a time when they were first married, when Nikki was first born. He was there and he watched as she pushed her way into the world and he and Eve had cried together, held each other and watched the first breaths of their child.

That had been the best time.

240

And for the first eight hours after the birth, Nikki had lain on his chest while Eve slept, while they all slept. A tight, centred family with a future that stretched ahead of them as clear and as bright as a December night at sea, with stars vividly distant in the night sky. They could see forever, and forever was perfect. Happy. Just the way both of them had imagined it to be.

The house on the Narragansett Bay rang to the sound of laughter, music, lovemaking and the cries and chuckles of their daughter. Those first three years had been so blissfully happy; so impossibly happy that neither of them could see the Evil that was hovering in the wings, waiting for the moment to strike when happiness was all there was and contentment was as natural as breathing for Jake, Eve and Nikki.

He had friends then. They had friends.

Every weekend during the summer, the house became a social centre for their circles of friends. Artists, musicians, writers; people from all backgrounds, both wealthy and poor met in the melting pot that was their home on the Narragansett Bay. It was stimulating, fun, exciting and yet some other element began to creep in their lives. A discordant note that initially sounded only now and again, eventually becoming a clamouring that refused to be ignored and their circle of friends grew smaller until they vanished altogether.

When and how it had happened, Jake still could not fathom.

It just seemed that one day, Evil woke up beside him and did not leave.

And in the turmoil of his inadequacies and fears, there was no room for friends.

In Frankie he had found a soul mate that was as tormented as he and they had forged a friendship in the lie of alcohol and denial. But there was a deep attraction between them that denied the lie and sought to find the purity in their lives. They had just never given it a chance.

"Perhaps with Eve gone we can live again. It's not an unfair comment and I think she would have agreed. The love we had couldn't allow any other love to exist. It was so strong. So powerful, so all consuming, and it destroyed us because we felt so threatened as individuals by the power of it." He began to cry, gently. Tears unashamedly streaming down his face as he looked at Nikki. "You are the testament to that love."

Nikki crawled across the raft and curled up against his chest, crying as well, feeling their grief blend as it should with a father and daughter for a lost spouse and mother.

*   *   *

"Sorry, Frankie. The first pattern couldn't find any sign of the yacht at all. We'll be flying another pattern further to the North as soon as the plane's refuelled."

It was not what she wanted to hear, but it did not surprise her.

"Thanks Art."

Some hours ago, exhaustion had overtaken her and she had fallen asleep in the chair. A dreamless sleep from which she awoke neither refreshed nor content.

Part of her thought that perhaps she was going insane, that finally her brain had overloaded and she had been reduced, just as Mary had said, to mumbo jumbo voodoo crap. But the other side of her, the stronger side, the spiritual side, denied that and propelled her across the room to lock the door, pull the drapes until the room was dark, lit only by a single candle placed in the centre of the large teak coffee table.

She spread a comforter on the floor and sat down, adopting a half lotus position, forming her fingers and thumbs into a triangle that lay comfortably in her lap.

This time she was more prepared, more purposeful and she felt the Truth of her existence powerfully as she sat and emptied her mind, centring her Being, until all that remained was the Essence of Life. It was an unhurried calm. Without fear. Without expectation. The void filled with a peace and a single presence that defied description.

And then she was free from her physical constraints.

As with the previous attempts she was flying over the ocean, but this time, instead of feeling a sense of panic and need, she allowed herself to be guided. Where she was, she had no idea and that was not what mattered. It was only important to be present.

Below she could see the ocean as the sun began to sink towards the horizon, the waves moving in sets as imperturbable as the breeze in the trees.

Long lines of light and shade moving slowly across the face of the earth.

Then there was a strong and powerful sensation that pulled her away to another part of the ocean and she went with it, allowing the force she felt was Jake to guide her until she saw the life raft rising and falling on the swell, occasionally swept by a breaker.

There was no emotion. She could not afford emotion for it would break the tenuous grip she had on her spiritual self. Instead she allowed herself to be guided, pulled towards the raft by the spirits that lay in its cold wet grip.

*   *   *

Jake was barely conscious. Injury and exhaustion had all but spent his reserves of strength and will to live.

He was delirious. He knew he was delirious.

Frankie was not here and yet he saw her clearly standing on the water ahead of the life raft, smiling. And a peace came over him and he knew that they were not going to die.

It was inexplicable.

"I love you Frankie. I want you to know that I love you. I've never told you before. I'm sorry Frankie. Sorry for everything."

He did not know whether he had spoken aloud or whether it was just his imagination.

It didn't seem to matter.

"This is my child, Frankie, and I love her."

He cradled Nikki's sleeping head in his arms.

Watched Frankie standing before him, feeling his mortality vibrantly fragile, his life held by gossamer threads of will power and hope.

This was his child and this was his lover and they both gave him a strength and power that defied all the efforts of the Evil that had been his constant companion for so long, to destroy him.

And he laughed softly in the face of his own death.

*   *   *

"Art I know where they are. Get me on the helicopter."

"I can't do that Frankie," he sounded tired. A sleepless night and Frankie's constant telephone calls made him want to leave the office and go home.

"Art. You do it because I know they're looking in the wrong place."

There was something in Frankie's tone that somehow penetrated the bureaucratic red tape. Either that or the Commander of the local Coastguard station had a secret he'd rather not share with the local community.

Within an hour she was strapped into the Coastguard helicopter as it lifted off the helipad and headed out to sea. The smell of jet turbine fuel strong in her nostrils, making her eyes water.

The crewman grinned as he made sure her safety belt was securely fastened.

"I'm Chuck."

He had given her a helmet and his voice sounded strangely hollow in her headphones.

She smiled nervously. "Frankie."

"So, they told us you know where the yacht is."

She nodded looking nervously out of the open door at the ocean flashing past beneath the aircraft.

"Which way?"

She closed her eyes, emptied her mind and concentrated. Within moments she could see the raft and turned to face the direction she knew they were. Opening her eyes, she pointed out across the empty ocean. "That way."

Whether the crew of the helicopter really believed they would find the life raft was hidden behind their professionalism. They had been ordered to take this woman and to listen to her directions, and that was exactly what they would do.

Chuck watched as Frankie stared out across the ocean, covering her nose at the smell of the aviation turbine fuel. He wondered who she was and what was so important that the base commander had personally escorted her to the aircraft. He had been on some strange missions, but this was definitely the strangest.

Frankie was oblivious to the scrutiny, letting her mind drift, knowing that they were flying closer and closer towards Jake and Nikki. The link was so tenuous she wondered if they would be in time.

*   *   *

At first he thought he was dreaming again.

He heard a sound like the fluttering of a thousand wings and saw a shadow drifting across Nikki's face as she lay across his chest.

The sun beat mercilessly down upon them, drying their skin, cracking open the flesh and he knew death was near as they bobbed helplessly on the rolling swell.

But in the distance, amongst the sound of the beating wings he heard Frankie's gentle voice calling out and felt her touch on his face.

"I love you Frankie. Forgive me," he gasped, his voice barely above a whisper.

And the wind howled around them with the beating wings that seemed so insistent.

He looked up, forcing his eyes to focus on the angel of death. But it wasn't as he expected.

The helicopter hovered fifty feet above the life raft and Frankie could see Jake slowly lifting his face to peer up at her. He looked confused and sick, barely hanging onto life, Nikki draped across his chest, her expression peaceful.

"Please Frankie. Move out the way." Chuck hooked himself onto the winch and swung out of the doorway, dangling above the life raft. Frankie watched as he was lowered towards the raft bobbing on the ocean as the now gentle swell flowed across the Gulf of Mexico to the Atlantic.

Jake saw the approaching crewman as a threat. Clutching Nikki to his chest. Ignoring the agonising pain and refusing to allow his daughter to be taken from him again.

"No. She'll never leave me now. Not now," he mumbled as the

crewman dropped into the life raft beside him.

"It's okay Mr Kimble. It's okay. You can let her go. She's safe."

Jake did not believe the man, but was too weak to prevent her from being prised from his arms, strapped into the harness and hauled towards the helicopter. Beyond her swinging body he thought he saw Frankie.

And then darkness closed over his mind

*   *   *

Nikki had not prayed since she was that little girl who knelt beside the bed with her father, her tiny hands held together and her eyes screwed shut as she concentrated on the words.

> `When I lay me down to sleep,
> I pray O Lord my soul to keep
> And if from sleep I should not wake,
> I pray O Lord my soul to take.
> God Bless Mommy. God Bless
> Daddy. And God Bless Nikki.'

The nightmare she thought was over was still with her, twisting its knife a little further in her soul as if trying to destroy her. But she refused to be destroyed and prayed even harder.

As she looked at Jake's pale lifeless face and the tubes snaking from his body into the respirator and the life giving plastic bags that hung on stainless steel stands beside the bed, she wondered what they had done to deserve this horror.

Nurses came and went unseen and doctors had long since given up trying to persuade her to rest. She would not until she knew he was out of danger and on the road to recovery.

For four days he lingered in a semi-coma. The operation had been successful in patching up his damaged lung, but the rib on his left side had torn his spleen and that had to be removed. Bleeding on the first night had required a second trip to the OR, but after that he made slow steady progress. Nobody understood how he managed to survive.

Nikki stayed by his bedside, alternating shifts with Frankie and when they were together they talked quietly, gradually getting to know each other and the threat that each felt for the other diminished to nothing, until their relationship became as sisters.

Finally, when she knew he was out of danger, she left and drove the Ferrari back to Rhode Island. There were many things to take care of, many arrangements to be made and her mother's body to bury.

It was a quiet funeral, just the priest and Nikki at the crematorium.

By the open door, Sam stood and watched, then he turned and slowly walked away.

As the coffin passed from view, Nikki felt her demons were finally laid to rest, disappearing with the smoke from the chimney up into the clear blue summer sky.

And when she returned to her home, the ghosts were no longer there. They left with the fresh air that swept through the house out through the open windows and across the Narragansett Bay.

As she looked she thought she saw Jake's yacht and she knew what she wanted for herself. Knew that the plan forming in her mind was not subject to one of Murphy's Laws. This time it was based upon reliable information and a resolute conviction.

Jake had no idea that Frankie and Nikki had discussed whether she should be there when he awoke and had decided that he should not have another crutch to lean on, that his recovery depended upon his own will to live, unaided by either alcohol or his daughter.

At first when he realized she was gone, he relapsed, but gradually his own sense of survival took hold and he reached into the reserves of strength that had been dormant for so long and slowly recovered.

Frankie was there when he opened his eyes and could see with a sense of reality instead of through a thousand gossamer thin drapes.

"I saw you. You were with us. I know you were."

She smiled softly. "I love you too Jake Kimble. More than you will ever know."

He smiled and nodded weakly. "I do know. I know."

As a part of his recovery, Jake spent the time working with Peter the water taxi captain, on the design of a new yacht. A modern, sleek, fifty-foot ocean cruising monohull, the hull built from cedar strip planking sheathed in fibreglass. The decks and bulkheads, honeycomb core sheathed in fibreglass. Once the design was finished Peter began the lengthy building process. She would be big, strong, fast and worthy of anything the ocean may throw at her and a fitting testament to Jake's own rebirth.

*   *   *

Frankie watched him from the foredeck as he walked along the beach beside the red brick walls of Fort Jefferson, lost in his own loneliness.

She had suggested that they charter a yacht and sail to the Dry Tortugas, so that he might finish the novel and allay the demons of the shipwreck while Peter built the new yacht. He agreed, but his concentration was not on the book.

Words and ideas would not come and she knew why.

But she let him alone, understanding that he had to deal with his ghosts in his own way.

There were times when he looked at a bottle of rum and she could see the thoughts running across his mind. At those times she had deftly steered him away and distracted him, until the urge to return to the bottle faded and he understood what she was doing, why she was doing it and thanked her.

But nothing could ease the pain in his heart.

He knew he had destroyed the illusion Nikki had lived with for most of her life. Even though she knew the truth, it was still a heavy burden to bear and he wished he could have lived the time over again and changed the events before they had happened. He had told her that, but returning to land had a way of reopening old wounds and the experiences would be hard for her to forget and forgive.

The sound of the Cessna overhead made him lift his eyes and cover them from the sun. It was the weekly run. He watched as the plane banked overhead and dropped down towards the still waters of the anchorage.

Last week Jake had radioed for a ream of computer paper, more for something to do than the need for more paper.

The Cessna touched on the water, sending up rooster tails of spray from the floats, gradually settling until it turned towards the land and the engine cut as the aircraft drifted to the dock.

Alvin jumped out onto the float and stepped neatly to the dock with the mooring line in his hand, which he quickly tied off, then reached in to help a passenger from the plane.

Nikki stepped down onto the dock and stood staring at Jake.

She looked beautiful.

More grown-up, her hair styled and the short pants and tee shirt accentuating her beauty. To him she was no longer her mother, she was his daughter, with an elegance and beauty that was uniquely hers, and his heart swelled with pride and love.

He muttered softly to himself. "So this is what it feels like."

She walked along the pier, jumped down onto the beach and sauntered slowly across to where Jake stood.

They smiled at each other and she leaned forward and kissed his cheek.

"How are you Jake?"

"Okay. Little slow, but okay." He held her at arms' length taking in her beauty and smiled. "I missed you."

"I missed you too. More than I ever had before," she said warmly and smiled again. "I love you Dad." It sounded good to him and felt easy and comfortable to her and she knew that finally she had come home. She turned and looked out across the anchorage to the yacht. "The yacht looks beautiful."

"Thanks."

Taking his arm, she steered him towards the dinghy. "So when's the wedding?"

"Wedding? What wedding?" Then he saw her mischievous grin and smiled back. "You made your peace with Frankie?"

"Sure. Long time ago. She's been keeping me up to date." As she pulled up the anchor and helped him push the dinghy into the water, it felt familiar and comforting. It felt like being home.

"What now?"

She clambered in and started the motor. "How about you write, watch Peter build the new boat, I collect conch and we all enjoy Frankie's cooking?"

"You know how to collect conch?"

"I had a good teacher."

He grinned and relaxed as she gunned the outboard and turned the dinghy towards the ketch.

It would have been wrong to say that the old urge to write was back.

It wasn't.

There was a new feeling, a feeling of relaxed contentment about putting the words and ideas that formed a story down on paper. An emotion he had not experienced, a calm, thoughtful emotion that was no longer associated with the desperate anger of his youth.

He knew now he could use that anger and his experiences to form a new emotion that would flow from his mind onto the pages and he no longer cared whether the publishing world was ready for him.

He would not write for them.

He would write for himself. Be true to his creativity. Be a reflection of the times as seen through his experience and not through the demands of others. Suddenly he was laughing happily, the sound echoing across the anchorage.

"Why not?"

FIFTEEN

May 26th 2002

Nikki had visited Key West many times over the years as Peter built Jake's dream yacht, and she had married the young boat builder on the foredeck of the newly named *SOLITUDE*. And she had seen what had happened to the old village where once sponge fisherman earned a decent living and that was the haunt of would-be Hemingway's and sailors in search of quiet cruising, and tourists came in search of somewhere different and untouched, to relax.

It had become like a frantic cauldron of a gay community in search of a life away from the social focus of the big cities; tourists in search of an excitement they could not define; college kids on vacation intent on blasting their minds into oblivion, and weekend racing sailors filling the bars after the frenetic regattas.

Perhaps these feelings were unfair and untrue, but Nikki thought back to the peace of the quiet beach where she and Jake had dove on the conch creeping through the sea grass. But the truth was that she had not spent much time actually in Key West and her perception was coloured partly by Jake's novel and Peter's whimsical longing for the romantic fishing village of the past, when Key West had declared itself *'The Conch Republic'*. Perhaps that was why he had settled so well into the sleepy town on the Narragansett Bay away from the rich racers on their expensive yachts, comfortable at the old fashioned shipyard.

All these thoughts rushed through her as she stared down through the aircraft window as they circled to the approach. She held Jake Jr. up to the window and whispered in his ear.

"Here's where I found my life, little Jake."

Now as she looked down at the devastation that Hurricane Joshua had wreaked upon the small island over the past few days, she knew that Key West would never be the same again. It would go through another transformation as the residents tried to pick up the pieces of their shattered lives and return to what once was but would never be again. She shifted uncomfortably in the seat; her body still sore from childbirth and the nurse who accompanied her glanced at her nervously.

"Okay hon?" Peter asked anxiously as sat down next to her having returned from the cockpit where he had spent most of the flight chatting with the pilots as Nikki and baby Jake slept. She smiled tiredly and nodded, not trusting her voice.

Chartering the private jet had been the only way to get down to Key West so soon, as the Airlines had refused to accept her and Peter had seen the stubborn thrust of her chin as he had tried to argue against flying so soon. The nurse had been a compromise.

Nikki turned back to the cabin window and watched the passing parade below and then stared out across the ocean, now serene after the storm, as the aircraft lined up to the runway and descended on final approach.

She thought perhaps she would feel dread at returning under such circumstances, but there was none of the anxiety she had experienced on her first journey to Key West all those years ago. Instead there was a strange peace as if with the birth of her child, her life had come full circle and the peace that spread through her was a gift.

The east end of Key West passed below the private charter jet as it flared for landing, the yachts like toys piled up against each other as the Hurricane had tossed them onto the land.

Nikki closed her eyes as the aircraft taxied to the ramp and the engines shut down, steeling herself, fearful of what she might learn now they had arrived in Key West. The heat washed into the air-conditioned cabin as the flight attendant opened the door and memories flooded through Nikki as she clutched Jake Jr. tightly to her. He whimpered in his sleep and made little sucking sounds, but settled down immediately.

Peter climbed down the steps, already sweating in the heat and humidity and helped Nikki to the waiting electric golf cart vehicle that took them to the terminal. Another cart followed with the bags. Nikki could see Mary and Owen waiting for them and smiled wanly, tired from the flight, glad to see them and yet not feeling like talking to anyone. Mary was smart enough to read the signs and after offering a brief kiss, hug and gentle touch for baby Jake, ushered them to the waiting car.

"I've put you in the apartment over the restaurant," she said briskly as she drove out of the parking lot. "It's about the only place that survived untouched. That and Owen's Bar of course."

Owen grinned self-consciously. He had not wanted to come to the airport, but Mary had insisted. *'We're family and she needs family right now,'* she had said and Owen knew from her tone that there was no arguing. "God works in mysterious ways, his wonders to perform," he muttered, more for something to say than for any religious belief.

"Silly old coot," Mary scoffed gently. "God didn't save your bar, you did." She looked at Nikki in the rear view mirror. "Broke his fingers fitting the storm shutters."

"It's nothing," Owen growled.

Nikki smiled and for the first time in two days, felt her body and mind relax, knowing that she was back in her second home. "Any news?"

"Not yet. The coastguard helicopters were damaged in the storm. They're waiting for replacements, but it's gonna take awhile," Owen said, shifting uncomfortably in his seat. "The Keys took a real beating. It's gonna take sometime before anything gets back to normal."

Nikki stared out of the window at the debris that had been cleared from the road and piled up on the sidewalks and vacant lots that used to be houses and businesses. Here at ground level the devastation was surreal, and she could see where the tidal surge had swept across the low lying Key and flooded through the buildings, sweeping some away and damaging others beyond repair. Her own personal problems seemed to pale into insignificance in the face of such a disaster.

Old Town Key West, Fleming Key and Key West Harbour had taken the brunt of the storm, and Nikki was amazed to see that Frankie's restaurant was the only building that had not sustained major damage. Protected on the east side of Key West Harbour, the building had received glancing blows from flying debris and the harbour wall had knocked down the storm surge so that the restaurant had only minor flooding that the sandbags had, for the most part, managed to contain.

Banyan trees, stripped of their foliage, stood like forlorn tangled sentinels of the disaster and the frangipani, hibiscus, wisteria, passion flowers and the myriad other plants that Nikki remembered had adorned the houses were gone, whipped away by the vicious wind.

Sticky mud churned up by the storm surge, caked the streets. Nikki was numbed by the destruction and turned to look at Peter and saw tears in his eyes as he stared at the remains of his adopted hometown. She reached over and took his hand in hers.

Owen had removed the boards from the apartment windows above the restaurant and Nikki could see out across the Harbour towards the anchorage where Jake's boat was usually moored. Some of the yachts had survived the onslaught and remained at their moorings while others had dragged and were thrown up onto Fleming Key and lay amongst the broken slash pine trees.

"Key West hasn't suffered this much destruction from a hurricane since 1846," Owen said quietly standing beside Nikki and looking out across the harbour. "Jake was better off out there." He tentatively put his hand on her shoulder. "They'll be okay. I know it. Peter built a good boat, you have to trust that."

"Thank you, Owen, I'm just tired that's all," Nikki said smiling at her father's old friend. Jake Jr. whimpered softly and opened his unfocused eyes, staring up at his mother. "Hush my little man," she said rocking him gently.

"If you need anything you know where to find me," Owen said awkwardly and turned away, shaking Peter's hand before leaving the apartment.

Mary smiled at Jake Jr. and stroked his cheek making soft cooing and clucking sounds. "He's so beautiful, aren't you little feller?"

"I wanted Jake to see him," Nikki whispered.

"He will. It'll take more than a hurricane to finish him, believe me. You wait and see," she pointed to a spot beyond the anchorage where the narrow channel led from the Gulf of Mexico into Man of War Harbour. "He'll come sailing in through there just happy as can be."

"I hope you're right," Nikki said without conviction.

"I know I'm right. Besides, Frankie better get back because I'm not clearing up all this mess on my own." Mary said briskly. "Now you just settle down and relax, you've got plenty of people to look after you."

Nikki turned from the window and lay back on the settee that already had pillows plumped so she could put her feet up, feed Jake Jr. and look out across the water just as Frankie had all those years ago when Nikki had *'stolen'* Jake away.

"Now I have work to do. I'll send up lunch in an hour or two, anything else you need just call." Mary turned to Peter. "Fresh juices are in the fridge along with some cold beers. Help yourself." Then she left them alone, closing the door quietly behind her as the nurse checked Nikki's blood pressure and temperature.

Nikki could feel the beating of her heart as the blood pressure cuff released and with it another beat, strong and vibrant and she knew at that moment that Jake was alive. Then exhaustion overcame her and she fell into a dreamless sleep.

Peter watched her and sighed deeply, feeling some of the pressure he had been under slide off him.

The nurse looked up and smiled. "She's fine. Get some rest, I'll watch her and the baby."

But Peter did not want to rest although three sleepless days and nights had left him physically and emotionally exhausted. He wanted to see the marina where his life in America had begun, to smell the air of the Keys and the warm breeze of the Gulf of Mexico.

It was only a short distance to Key West Harbour, but walking through the battered streets brought home to him the intensity of the hurricane. Gone were the smells of the frangipani blossoms, hibiscus, bougainvillea, bromeliad, orchid oleander and other tropical plants that used to fight for dominance in the small gardens of the Old Town houses. Instead, the air was filled with the smell of sticky mud, decomposing fish, backed up sewage and already rotting wood. Mud caked cars lay like discarded children's toys, strewn haphazardly amongst the backyards, vying for prominence with the shattered dinghies and small boats.

Peter could see the mildew already forming inside the broken homes that looked like a photograph of bombed out buildings of the Second World War. The wastewater treatment plant on Fleming Key had suffered a direct hit and the local facilities were not yet back online. The few people he met looked at him with a vacant expression, staring straight through him as if he wasn't there, before turning back to clearing the debris from their battered homes.

The beauty of the day, cloudless sky and impossibly blue water seemed at odds with the broken coral and sand island. He walked on until he reached the west end of the harbour, where he could walk on the breakwater and look out across Man of War Harbour to where the moorings used to be and he drove the water taxi.

Exhausted he sat down, his mind blank, trying to soak in the heat and the sea smells that still drifted across from the outlying keys and blot out the awful probability that Jake and Frankie did not survive.

The rising blast of the siren atop the Coast Guard station at the North West end of the harbour, and boom from the cannon shook Peter from his torpor.

The cannon boomed again, echoing across the water and the siren wailed, rising and falling in the vapid, humid air. He saw figures running from the station building towards the small twenty-five foot inflatable cutter that had survived the hurricane and jump in, firing up the outboard engines and throwing off the dock lines. Within moments the cutter was blasting across the harbour towards the breakwater entrance and out into the channel.

Peter strained his eyes to the horizon to try and catch a glimpse of what they were racing towards. At first he saw nothing and then thought he saw a low silhouette on the horizon. He blinked, rubbed his eyes and looked again as the Coast Guard cutter closed the distance to the object and then his heart missed a beat and the horizon tilted as he felt a wave of dizziness and light-headedness sweep over him. When he could focus his eyes again he knew what he saw.

The shape of the yacht was unmistakable, crafted by his own hands.

And he began to cry.

Then shout and scream as exhaustion left his body in the euphoria of seeing Jake's yacht, battered, damaged but proudly motoring down the channel towards the harbour. He ran down the breakwater to the entrance, waving and yelling, not caring that they could not hear him at this distance.

Aboard *SOLITUDE* Jake held Frankie close as he steered the yacht slowly towards the approaching cutter.

The ordeal of the past three days had taken a toll on both of them and they were hollow eyed from lack of sleep and fear, but even so both felt exhilarated that they had overcome the storm and survived due to their skill and their will to survive. Jake patted the wheel thanking the yacht for taking care of them and not floundering and giving up to the hurricane's might.

"We're home my darling," he said softly, looking into Frankie's eyes.

"This yacht is our home, Jake," she replied, smiling through her tears. "I know that now."

Jake nodded and lifted his eyes to the cutter as it came alongside, the skipper grinning from ear-to-ear.

"Welcome home, Captain," he said saluting smartly. "It would be our privilege to escort you into the harbour, sir."

"Cut the crap, Johnny," Jake laughed. "Just buy us dinner."

"My pleasure, Jake. Follow us in, the channel's changed a little since the storm. We'll berth you at the station dock, it's about the only one that's not been destroyed."

"Lead the way, young man."

Out of the corner of his eye, Jake caught sight of a figure on the breakwater waving his arms and jumping up and down. It took a moment for him to recognize Peter and he stood and waved, yelling across the two hundred yards that separated them.

"PETER. PETER. WHERE'S NIKKI?"

"SLEEPING. I'LL SEE YOU AT THE STATION." Peter turned and started running back down the breakwater. It would take him some time to get around the whole harbour, but he didn't care. Happiness and joy lent strength to his legs and he ran as if his life depended upon it.

*   *   *

The sound of the cannon echoed through Nikki's sleep and she thought she was back in the Dry Tortugas when the cannon sounded to warn of the approaching storm. The air felt similar, but there was a subtle difference she could not fathom in her half sleep. Perhaps it was the soft touch on her forehead as if someone was smoothing the hair away from her face, an act she had performed herself on her mother's body.

Perhaps she was dead and Peter was doing the same thing.

But there were other sensations and sounds that did not seem to belong to a funeral parlour.

Voices, the sound of laughter and a baby's cry.

Then Jake's face drifted into focus and she still thought she was hovering in the twilight of death, but gradually the room came into focus and she saw it was Frankie's apartment and there Frankie was standing beside Peter smiling with baby Jake in her arms, laughing through tears.

"Jake?"

"Hi sweetheart. I hear you had a rough time of it," he said gently, still stroking her forehead.

"We have to stop doing this. It's getting really old."

He laughed loudly and took her in his arms, squeezing her tightly to his chest. "We were fine. Your husband's a great boat builder. Little scary at times, but nothing we couldn't handle. I would have called but the sat-phone got drenched."

"What do you think of your grandson?"

"I think he's a lucky little feller."

"I suppose you'll want to teach him to sail."

"Not unless he wants to."

Nikki grinned. "Between you and Peter he's got no chance."

Jake smiled gently. "I hope you're going to stay for a while. A few days at least. It looks like you need to rest."

Nikki looked at Peter, who nodded. "We've got time," he turned to Jake. "Besides I'd better check out the boat, see what you've done to my handiwork."

Three days after *SOLITUDE* sailed back into Man of War Harbour and Peter had repaired the minor damage wrought by Hurricane Joshua, the yacht bobbed gently to anchor in fifteen feet of clear, turquoise blue water. It was as if the storm had never occurred here near Jake's favourite conch beds in the little bay where he had first brought Nikki all those years ago.

Close by, Jake snorkelled with Peter and Frankie, diving down every now and then to swim along the bottom where the sea grass gave way to the sandy bottom and the conch crawled slowly. Multi-coloured reef fish darted past in brilliant shoals of flashing light and in the distance a pair of barracuda hovered just on the edge of vision, before deciding there were too many people in the water to investigate further and vanished with a flick of their tails.

Bubbles wobbled to the surface as he slowly let his breath out and Nikki could see him clearly in the clean water of the small bay. She lifted her eyes and saw that the shack was still standing, sheltered from the hurricane by the tangled mass of slash pines, mangrove and casuarina. A slight welcome breeze ruffled the dry leaves, sending a rustling sound across the bay, before dying away to leave the perfect silence of their private anchorage.

For a moment she could see Jake and herself twelve years earlier, sitting uncomfortably on the sand with the raw wounds of confusion and anger tearing at them. And she reflected briefly on all that had happened to bring them back to this place at this time. Then the past washed away into the distant closet of memories and she smiled contentedly, because now she finally knew who she was and where she belonged.

Baby Jake shifted in his sleep and opened his eyes, looking up at his mother and whimpering softly. Nikki reached down and picked him up, turning him so he could see his grandparents and father swimming in the warm water.

Jake broke the surface holding up a beautiful pink conch, perfectly formed, its curved mouth delicately coloured and swam to the dinghy, leaning over the tubes and placing it carefully on the floor before swimming back to join the others.

Nikki laid Jake Jr. in the crook of her arm and let him feed while she reached for his grandfather's book. She opened it to the last page and read quietly to her son, who stared at her face intently as if he understood exactly what she was saying.

> *In the end, Monroe was what he had always wanted to be.*
> *A Conch Collector.*
>
> *The burdens of his life distilled into the size, shape and beauty of each of the complex yet simple creatures he watched and on occasion harvested.*
>
> *Some days the problems amounted to no more than the decision whether to dive, or whether to make love to Sigourney.*
>
> *And each day he smiled, for he had discovered that the Essence of Happiness was no more than a Celebration of Life Itself.*

Other Books by the Author

autobiography
CONTACT

literary fiction
AN UNQUIET AMERICAN
COLLISIONS

dystopian satire
THE BOOK OF BAKER Part One: *Dreams from the Death Age*
THE BOOK OF BAKER Part Two: *Armageddon*

thrillers
THE ORANGE MOON AFFAIR (A Thomas Gunn Thriller)
THE JONAS TRUST DECEPTION (A Thomas Gunn Thriller)

These books are available in the Amazon Book Store and Amazon Kindle Store

I hope you enjoyed this book and would very much appreciate it if you would post a review on my Amazon page. To learn more about the author, or new releases and special offers please visit our website and leave your email address on our secure form.

www.afnclarke.com

www.ingramcontent.com/pod-product-compliance
Lightning Source LLC
Chambersburg PA
CBHW030126180626
46812CB00002B/573